LENA KENNEDY

The Dandelion Seed

HODDER

First published in Great Britain in 1987 by MacDonald & Co
(Publishers) Ltd

This edition published in 2013 by Hodder & Stoughton
An Hachette UK company

1

A CIP catalogue record for this title is available from the British Library

Paperback ISBN 978 1 444 76737 7
Ebook ISBN 978 1 444 76738 4

Printed and bound by Clays Ltd, St Ives plc

Hodder & Stoughton policy is to use papers that are natural, renewable
and recyclable products and made from wood grown in sustainable
forests. The logging and manufacturing processes are expected to
conform to the environmental regulations of the country of origin.

Hodder & Stoughton Ltd
338 Euston Road
London NW1 3BH

www.hodder.co.uk

Foreword

It is strange how a tiny plant seed, so minute and hardly discernible will survive any conditions no matter how much we ignore it, try to destroy it, or even protect it. Regardless of what we do, out of a batch of seeds, at least one will always survive.

As I sit in a green meadow, the birds are singing around me and the tall grasses rustle in the wind. In the distance I can see a clump of golden dandelions, the most common of our wild flowers. 'Piddle-beds' we called them when I was a child and played in this same meadow. 'Don't pick them,' my friends would say. 'If you do you will wet the bed tonight.' With the wilful obstinacy of youth I picked a good bunch, and then wondered why I had not wet the bed that night, as my companions had claimed I would.

Now I sit and dream in this peaceful meadow and watch the tiny dandelion seeds float off on the swift breeze in the direction of the sea, taking their own flight towards the shore where they split up, sending the tiny umbrella-like shapes on to their individual destinies. I began to wonder how far they would float on the waters. Would they soar over the sea to be lost in the ocean or would each one have its own place to rest and take root? Perhaps it would land in some meadow like this one, or in some suburban garden, a clump of golden blooms coming forth to strike annoyance in a dedicated gardener who would dig them up and curse the wind that brought them.

Dandelion seeds have been in existence for almost as long as man. When and where did they come from? When the Pilgrim Fathers sailed for new lands, did the dandelion seed sail with them? As I lie on my back deep in reflection and chewing a piece of grass, I am inclined to think so . . .

I

The Brook

Over the flat Essex marshland, runs the River Lea. The rider crossing the marsh on this dark February night felt cold and dejected. In spite of his thick warm cloak, the chilly white mist seemed to get to his bones. Even his horse was getting weary and slowing down as if the cold were seeping into its limbs. The rider would not be sorry to get to London. He had ridden from the coast, travelling since early morning through miles of deep forests and tiny hamlets. With a shiver he pulled up the collar of his cloak about his ears. 'It would have been better if I had stayed overnight at Higham Hall,' he thought to himself. 'I would have been made welcome there, but in this desolate waste, there is no place I know.' Thomas Mayhew had begun to feel quite sorry for himself.

As he reached the crest of the hill he could see a little brook dancing over the meadow to join its big sister the River Lea. Dismounting, he led his horse to the clear rippling water. As the horse drank, Thomas stretched his legs, only realising then how very saddle-sore and weary he was. For a moment he was heartened by the sight of a dim light to the left. But then realising what it was, his heart sank. 'Brook House,' he muttered. 'No good going up there. Robert Carr and the Brook family were not exactly friends, so they'll not welcome me.'

Thomas looked across the wet green fields ahead of him and stroked his black pointed beard. It was dangerous country, this Lammas land, he thought. People talked of witches who danced out there at Lammas Tide. Again he shivered and pulled his cloak tighter around him. Better ride on, he thought, turning to his horse to remount.

Through the still air came a sound like the whimpering of an animal. Peering towards the long grass at the side of the brook, Thomas suddenly saw a young girl lying there, and sobbing as though her heart would break. He went over and gently lifted her up.

'What's the matter, lass?' he asked softly.

The girl did not answer but her thin shoulders shook with distress. She tried hard to pull away from him but he held her firm.

'What are you doing out here all alone?' he asked. 'Has your lover deserted you?'

The girl struggled under Thomas' hand. 'No, no,' she sobbed. 'It's my mother.'

Thomas took hold of her arm. He held her firmly but continued to speak softly. 'Come now, let's go and find your mother. It's much too cold to be out here.'

'They will kill her when dawn breaks!' The girl's voice rose hysterically.

'Who will kill her?' Thomas felt himself losing his patience. Soon it would be dawn and the air had got colder. All he wanted was a warm bed. 'I can't leave you out here, that's for sure,' he muttered.

Reaching out, he lifted her small thin body up on to his horse, and then remounted himself. And with the girl's shivering body pressed close to him, Thomas turned towards the rising sun.

As they rode across the wet grass, he glanced down at the tear-stained face at his shoulder. She was not a bad-looking little girl, he thought – thin with long delicate features, which were not at all usual among the common people. She looked about thirteen, and he wondered who she was.

After a while the girl's shivers stopped and she began to talk. 'Oh dear, good sir, please help me,' she pleaded. 'They have dragged my mother from our bed and done terrible things to her. They say they will drown her in the pond today at daybreak.'

Her hazel-brown eyes stared pathetically up at him, and Thomas felt a sudden surge of protective anger. 'What devils!' he exclaimed. 'But why?'

'They say she is a witch,' the girl wailed. 'But it is not true. She is the dearest mother in all the world.' The sobs came forth again.

Thomas had begun to feel doubtful. Perhaps he should have left the girl where he had found her. He couldn't afford to get mixed up in a witch hunt.

'Where's the nearest inn?' he asked.

'The Duke's Head at Hackney. It belongs to my stepfather.'

'Well! I'd better return you to him,' Thomas replied with a feeling of relief. At last he knew what to do with her.

'But my mother . . .' she begged. 'Please, you must help her!'

'We will see,' he muttered soothingly to try to keep her quiet. Luckily, she seemed content at this answer and settled down against his chest.

Thomas drew her closer and was surprized to realize that he felt a strange affinity with this young maid, who sat waiting so confidently for him to help her.

At last the sun came up in the east, a huge red ball of fire. They crested the hill and went down into a green valley, which was grey in the misty morning sun.

'Down there! That's where they are!' The girl pointed excitedly as they rode down towards a small village.

'What's your name?' asked Thomas.

'Marcelle,' she replied, 'Marcelle de la Strange.'

'Isn't that French?'

'Yes, we came here from France last year, but my father's enemies followed him and killed him, out there beside the brook.' Her voice wavered as she added: 'That's why I ran to the brook, to call on the spirit of my father to help my mother in her distress.'

They reached the bottom of the slope and there was no mistaking the sound of a mob – the mutters and moans of angry excited voices and above them every now and then rose a piercing scream.

Marcelle held on tight as Thomas whipped up his horse and charged down the hill. A large group of people stood around a pond screaming and jeering at a woman in the water. As she struggled to get above the water, she was pushed down again with long sticks. Her screams were terrible. The crowd were not only trying to drown her but were throwing bricks and filth at her as well. Marcelle pressed her little face close to his chest as Thomas rode into the crowd, drawing his sword and striking all around him. When he had pushed them back from the edge of the pond, he dropped from his horse's back to the ground and waded into the water. Grasping the poor bedraggled bundle he pulled her out and laid her onto the grass. But he could see it was too late. The woman's hair had been torn out in lumps, and her face and body were a mass of wounds. They had tortured the poor defence-less woman literally to the point of death.

Thomas felt sick, and trembled with rage at the sight of the dead woman. But who had been responsi-ble for this terrible deed?

The crowd drifted off, still hurling insults at the man who had spoiled their fun. As he turned again to the sodden body on the ground, some manservants, saying that they came from Brook House, offered to help. 'We will take her inside until someone claims the body,' said an old man in coachman's livery. He lifted the poor ragged burden from the ground, but Marcelle clung on to her mother's arm, which was almost as thin as her own.

'Oh, don't leave me!' she cried out. 'Please don't take her away.'

But firmly the old man carried the wet body off and Thomas held Marcelle in his arms until her weeping had died down. 'Let's go and find this stepfather of yours,' he said gently. He lifted her back on to his horse and rode with the sobbing, shivering girl towards Hackney.

It was a rural village, Hackney, with a Norman church. On the village green stood stocks in which Marcelle's poor mother had spent her last night.

'It's here,' Marcelle whispered. 'This is where I live.' They were heading towards an inn lying back off the main track. A big gateway opened on to a cobbled courtyard and above it a sign swung in the breeze. 'The Duke's Head'. It was very quiet and no one was about, but as soon as Thomas had lifted her down from the horse, Marcelle gave a terrified glance at the door. 'I'll not see him!' she cried and scuttled off around the back of the house like a young rabbit.

Thomas Mayhew was astonished and stared after her. Taking off his round flat hat, with Robert Carr's crest embroidered on it, he scratched his head and rolled his eyes.

'Well, there's gratitude!' he chuckled. 'Well, I'll need to rest up, anyway.' He whistled and a bent old ostler appeared to take care of his horse.

Thomas went inside the inn. It was very dark inside. As his eyes became accustomed to the light, Thomas could make out a long low tap room and sawdust on the floor. Stalls, tables and trestles were dotted here and there about the place. Only two people were there – the landlord and a customer, a small, shrivelled old man wearing a smock. The landlord was big and brawny. Without a word, he served Thomas with ale and then turned back to his other customer. Thomas wondered whether to tell him about Marcelle and the death of his wife, but he decided to remain quiet. From his corner he drank the strong ale and listened to the conversation between the landlord and the old man.

The landlord looked like a rough customer. He had a recent cut on his head and his eyes were red-rimmed and raw-looking. He was not, Thomas thought, a very prepossessing fellow. He had a full, brutal-looking mouth and his unshaven chin was prickly with bristles.

The old man spoke in a hoarse whisper that was so loud Thomas could hear every word from where he sat.

'They got your woman.'

'Oh, yes?' the landlord shook his head. 'Upset me, I can tell you.'

'I thought you wanted to get rid of the missus,' piped up the old man.

'Shh!' hissed the landlord, glancing from side to side. But then he spoke in a louder voice. 'But she were a witch, right enough. See what she did to me . . .' He touched the recent cut on his head. 'Threw sawdust in me eyes and pushed me down the stairs. Wonder I live to tell the tale.'

The old man chuckled. 'I thought you fell down and she chucked sawdust 'cause you were trying yer old tricks on that little girl.'

The landlord's fat face went dark red. He squinted in the direction of Thomas, who was sitting perfectly still and pretending to doze. 'Shut your great mouth, old Jem,' he said, 'or else I'll shut it for you.'

Nattering and muttering, Jem made his way to the door. 'Made a fine mess of her in the stocks, they did,' he said with relish. 'I expect they have drowned her by now.' Shaking his head he disappeared.

The landlord began to polish the tankards in a fierce noisy manner until Thomas opened his eyes and asked the time of the day.

''Tis nearly nine o'clock,' the man replied, all smiles. 'Would you like something to eat, sir?'

'No, thanks,' said Thomas. 'I am on my way.' He felt a wave of anger at the ugly rogue in front of him, and wondered what had happened to the little girl. But it was not his business and he was expected at Whitehall. So he got his horse from the stables and continued his journey towards London.

He left Hackney and rode through the pretty hamlet of Kings Hold, passing another great manor house surrounded by green meadows. For some reason he could not stop thinking of that little girl. His shirt front still felt damp from her tears; perhaps he should have stayed behind and tried to find her. He felt sad, but at the same time he knew that it was no good sticking his head into other people's trouble. In times like these, no one was safe. And if he had not been such a fool in the past, he might have been in a better position today, instead of riding messenger for the despicable Robert Carr.

Thomas reached Bow Bridge and entered London. A foul smell hit his nostrils. It was disgusting and hung over the whole city. Londoners said it was the plague that brought it, but any foreigner knew that it was caused by the dirt and filth the Londoners lived in.

Already Thomas was longing for a breath of clean

air from his beloved Dorset, for the undulating moors and the golden sands down at Lulworth Cove, where he had first become aware of his urge to go to sea. In the distance was the grey Tower, where Sir Walter Raleigh, his old master, had been cooped up for the last ten years. Thomas' own father and brother had died in the service of that great man and Thomas knew that he would never have a master like that again.

The streets were getting narrower and more crowded. Crowds of people were swarming all over the place and ragged little children ran under his horse's hooves, begging for bread. Thomas felt sickened. What a desperate place it was by day, this poor part of the city!

As he approached the Fleet prison, he passed a horsedrawn cart guided from behind by a man carrying a long whip. Tied to the back of the cart was a man whose battered body showed that he was just completing a part of his punishment of being whipped at the cart's tail for four days. Thomas felt nauseous at the sight of it. There was no such sympathy from the crowd. People ran behind the cart shouting and jeering at the poor fellow tied to it, and each time the whip descended there were roars of delight and screeches of laughter. It was pure entertainment to them.

Thomas' strictly Puritan mind was shocked. It was all the fault of that Scottish devil King James! But it had not always been so. He could well remember when he had been a young page in the court of the great Queen Elizabeth. Recalling her last days, he could still picture her sitting propped up on the floor, her face yellow and wrinkled with pain and old age. But that astonishingly dominant spirit still shone out and the greatest of men were reduced to shivering wrecks by one angry look.

The Queen had been a real sovereign, someone to respect and look up to. But what had they now? This Scottish fellow did not command any respect, with all his pimps and hangers-on. He threw the country's good money away and toadied up to foreign powers such as Spain. Thomas felt his anger rise welling inside again. He was damned if he would not ask for his release and go off to Virginia again!

Soon he had skirted Saint James' Park and entered the Holbein gate of Whitehall. Fantastically dressed courtiers minced past him, Thomas frowned disapprovingly. 'More like foolish women than men,' he muttered.

Jumping from his horse and handing it over to the servants, he quickly went to the anteroom to wait to be called by his master and the King's favourite, Robert Carr. He sat quietly as other ushers and messengers sat about talking, and pages trotted in and out. The lofty room echoed with the sound of voices. But Thomas did not talk. He had not been nick-named, Dour Thomas for nothing. He had no use for talk of lechery or of the foolishness of the King, the usual topics of conversation at court, so he kept himself to himself.

Soon the call came and he followed the page to the sumptuous apartments of the effeminate Robert Carr. Thomas' master had hair as golden as a young girl's.

He was slim-waisted and elaborately dressed in velvets, braid and beads, lace and frills. He opened the letter Thomas had handed him and his face paled slightly as he read it.

'Stay around, Thomas Mayhew,' he ordered. 'I will have need of you to ride to Essex with me in a few days.' Then with an airy wave of his hand, he dismissed him.

Thomas walked to his lodgings. It had been a most depressing day. The image of Marcelle's little face lingered in his mind; he could hear her weeping and feel the soft brown sweep of her hair, like a sparrow's wing. That's it! She had been like a little bird. Would he ever see her again? he wondered.

When Marcelle had dropped from Thomas' horse, another terrible fear made her little body tremble. *He* was in there, that monster who had caused her mother's death, the pig who had made their lives hell these last three months. She knew she could not face entering that inn again, so she ran to the only person she knew, along a narrow alley, and between two hitching posts where tall wooden houses leaned lopsidedly over the street.

On the steps, taking in the air, sat Betsy. She was half dazed and clearly trying to get rid of the effects of last night's rendezvous with the bottle. It had been a busy night for Betsy up in the city. The gentlemen were always ready for a quickie in the alley and never minded paying. But a little drink always helped, and gave her a bit of Dutch courage. She was not a bad-looking girl, but to look at her she would have been taken for about twenty-five, when she was in fact only eighteen. Obliging the gentlemen since she was fifteen had aged her a lot, but she still had that fun, over-blown beauty. Blonde, with china-blue eyes, she had the sort of good looks that fade very quickly.

Betsy was Marcelle's only friend in England. They had met at the inn where Sam, her stepfather, employed Betsy when he had a rush of customers, and the two girls had become friends. So in the daytime, Betsy would sit on her steps on call, and when the situation at home became unbearable, Marcelle would seek her out and sit outside with her. With her rough-tough humour and love of life, Betsy was just what the gentle, confused little Marcelle needed. And now in her anguish, she ran to Betsy, jumping on her as she dozed.

'Blimey!' said Betsy, waking up with a start. 'That you Marci? You gave me quite a turn.'

'Oh! Betsy, Betsy.' Little Marcelle hung on to the older girl's greasy petticoats and laid her head on her lap. Here was a place of safety at last.

'What's up, love?' Betsy asked. 'Old Sam been up to his tricks again?'

'No, it's my mother,' Marcelle whispered in a small frightened voice. 'They have killed her.'

Betsy jumped to her feet. 'They haven't!' she exclaimed. 'My God, Rolly come down here!' she shouted into the hallway behind her.

Moments later, from the darkness came the tall gangling figure of Betsy's brother, Rolly. The boy's head lolled to one side and he drooled from his wide, open mouth, but his physique was magnificent. He was at least six foot tall, with huge shoulders and chest, giant hands and feet. He was truly a formidable figure. As he came outside, he looked sheepish, like a little boy caught stealing apples. One eye was damaged and a piece of flesh was missing from his ear. Betsy looked at him angrily.

'Rolly, what's all this about Marcelle's muvver?' she demanded.

'I dunno, he said.

'What you mean, you dunno? You was here watching out, wasn't yer?'

'Yus, I saw 'em but I never joined in, honest I didn't,' Rolly protested like a small child.

'Why didn't you wake me up, you stupid sod?' yelled Betsy.

'It was no good, they took her before you was home,' he muttered into his chin.

Betsy, arms akimbo, looked at Marcelle for confirmation of this.

'He's right,' answered Marcelle. 'They took her last night and they drowned her at dawn.'

'The bastards!' yelled Betsy, her pretty face flushed with rage. 'The dirty bastards! Rolly, go and find out who rounded them up, and don't come back till you do,' she shouted after her.

Rolly's tall shape ambled off down the alley immediately. He knew he had to go at once rather than annoy Betsy by hesitating. Theirs was a strange brother and sister relationship. He protected her physically, while she with her brains looked after him.

'Come indoors with me, love.' Betsy took Marcelle by the hand and they went inside the building. A long passageway led to Betsy's one room. Children played about and old folk lay in this corridor as if it were the last place to rest from a world that had no further use for them. The air was heavy with the rank smell of sweaty bodies.

Betsy's room was very bare, with only a rickety homemade table in the corner and two straw pallets on the floor. A brown jug stood on the table and beside it a tin cup. Betsy poured a drink for herself and knocked it back quickly. Then she poured one for Marcelle. 'Drink it, love, it will do you good. It's rum. A sailor gave it to me last week. He didn't have no money, so I took the goods.' She started to giggle and Marcelle's frightened eyes glanced around the poverty stricken room.

'Tain't much of a place, is it?' said Betsy. 'But never mind, it's better than the river arches. I made do with them till I got this room.'

She pulled out a little stool for Marcelle to sit on and from the corridor she found a wooden box for herself. As she sat down, she hitched up her skirt to reveal the scarlet quilted petticoat that she was so proud of and settled back with her legs wide apart and her bare feet on the dirty floor.

'You know, Marci,' Betsy said, 'you think it's a terrible world out there, but it's much worse down in the city, I can tell yer. Me and Rolly came up here when our folks died in the plague. And I ain't sorry. It might be a long walk down the town to earn a few shillings, but it's cleaner and safer up here.'

Marcelle felt warm and fuzzy with the fiery rum inside her. She sat hunched up on the stool, still feeling quite dazed by all that had happened to her.

Betsy looked at her sharply. 'For a girl like you it ain't going to be easy,' she said. 'I think you had better stay here.'

Marcelle looked around the hovel, and felt afraid. It was so stark and squalid, and Rolly slept here as well. Besides, her stepfather would find her soon enough. 'No, not here!' she stammered. 'I can't, but I can't go back to the inn, either. I'm too scared. He will get rid of me. I know too much about him.'

Betsy looked thoughtful. 'Not if I come with you,' she said. 'When Rolly comes back we'll go and see him. Rolly will stay here, otherwise he will be off down the cockpit and get himself all chewed up again. I have to keep an eye on the bleeder.'

Ten minutes later, Rolly came sidling in.

'Well,' demanded Betsy. 'What have you found out?'

'Sam paid men from London. The villagers never done it. That's what they say, Betsy,' Rolly replied.

'Where's old Sam now?'

'Gone up Brook House to see the lord. Says he's going to claim damages for the loss of his wife.'

'Bloody old hypocrite!' Betsy looked down at the frightened girl. 'Never mind, Marcelle, we will go back to the inn, and you must lock yourself in your room. I'll settle Sam, the old devil. Now, Rolly, don't you dare leave this alley! I'll be watching to see if you do.'

It took a bit of persuasion to make Marcelle move, but in the end, with Betsy holding her arm and Rolly dawdling along behind them, they walked down the alley towards the inn.

'How can we get in if it's shut up?' asked Betsy.

'Through the stables,' Marcelle replied.

They crept through the stables to a back door that led to the kitchen. Betsy's round blue eyes looked hungrily at the food left on the table. 'Crikey! Let's have a good tuck-in before old Sam gets back.'

Betsy busily cut off chunks of beef and pulled away hunks of bread, passing Rolly's share out of the window to him as he waited in the alley. Betsy wolfed down the food and belched loudly with a wide grin. But Marcelle was not hungry. Betsy shrugged and ate Marcelle's share as well, so hungry was she.

Marcelle quietly poured herself a mug of milk and took it upstairs. Betsy followed and tucked her up in bed. 'Now don't move or make a noise, luv, whatever you hear. Just trust old Betsy. I'll settle Sam, and I won't half enjoy doing it,' she said with a wink.

She closed the bedroom door and locked it, putting the key in her pocket while little Marcelle placed her weary head on the pillow and was immediately asleep.

Down in the alley, Rolly was playing with the children. He may have been very simple minded, but he had the physical strength of two men when roused. Confident of her brother's protection, Betsy stood in the doorway with her arms folded, waiting for Sam's return. Her sharp mind was ticking over quickly. At last she had got that old fool where she wanted him, she thought. He often employed her somewhat bizarre talents to amuse his customers, but the bloody old skinflint always took half the profits. Betsy had every intention of getting even with him and of taking care of little Marcelle at the same time. Feeling determined and tough, Betsy awaited the landlord's return, as she watched the kids chasing Rolly in the dirt.

2

Audley End

In the great dining hall of Brook House Sir Fulke Greville had finished his dinner and was now standing by the blazing log fire with a tall goblet of wine in his hand. He looked exceedingly annoyed. 'Well, what is all this business?' he demanded of a terrified-looking lackey. 'Am I always to be plagued by these devils while I eat a meal?'

'It's the husband of the woman Father Ben buried this morning, sir.' The servant looked nervously from side to side as he spoke. Priests were something one hardly dared mention nowadays since the gunpowder plot, though Brook House still sheltered Father Ben, their old Jesuit family priest. With money and influence most families were able to do this and the Grevilles was one family that had remained Catholic. But priests had to be kept hidden and have contact only with the old devoted family servants who looked after them.

When the body of Marcelle's mother was carried into Brook House, Father Ben had found a rosary and a locket sewn into her skirt. He had promptly given her a Catholic burial in a secret part of the grounds.

Sir Fulke was furious that now this damned heretic

husband had arrived to poke his nose in and cause trouble. He had to be silenced. 'I'll attend to him,' he said, moving towards the door. 'Bring two men to the entrance hall.'

Sam was grovelling on the black-and-white marble floor as two lackeys stood over him. 'My poor wife, your honour, dragged from her sick bed. I am left destitute, with no one to help me run the inn. And I have no money to buy help or bury her.' He crawled like a dog almost to Sir Fulke's feet.

The nobleman stared at him in disdain. 'Why did you not take better care of your wife, you rogue?' Sir Fulke roared at him. 'I've a good mind to have you punished for your carelessness.'

'They took her from me, your lordship,' Sam whined piteously. 'What am I to do, sir? I'm sure you understand that my livelihood depended on her, sir, and I loved her more than I can say . . .' He wiped his eye as if to clear away a tear.

Sir Fulke stared at this grovelling creature, not quite sure of how to respond. He was a sympathetic man at heart but also shrewd. He guessed that Sam the landlord would prefer a purse of coins to cheer him up rather than condolences or an arm around the shoulder. He was also eager to get him out of the house so that no more attention was brought there with its risks to Catholic sympathisers such as he.

Pulling a leather pouch from his belt, Sir Fulke dropped it on the floor where Sam still knelt. 'Take that for your loss, you rogue,' he said. 'Now, be off. And I never want to see you here again.'

Sam scrambled to his feet, bowing and scraping. He could hardly believe his luck. 'Thank you, sir, thank you,' he gasped, backing towards the door. 'My dear wife cannot be returned to me but your kindness goes a long way towards comforting me . . .'

But Sir Fulke had already turned and disappeared down the long corridor.

Sam stared at the purse for a moment, tossed it up and down gleefully, and then practically skipped back down towards his inn.

At the Duke's Head, Betsy was serving the customers when Sam walked in. He look astonished to see her in charge and stood by the door speechless for a moment.

Betsy put her hand on her hip and sidled up to him. 'I heard you was needing a woman about the house,' she said with a slow smile. She ran her hand over his buttocks. Sam backed away, astonished. 'I'll help you out in every way,' Betsy crooned. 'I'm very obliging . . .'

Still unable to believe his eyes and ears, Sam grinned stupidly and nodded.

And so it came about that Betsy installed herself as the lady in charge at the Duke's Head, willing to become Sam's bedmate in order to be Marcelle's protector. A kind-hearted girl, was Betsy, even if her method of going about things was a little unorthodox.

Everyone seemed settled and relatively happy, except little Marcelle, who crept about the building like a mouse, a scared look in her eyes, always watching in case she met Sam.

'Get that bloody girl working!' he would yell at Betsy, and Marcelle was given the most menial tasks to do. Betsy was kind and kept Sam away from her, but even she had always had a rough life herself and could not understand Marcelle's aversion to the life she lived.

Marcelle could hardly bear it, scrubbing wooden tables, washing dirty clothes and lighting fires from morning till night, until she fell into bed, often too tired to sleep. Under the thin blanket she would toss from side to side, praying desperately that God would be good to her and take her to her mother in heaven. Her little face got thinner and her shoulders grew rounded as her mind revolved continuously on how to end her life. She could not do it herself; to commit suicide would condemn her soul to hell. So she could only pray that God would be good and somehow let her die. Betsy frequently tried, as did Rolly, to make Marcelle laugh, but neither ever managed to raise even a flicker of a smile on her lips.

'Like a bloody scarecrow,' roared Sam when he caught sight of his stepdaughter one day. 'Just like her old mother, she is, a bit barmy.'

Betsy glared at him contemptuously. She was beginning to get a bit sick of him but her pockets were well lined. And on the nights when old Sam was drunk, Betsy went back to her old profession. Once Marcelle came upon her in a dark corner of the passage. Betsy's petticoats were up around her waist and a heaving, groaning gentleman was forcing her up against the wall. Poor little Marcelle was terrified and she felt quite sick. She had often heard whispers that Betsy was of easy virtue, but she had never known exactly what that meant. After seeing this sight, Marcelle hid in her room for days, until Betsy came to find her.

'What's wrong, darling? Do you feel ill?' Betsy asked.

Marcelle drew away from her. That terrible heaving image was still in her mind.

'Now come, love, you have got to pull yourself together,' Betsy implored her.

'Oh, how can you sleep with that disgusting man after the things he did to my mother?'

Betsy stroked the girl's hair gently. 'Hush, love, don't worry, I only do it for gain. It's nothing to me. And I think 'tis better for you to take a man and then you wouldn't feel so unhappy. I had men when I was thirteen,' she added almost proudly.

But Marcelle threw herself on her knees beside a little statue of the Virgin Mary. 'Oh dear good lady, mother of Our Lord, shut my ears from this talk. Help me to come to you.' She prayed wildly.

Betsy went to the door. 'Well, you're a strange one,' she said. 'And no mistake, I suppose you want to be a nun, but you can't, my love. Old King Jamie killed off all the priests and their lady friends as well.' With that she went off to the taproom, leaving Marcelle to her prayers and her misery.

Sam was down in the taproom and glared at Betsy when she came in. His vicious face was almost blue from the ale he had consumed. 'Where the hell have you been?'

'Up to see Marci, she's not well.'

'She never is – like that bitch of a mother.'

Betsy filled Sam's tankard from the barrel. 'How did you come to marry 'er?'

'Never did!' he roared with laughter. 'But she didn't know that. She wouldn't let me have it until I married her, but she had a nice little packet of money and jewels, she did.' Sam paused for a moment, gloating at his cleverness. 'So I got the blacksmith to perform the ceremony. Silly old bitch, didn't speak enough English to know the difference.'

'What happened to her first husband?' Betsy wanted to get the truth out of him while he was drunk.

'They arrived one foggy night about a year ago, just three of them – man, woman and the child. They looked like they had travelled a long way. I gave them a room and after they retired, two strangers came in and asked if I'd seen them.' Sam's face assumed a very crafty expression. 'Well what was I to do? They paid me well and I took up a message for him to meet them. He left his wife and kid here, and rode out and never came back. The watch found his body out on the marsh. Put up a good fight, he had, but he was hacked almost to pieces. So me, with me kind heart, I looked after that little widow, I did.' As he began to cackle uncontrollably, Betsy looked at him with hatred in her eyes. One day he would get his come-uppance.

Hanging about in Whitehall was getting on Thomas Mayhew's nerves. For days he had been waiting for that effeminate pimp Robert Cart, and still he was shilly-shallying, changing his mind five times a day. 'Tell the messenger to stay,' Carr had first ordered. 'I'll go to Essex tomorrow.'

Three days had passed and Thomas Mayhew was still sitting in the antechamber watching the other retainers play dice and go off to spend mornings at the cock-pit. Bear-baiting and cock-fighting were popular sports, as was wrestling between men who would almost kill one another. No matter how much he tried not to, Thomas hated all these cruel sports and refused to join in with the crazed shouting from the excited audiences.

As he sat there, his mind travelled back to those pleasant evenings beside the cool rivers of Dorset, when he fished with his master's son, Cary. How gently the tiny fish had been removed from the hook, and how glad he had been to see them thrown back into the swift-flowing river. 'I must be a weak-minded fool,' he muttered to himself. 'I've no stomach for these blood sports.' He glanced about him and reminded himself that he had better be careful or one day he would speak his mind about more than blood sports. And undoubtedly it would be regarded as treason. His head would then decorate London Bridge, or perhaps would swing on the gibbet on top of a hill until his bones were bare of flesh . . . Occupied by these morbid thoughts, he stared out of the window and watched the young Prince Henry playing tennis out there in the gardens. The prince was tall and graceful, and the sun shone on his golden hair. He played with quick elegant poise. He was a grand lad, this sixteen-year-old heir to the English throne, and so different from his coarse bawdy homosexual father.

'Thomas Mayhew!' called a little page. 'Thomas Mayhew!' The words echoed down the stone corridors and Thomas quickly pulled himself together. So at last dear Robert was ready to ride, he thought with relief. About time! With long strides, his sword clanking at his side, Thomas headed towards the fabulous apartments of the King's favourite, and entered.

Amid the gold and scarlet brocade hangings of an enormous carved four-poster bed, sat Robert Carr. His pale face looked more worn than ever, and his long blond hair, elaborately curled, flowed about his head on to a silken pillow.

'Oh dear!' he sighed, sniffing at the bundle of herbs he always had to hand to ward off germs. (Robert Carr was terrified of germs; if someone sneezed he quaked in his shoes, in dread of catching some disease.) 'Stay there, don't come too close,' his high-pitched voice warned Thomas.

Thomas remained just inside the door, with a dour expression on his face. The smell of this room disgusted him. French perfume and some strong smelling herbs hung heavily in the air.

'Oh dear! I am sure I've been taken with something, I feel so ill,' Robert Carr held the herbs to his nose and lay back on his pillows, his eyes closed. He looked just like a swooning woman, thought Thomas with contempt.

'Give him the letter, Sobey,' Robert ordered his

secretary, who was sitting in the corner at a small writing desk.

The small dark gentleman handed Thomas a heavily sealed package. 'It's very important and very confidential,' he said. 'Go straight to your destination. If there is any trouble, you must see that it is destroyed.' There was an amused glint in Sobey's eye as he glanced over at dear Robert lying in the bed, for he knew exactly what was wrong with their master. He had annoyed His Majesty and was in the doghouse. But as soon as the news reached the King's ears that dear Robert was ill, he would forget his earlier irritation and trot in to Robert's apartment with a trayful of cossets to doctor and fuss his friend as he liked to.

So it seemed that this time Thomas would have to travel alone just to deliver a message. He glanced at the package – it was addressed to Frances Devereux, Countess of Essex, Audley End, Essex – tucked it under his arm, and left with a smart bow.

The following morning, at the end of February in the year 1610, Thomas Mayhew rode once more out of London. Dawn was just appearing and the city was beginning to wake. It had become warmer and there was an unexpected spring freshness in the air as Thomas passed through Bishopsgate. The carts laden with winter vegetables had begun pouring into the markets. Soon the streets would be alive with people, and no doubt there would be a prison hanging or a whipping for their further entertainment.

Thomas was not sorry to be leaving the squalor

behind but as he rode briskly along, his thoughts settled back on the inn where he had left little Marcelle. Surely it was somewhere along this road. He wondered again what had become of her, and he felt a faint stirring in his breast as he remembered her soft little body trembling like a trapped wild bird, pressed close to him for comfort. He glanced towards the green fields to his left, noting his route. If he kept to this road he would certainly pass the inn, and perhaps he would call in there. It would hold him up for a time, but Sobey had not said that the letter was urgent. Then he remembered the forest road after dark and changed his mind. No, he would call on the way back. So he quickly turned his horse's head, aimed it at the stile in the hedge and kicked into a gallop. His horse cleared the stile and cantered steadily over the soft meadows towards Epping Forest. Leaving the flat land behind, Thomas was soon high up on a hill and, looking down, he could see the dim shape of London and the river Lea, with its little sister the brook running alongside. He would definitely return.

The memory of little Marcelle would bring him back here. Spurring his horse, Thomas shifted his thoughts to Robert Carr. What was he doing writing to the Countess of Essex? Frances Devereux was a well-known bitch. Thomas knew her and had seen her at Whitehall many times, with her white hard face, which was strangely cold and beautiful at the same time. It had been rumoured that Prince Henry had been in love with her, which was why she had been married off so quickly. But still, at thirteen, she had been too young for marriage, Thomas thought. What did a girl of that age know of life? His mind drifted back to Marcelle. She was only about thirteen. He would like to marry a virginal girl, if ever he wed, he thought, but having seen the antics of the married ladies at court, he would have to make sure that he never lost her from his sight. Women were easy enough to get, even in his modest station in life. But most of them were riddled with pox, caught from some high and mighty lord. Thomas shuddered. Perhaps he could do without love.

He rode furiously through the forest, stopping only to water his horse. The deer ran out and dashed along the path in front of him. Once he spotted a pure white fawn. It was a rare sight and it seemed like an omen. But good or bad, he was not sure.

The forest thinned and there at last, nestling in the valley, was Audley End, home of the countess' parents. He rode through the tall iron gates and drew nearer to the beautiful house. It had belonged to one of Elizabeth's greatest courtiers, and money from the gold they brought from the Indies had been poured into building the house. Clipped yew hedges lined the wide drive. The entrance hall had a flight of marble steps leading to a great hall with a high carved ceiling in gold, red and green. Thomas held his breath. The old master's house at Sherbourne was impressive, but it was nothing compared with this. He gazed up at the vast oil paintings in the great hall – grave-faced Elizabethans staring down haughtily, in their white ruffs and red and purple velvets.

'Are you well, Thomas Mayhew?' The young countess greeted him as she sailed swiftly and gracefully down the ornate carved staircase. She was a Devereux by marriage only, if it could be called a marriage. Frances was a Howard from the blue blood of the land. She was tall, slim, and fair, with a dead white face. Her small mouth was set in a grim line, but large dark unhappy eyes stared out mockingly from this pale mask. She was not yet seventeen, but had been married to the Earl's son, Robert, for nearly four years. The weary look which came from those eyes could have belonged to a woman of forty.

Thomas knew the countess fairly well. He had known her as a child when she played in the Whitehall Gardens with the King's children, and he had been in the escort that had taken them to the Queen's Palace at Greenwich. He had often thought that Prince Henry and Frances Howard made a very good-looking pair. They were almost the same age, and he had a red gold head to contrast with her pale gold one. But the Prince's marriage into a great Catholic family such as the Howards was unthinkable.

Frances now escorted Thomas to a small side room and told her ladies to wait outside. In the room she turned and held out her slim white bejewelled hands, eager to get the package he had brought her. Thomas stood by the door while she read the letter. The room was a cosy little parlour. It had oak panelled walls, with large carvings of a Tudor rose and the gilded lily entwined. Bowls of freshly picked snowdrops were arranged round the room, and on the central table was a huge oriental vase containing winter jasmine. It was a pleasant, fresh-smelling room, and it reminded him of Frances herself – cool and calm but not sweet. Frances could never be sweet. The still coldness of death hung over Frances. Thomas shivered. He would not be sorry when this job was over.

'My ladies will take you to the servants' quarters to eat and rest.' Frances' bell-like voice rang in his ears. 'Return before the evening. I have another message for you.' With an imperious wave of her hand, she dismissed him.

Thomas went down to the warmth and the chatter of the kitchen, where people were working, eating and laughing. He felt very relieved to be in the company of sympathetic people after being with the iceberg Frances. The kitchen staff had another guest – an old friend of Thomas, called Will. Will was a flute player who sang for his supper. On his travels up and down the country, Thomas often met Will, who was a strange young man – part-preacher and part-minstrel. No one knew his background, but it was rumoured that he had been brought up in a monastery. But since the monasteries had been dissolved, he had wandered the countryside, playing and singing and preaching a strange religion which no one took seriously. He loved poetry that flowed almost involuntarily from his lips and he was known to have some powers of healing. Certainly, many poor people had great faith in his powers. His age was hard to define and his head was shaved so that it was smooth and completely white. And he always wore the same drab garments. Now in this warm kitchen, he sat astride the table and played wonderful songs such as 'The Merry Month of May' and 'Under the Green Wood Tree'. All the serving men and women sang in chorus and Thomas quickly joined in. Warm and safe in this merry company, he soon recovered his good humour.

3

The Duke's Head at Hackney

'Riding through the forest tonight, Thomas?' asked Will.

'Aye, I'll be returning to town before dusk,' replied Thomas.

'Then I'll ride with you,' answered Will in a soft gentle voice.

The kitchen staff found this conversation a great source of amusement. 'Tis no good, Will,' said one. 'Dour Thomas will not ward off the devil, he's too good a friend of his.'

Thomas was not too anxious to ride along with Will and his slow-winded old nag, but the man was good company and at night it was a lonely road. 'You are welcome to join me, Will,' he said. 'I'll be leaving soon.'

A manservant, in his gorgeous livery, was already waiting to conduct Thomas to the countess Frances who stood in the great hall with its black-and-white marble floor. She had dressed for supper in an emerald green gown that shimmered as the silken folds fell to the ground. There was a snow-white ruff at her neck and the front of her gown was cut very low so as to expose the top half of her creamy bosom. A little jewelled cap held her hair back from her face. Her strange eyes stared at Thomas insolently as she held out a package to him. 'Have I your attention, Thomas Mayhew?' she asked.

He nodded and bowed low over her hand.

'I want you to break your journey to deliver an important message for me. You will be well rewarded.'

'It is my pleasure, gracious lady,' returned Thomas courteously.

'Do you know a house called Craig Alva?' she asked. 'It is on the road to Leaford.'

'I do, my lady,' replied Thomas. 'I have delivered a message there before, for my master, Robert Carr.'

'Good, take this package to Mistress Lane and she will then give you a package for Robert Carr. Remember, it is very important and no one else is to know. I hope, Thomas Mayhew, that I have your loyalty.' She added the last sentence with a warning note in her voice.

'I have ridden as a royal messenger for ten years, my lady,' replied the unsmiling and rather annoyed Thomas.

Frances' lips twitched. 'No wonder they call you Dour Thomas,' she said, handing him the package. 'I'll see you get your reward.' Slowly and graciously, she retired.

Soon Will and Thomas were riding towards the sunset. The sky stretched red and yellow in the west. The sun, a golden ball, gradually sailed out of sight, and a hush descended on the forest as the birds settled in their nests. A blackbird gave its last glorious song of the evening and a young fawn suckled close to its mother's belly.

As they rode along Will sang in a soft melodious voice. They were strange tunes that just came into his head, with no rhythm and not a lot of rhyme. But they rolled off his lips like the whisper of a warm breeze.

> *It seems to me that the night is long,*
> *Dreams are mostly what goes on,*
> *I don't care, I'm running free,*
> *I'm the way a man likes to be.*

Thomas seldom smiled but his dark eyes gleamed with amusement as he now listened to Will's crooning.

> *Fair maiden is looking fine,*
> *Very glad she is no friend of mine.*

'If you mean the countess, Will,' said Thomas, 'she is no maiden. I think you must have run out of rhyme.'

But Will only chuckled and went on singing,

> *Ain't love true, go on do,*
> *Oh! why can't you?*

'So you have heard the rumour,' said Thomas. 'She is asking for a divorce.'

Will's reply still in rhyme came back:

> *Don't tell me, sire, it ain't true,*
> *Why can't I do what other men do?*
> *Poor Robert don't know what to do,*
> *But my lady knows the right sort of brew.*

'Be careful, Will,' warned Thomas. 'Remarks like that will likely lose your head for you.'

But Will just smiled gently and lapsed into silence.

'A son of the great Essex – impotent,' muttered Thomas. 'It hardly seems feasible.'

Then Thomas began to think of the package in his wallet and the break he had to make in his journey to Annabelle Lane's house. She could well be up to something, he thought. You never could trust these aristocrats. Still, it was not his business, so he cast it from his mind.

Now Will was singing 'Drink to Me Only', and Thomas hummed in tune with him until they left the forest behind them and came to the open land again. The full moon was high in the sky and shone down on the meadows giving them a silvery gown. The trees loomed tall at the road side, but there was not a sound in the still air except the soft drone of Will's voice and the steady clip clop of the horses' hooves.

Turning off at the top of the hill, Thomas asked, 'Are you coming with me, Will?'

'To sweet Annabelle's? Indeed I am,' trilled Will.

Thomas wondered vaguely how Will knew that he was going to see Annabelle Lane, but then with Will one would always wonder.

A gibbet at the top of the hill creaked and groaned in the soft breeze as the long-bleached bones swung to and fro in their chains.

'How do you do,' said Will, raising his little hat to the grim remains. 'An old friend of mine, he was, a wonderful friar.'

Thomas laughed with grim humour.

The large timber house soon came into sight appearing black and white in the silvery moonlight. Two tall chimneys stood guard on either side as the house lay back from the track surrounded by a lovely garden.

Their feet crunched on the rough path as they led their horses clopping round the back of the house to the stables. For several minutes Thomas then threw pebbles up at the first floor window until a head wearing a red nightcap appeared.

'Is that you, Thomas Mayhew? And is that Will with you?' a hoarse voice called from above. 'I will throw out the key and then you can make yourselves comfortable around the fire.'

A bundle of large keys was thrown out of the window and the head with the long pointed nightcap disappeared from sight.

The weary travellers let themselves into the tavern. It was warm and cosy in Annabelle's kitchen, with its well scrubbed tables and brightly polished brass pots. Will poked the dying fire to revive it. On one side of the brick oven they found a pot full of soup. The smell of mutton and onion broth was appetizing and irresistible. Thomas found two wooden bowls into which he ladled the broth and after this warming meal they settled down on the sheep skin rug to sleep.

In Annabelle Lane's hospitable home, travellers were seldom turned away. There was always a good fire and some hot food waiting for an unexpected visitor in the cold of winter. At five o'clock the next morning, the house came to life with the chatter of the local milkmaids, who awoke the two men asleep on the sheepskin rugs. While Will went out to the barn to chat to the maids as they did their milking, Thomas washed under the pump in the yard. Afterwards he stood by the window looking down into the sunlit valley towards London. He decided that he would stay for a meal before he set off again.

Old Abe Lane, the owner of the nightcap was now downstairs in the kitchen pottering about preparing a tray for Annabelle, who liked her breakfast in bed. Thomas had visited this house before but certain things about it always puzzled him, such as the warmth and hospitality of the place and the fact that the Lanes were never short of food. It all seemed to run on well-oiled wheels, very unlike some of the places he had stayed in.

Annabelle was fair, amiable and so obviously a lady that Thomas puzzled about what the attraction between her and Abe. He was so much older and very earthy – a citizen of the North Country, Thomas guessed, by the tone of his voice. Abe spent much of his time below stairs, fixing dainty dishes for Annabelle and waiting on her like a servant. Yet he was supposed to be her husband. And all the while, Annabelle, so gay, pretty and always so smart in her gowns, entertained the ladies who came to visit her in her private sitting room. Annabelle certainly had plenty of friends in the right places. She and Abe chose to live out here, a long way from the nearest town. And now here in

Thomas' wallet lay a letter for Annabelle from the Countess Frances. He could not but wonder what was behind it all.

Another odd feature of the Lane's house was Merlin, who lived in an attic at the top of the house. He was a strange creature who only appeared occasionally at meal times, as he did this morning as Thomas and Will sat in the kitchen. Merlin was tall and thin, and he always wore a long flapping gown which was covered with paint spots in multitudinous colours, oil and grease and even ink. Indeed, it was impossible to tell what the original colour of the garment was. His hair was long and he sported a straggly beard which was also stained with many colours, while his eyes, shining like black shoe buttons, never missed a thing.

'Morning, Merlin, got up nice and early,' chattered Will.

Merlin grunted and examined the shape of Will's shaven head very carefully, feeling and touching it all over. Then he pulled from a pocket a small trumpet-like object with which he proceeded to listen to Will's heart. 'The head's the same,' he muttered as he passed over to the stove and helped himself to porridge before toddling off again.

'I'll send you my head when I am dead, Merlin,' Will called out after him.

''Twill be sooner than thee thinks,' retorted old Merlin as he disappeared out of the room.

Annabelle had eaten her breakfast and was now up and about. She came forward to greet Thomas looking very attractive with her wide smile and tip-tilted nose. But she always looked good, a fact that Annabelle was very much aware of. She always flirted with any male she fancied, and it usually worked. Even Dour Thomas had fallen under her spell and liked Annabelle very much.

'How is my Lady?' Annabelle now asked Thomas brightly as Thomas handed her the letter.

'As fair and as far away as ever,' replied Thomas.

'Poor unhappy little thing. It's terrible for her in that great house away from the court and her devoted family.' Annabelle wiped away an unconvincing tear.

Thomas did not answer. He was not concerned with such things. His task was only to deliver the message, collect Annabelle's message for Robert Carr, and be away again.

'I must go to Merlin,' Annabelle said, turning away from Thomas. She then hurried across the floor with her black silk gown rustling, and her little embroidered cap sitting jauntily on her fair curls.

Old Abe swept the red brick floor of the kitchen with a broom of birch twigs. He did not say a word, merely glancing up from under his bushy brows as Annabelle swept past him.

'They say the plague is returning to London,' Abe told Thomas when his wife had gone.

'I had better stay here,' said Will caressing a young milkmaid.

'So you'll stay here then, Will?' Thomas got up from the bench.

'Yes, I'll stay for the spring fair. Mind how you ride Thomas.'

Astride his mount once more and the precious sealed package for Robert Carr, which Annabelle had slipped him before he left, in his wallet, Thomas rode down into the Lea valley until he came to the familiar little brook. This he followed as it rippled and gurgled on its way through the marshland until the tall tower of Brook House came in view. Then he was on his way to the Duke's Head in Hackney.

There had been quite a bit of excitement at the Duke's Head recently. Betsy had not been her usual good-tempered self at all, the reason being that the previous night her brother Rolly had run off. He had seen the Mummers marching by and, like a little child, had gone marching with them. He often did this – the call of the ring was too strong for him – and now he was off to Shoreditch, to the spring fair. Betsy was worried, for although she knew that he would come back, he would possibly be beaten to a pulp from fighting and wrestling for wages which no one ever paid him. Sometimes, on these occasions, he even ended up in the Fleet Prison and it cost a lot of money to get him out. Now Betsy was in two minds about whether to hitch up her skirts and run over the fields to get to town before Rolly did. But Sam, lord and master, had other ideas, and she and Sam had quarrelled incessantly all day long.

Marcelle was looking thinner and paler than ever, as she went about her tasks, trying hard to shut out the shouting and swearing that was going on around her. Over and over again, she recited the Lord's Prayer as she knelt down on her knees on the steps, scrubbing the entrance to the inn.

By nightfall, after the inn had closed and guests were all asleep, Sam and Betsy had started their fighting again. From downstairs came screams and shouts, and the sound of breaking glass, and thuds as objects were thrown about. Finally Betsy fell into Marcelle's room beaten to a standstill, since Rolly had not been around to defend her. Marcelle quickly locked the door and pushed a heavy chest up against it. Outside, Sam was drunk and vicious, stumbling down the corridors shouting and yelling.

'Send that skinny bitch out here!' he yelled. 'It's time she earned her keep. I'll learn her, she'll soon know what life's all about . . .'

With her legs weak and buckling, Marcelle knelt down to help poor Betsy whose nose was pouring blood. One of her eyes was closing, and her clothes were in ribbons. Her whole body seemed to be a mass of bruises from Sam's well-aimed boots. Sam continued to rant and rave outside Marcelle's firmly locked door until one of the guests, woken by the racket, called out angrily: 'Pox on you, landlord. Do I pay good money to listen to your drunken rages all night?'

It was only then that Sam calmed down and finally left them in peace. In bed, Marcelle cuddled the weeping Betsy to her.

The next morning, the bright sunshine shone through the bedroom window and brought in sounds of movement from the road outside – the clatter of carts taking produce to the city, the singing of the flower girls and the cries of the water carriers. Marcelle lay motionless in bed, gazing down at Betsy's poor battered face. Betsy lay on her back snoring. There was dried blood all around her mouth, her eyes was extremely swollen and her blonde hair, spread out over the pillow, was bloody and tangled. She was not a very nice sight to see so early in the morning, but Marcelle looked at her with pity in her eyes, and only saw her friend's pathetic, tear-stained face, not blousy Betsy. She turned towards the little statue of the Virgin, which had meant so much to her on those unhappy days. The Madonna had long golden hair and a bright blue dress painted on her wooden form. She seemed to smile sweetly at Marcelle. To this little virgin Marcelle always prayed, telling of her secret fears and kneeling long hours before her when her mind was troubled. This morning, however, suddenly seemed a special day and there was nothing to worry over. The Virgin's sweet smile on her little wooden face gave Marcelle confidence; there was nothing to worry about.

She crept out of bed and rearranged the little posy of wild flowers she kept beside the statue. As she did so, her thoughts flew back to another place where there were lots of flowers – fields of them – and with her was a woman with shiny black hair and rings in her ears. She could still hear her gay laughter and see the even white teeth as they flashed in a smile. Where was that place and who was the lady? Many times this memory picture came to Marcelle's mind, and she was sure that it was her old home in France. All she could remember of her journey to England was horses galloping, riding through the night, and a sense of apprehension. That was all. She would never know more now, for there was no one left to tell her. Now trapped in this terrible house, it was the end of her road. For a moment, tears of self-pity welled up in her eyes but then again she was given strength by this strange sweet sense of hope and happiness which returned to her. The little Virgin seemed to be trying to say that all was not lost. Pray, Marcelle, she seemed to say, and you will be guided. Marcelle fell down on her knees, hope and faith seemed to burst from her young heart.

Betsy stirred in the bed. 'Christ!' she muttered. 'I can't bloody move. I'm stiff and sore all over.'

With a little shudder at Betsy's swearing, Marcelle rose from her knees and went over to the bed.

'Got anything to drink, love?' asked Betsy.

'I'll get some water,' Marcelle replied gently.

'Gawd!' groaned Betsy. 'A lot of good that will do! Sneak down and get a jug of ale or some gin, can't seem to move. That swine has done for me.' She sat up holding her head in her hands.

Marcelle was frightened by the thought of going downstairs alone, and she hesitated. But Betsy's groans were getting louder as she called out: 'Go on, love, he will be in the bar this time of the day. Creep into the kitchen, there's a jug down the bottom of the larder.'

Glancing nervously from side to side, Marcelle crept slowly down the wooden stairs. It was very quiet in the kitchen but the room looked as if an earthquake had hit it. The pine table was overturned and stools lay on their sides. Broken crockery lay everywhere, and the walls and towels were all splattered with blood. A dreadful fear gripped her, paralyzing her like a rabbit trapped by the light of the torch. The dramatic signs of the violence of the night before made her feel weak with fear.

Next door in the bar, Sam leaned heavily on the counter. He did not feel too good himself this morning and his eyes were bloodshot. It was with a shaky hand that he served a dark young customer with ale. 'Sorry, sir,' he said, 'There's no food ready yet, my wife is a bit poorly this morning.'

Thomas Mayhew stared at this brutish-looking man, taking in with disgust the red-veined eyes and the purple bristly chin. He noticed that the landlord's crumpled shirt was filthy and blood-stained and certainly looked as if it had been slept in. Thomas was disgusted by the way Sam leaned over the counter, with the greasy bare flesh of his fat stomach bulging out of the space where his pants and shirt should have met.

It's just as well there's no food, thought Thomas. He never fancied eating in this place anyway. Thomas did not suppose it would be much good to ask after Sam's step-daughter. Indeed, he scarcely looked sober. Perhaps it was best just to drink his ale and be on his way.

Engrossed in these thoughts, he did not notice that the landlord had left the bar, until a shrill piercing scream came from another room. Thomas jumped to his feet and his hand shot up to his sword hilt. The scream came again and this time he recognized the voice. It was Marcelle. 'Betsy! Betsy! Help me!' she was crying, and suddenly two people rushed to her aid.

Downstairs tumbled a half-dressed Betsy just as Thomas vaulted the bar and rushed through the door with his sword drawn. As they entered the kitchen at the same time, what met their eyes was the sight of Sam holding Marcelle by the hair, his great hands jerking her head back viciously. Her dress had been torn from her thin shoulders. It seemed that he had crept in while she was busy pouring out a drink for Betsy, and he had pounced on the helpless girl.

'Steal from me, would you?' he had snarled. 'The law can have yer when I have finished with yer, skinny bitch.' He had grabbed her and started to tear off her clothes at which point she had screamed with mortal terror. It was this that both Thomas and Betsy had heard.

Arriving on the scene together, Betsy ran up and caught hold of the half-conscious girl, while Thomas, with the flat of his sword and the weight of his body, knocked Sam off balance. Down Sam went with a resounding crash that literally shook the floor, but he was up like a shot with a knife in his hand. 'A fancy man, aye?' he snarled. 'That's what she's up to!' With a roar, he lunged at Thomas.

Betsy screamed insults at Sam and encouragements to Thomas as they both dodged back and forth around the room. Suddenly the back door opened and Rolly's enormous figure shot in, throwing itself on the landlord's back and bringing him down with a loud crash to the floor. As this happened, they knocked Thomas' sword from his hand. There was a loud groan and a squelch as Sam rolled over, the point of the sword buried deep in his fat stomach.

The others all stood staring in silence at the gushes of blood and the little white balls of fat that burst out of the skin where it had been gashed.

Betsy turned from Sam's lifeless body to her brother. 'You silly fool!' she screeched. 'What yer want to do that for?'

Rolly looked sheepish. 'Sorry, Sis, I thought he was going to hurt you.'

'Well, he's done that for the last time,' replied Betsy. Now she was down on her knees and helplessly trying to stop the flow of blood with a cloth.

Thomas held the silent pale-faced Marcelle close to him. 'There's nothing to be done. He's dead,' he said flatly. Feeling somewhat sick, Thomas suddenly remembered the important message in his wallet. He went forward and locked the doors to the inn. 'We had better get him out of sight,' he said. 'Give me a hand here, Rolly.'

Together the men got Sam's heavy body down into the cellar while Betsy cleared up the mess in the kitchen. Marcelle was silent and boiled some water to make them hot spiced drinks.

As they sipped the steaming drinks, the four conspirators sat facing each other round the kitchen table contemplating what they should do. Thomas' pale calm face contrasted sharply with Betsy's frightened red visage. Rolly quietly looked from one to the other.

'What are we going to do?' asked Betsy.

'Well, I am not sure,' replied Thomas. 'If we say anything they will take you in for sure. I suppose we might say we found him dead.'

Suddenly Marcelle spoke. They had almost forgotten she was there for she had not said a word in all this time. But now she spoke with venom in her voice. 'He deserved to die,' she hissed. 'He killed my mother. I am glad he is dead, and I don't care if they hang me.'

Rolly gazed around him, goggle-eyed, at the thought of being hung. But Betsy's shrewd mind was ticking over. 'Look here, no one knows but us. We must just all trust each other. Rolly will get rid of the body tomorrow. Can we depend on you, sir? I don't know you from Adam and you wear the Royal Badge, but how do we stand with you?' she questioned Thomas sharply.

'I came to see if the girl was all right,' he said. 'I dare not be found here, for I carry a letter of Royal Command.'

Noticing the fanatical look in Marcelle's eyes, Betsy bit her lip thoughtfully. ''Tis the lass that's the problem,' she said to Thomas. 'She will tell all. She has religion and won't be able to help it.'

Thomas gave an understanding nod. 'She can come with me,' he said simply. 'That is, if she will. I will find shelter for her.'

'That's it!' declared Betsy. 'You take Marci and I'll take care of the rest. I ain't letting Rolly get shut up in a cage if I can help it.' Marcelle sat pale and still on a bench, muttering her prayers. She seemed not to care any more.

Betsy wrapped Marcelle in her warm cloak and made a parcel of the poor girl's few belongings. A frown creased Thomas' brow as he had a good look at Marcelle for the first time. She seemed to have become even thinner than he remembered her, and she looked like an imbecile with her eyes staring in front of her and her lips moving silently. Thomas went over and knelt beside her. Taking her hand in his, he said: 'Don't you want to come with me?' His voice was soft and gentle.

Marcelle smiled at him for the first time. 'I want to more than anything else in the world,' she said softly. 'I am praying to thank Our Lady for sending you to help me.'

Thomas wrinkled his forehead. What a strange child she was. Yet she was almost a woman, and not a bad-looking one either. His thoughts were very jumbled. What the hell was he getting into? And where should he take her? Certainly not to his lodgings. It was then he thought of Annabelle Lane's bright, happy house. Yes, he would ride back to Craig Alva. Annabelle would not turn the girl away, of that he was sure.

At mid-day, Thomas rode back down the road with

Marcelle tucked up warm and close beside him. His heart thumped madly, though he was not sure why. As he looked down at her fine, pointed features, she gazed up at him from under a dark green hood. Her bright eyes looked up at him trustingly and he felt a strong urge to stroke that shiny, nut-brown hair. He cuddled the girl close as they rode back down the Lea Valley to Annabelle's house.

The morning had been fine but was now growing colder, but Marcelle, feeling warm and cosy, neither knew nor cared where she was going. They followed the little brook over the marshland and, once over the wooden bridge that crossed the Lea, the road wound upwards and the air became fresher as they came towards the forest.

Marcelle's thin nose gave an appreciative sniff. 'It's lovely to leave the smell of the town behind,' she murmured.

''Tis a fine place out here in Essex. It reminds me of my home in Dorset,' replied Thomas.

Soon the thatched roof and the black timbers of Craig Alva came in sight. As they rode towards the house, they passed the old church at Chingford, which stood squarely built with its Norman tower. It had not been neglected as many of the churches in town had been since the Reformation, but was cool and peaceful looking. It was in good condition and even the stained glass windows were still intact. Marcelle stared at it with interest. 'Is that a Catholic church?' she asked.

'No, lass,' replied Thomas. 'Now you must forget

your Popish religion. Today it is Anglican which is as near to Catholic as you will get.'

Marcelle looked longingly at the church as they passed by. How she would love to go regularly to church once more, as she used to with her parents before they all came to England.

As they drew near to Annabelle's house, they spied Will sitting on the lawn. With him were two milk-maids in white caps, sitting beside him as he strummed on his viol. They listened to his sweet voice and made garlands of laurel leaves to hang around his neck.

When Thomas rode up, a grin crept across Will's face as he chanted: 'The Royal rogue has returned, for the little white fawn he brings, he yearns.'

'Is that how you earn your keep?' growled Thomas as they passed.

Abe Lane was busy in the kitchen but greeted Thomas cheerfully. 'Back so soon, Dour Thomas? And who is this, your mistress?' From under his bushy eyebrows, he stared at the shy Marcelle.

'No, 'tis my kin,' lied Thomas. 'I want her to stay a while. Can I see Annabelle?'

'She's in the parlour at this time of day,' Abe replied, bringing a glass of cool, foaming milk for Marcelle. 'Drink this, little one,' he said kindly. 'It will refresh you, you look so tired.'

Marcelle thanked this funny looking old man. How kind and thoughtful he was. The gentle atmosphere in this house helped to dispel her fears.

While Marcelle sat with Abe Lane in the cosy

kitchen, Thomas went off to find Annabelle. She was in her parlour getting it ready for the great ladies who visited in the afternoons. Annabelle was brought up on the Howard estate and, as a young girl, had been a maid to Frances Howard. Thus she had been under the influence of Frances' notorious step-mother, the Duchess of Suffolk, who was generally known to dabble in the black magic arts. Annabelle shared the dark secrets of this famous Howard family and now lived in semi-retirement with Abe at Craig Alva. The court ladies came to visit Annabelle because of her knowledge of love potions and evil concoctions. And now in her parlour she stood by the window with the sun shining down on her brassy blonde hair. When Thomas entered, Annabelle was arranging tall sprays of jasmine in a bronze jar. Her dainty artistic hands almost caressed the blooms, but her brown eyes seemed to grow darker and her face grew pale when she saw her visitor. The sweet smile died on her lips and her face was suddenly hard and questioning. 'Back so soon, Dour Thomas? Is there anything amiss?'

'Be calm,' Thomas raised his hand as if to reassure her. 'There is nothing wrong. I have returned for reasons of my own. The despatch is still safe in my wallet.'

Annabelle visibly relaxed and the sweet dimples returned as she smiled at him. With her little turned-up nose and the snow-white cap on the back of her head, she was an appealing sort of person, whom kind men loved to protect, but under that golden thatch of hair lay a brain of amazing quality. A shrewd bargaining brain combined with a gay appraisal of life that gave her such power over the less intelligent well-brought-up ladies of the land. It allowed her to live comfortably and be independent.

'Be seated, Dour Thomas,' she said. 'If that's all your mission is, I am content.'

Thomas sat on a low embroidered stool and Annabelle seated herself facing him in a carved oak chair. Her black silk dress with its white ruffs at the neck was immaculate.

Thomas was fond of Annabelle but he never felt quite at ease with her. He often felt that those clever brown eyes delved deep into his mind. 'I have a special favour to ask you, madam, and then I must be away, for my master will be getting concerned.'

'Well then, what is it? A love potion or worse?' Annabelle joked.

'I have brought a young lady back here and I want you to shelter her for a while.'

'A mistress, Thomas?' Annabelle smiled and raised her eyebrows. 'I am very pleased for you.'

Thomas wanted to keep up his lie. 'No, just a cousin in distress,' he said. 'She is well born but has fallen on hard times. I will pay for her keep, and I can assure you she is trustworthy.'

'Well, where is she?' Annabelle asked brightly.

'With Abe at the moment. Shall I go and fetch her?'

'No, I will come down. I am finished up here for a while.'

Gracefully, Annabelle led the way down the wide oak stairway to the kitchen where Marcelle was still sitting with Abe. A small kitten lay curled up on her knee, and the colour had returned to her cheeks. As she stroked the little cat's sleek fur, she looked very calm and content.

When Annabelle saw Marcelle, her brown eyes softened, noticeably. The girl reminded her of her own daughter who had died of smallpox at the age of five. She would be fifteen now, had she lived.

'Hullo, my dear,' Annabelle greeted Marcelle. 'You are most welcome. Your home is with me until Thomas and you are wed.'

Thomas cast a surprised look at Annabelle. She still had the wrong idea but there was no sense in arguing. As a matter of fact, he had no serious intention of ever being married.

Marcelle looked quickly up at Thomas, the same question in her eyes, and he patted her hand. 'Must be off. I will be in to see you the next trip,' he said. 'Farewell for the present.'

So off rode Thomas once more. Now he did not notice the scenery about him but thought only of Marcelle and her warm little body so close to him on the horse when they rode together. He realised that he felt good, warm and peaceful. Something odd was happening to him but he did not mind at all. He turned towards the fields and urged his horse on, to gallop like mad, leaping ditches and fences on their way to London.

The journey seemed much quicker than usual

and, when the effeminate Robert Carr snapped and snarled at him for being so late, Thomas only grinned. 'My mount went lame on me,' was the only excuse he gave.

4

Craig Alva

After Thomas had left, Marcelle found that she was not alone in this cheerful home. How could she be? The bright surroundings and pleasant people all reminded her of that home in the distant past of which now her memory gave her only fleeting glimpses.

Most of that afternoon, she played with the kittens. There were three of them, all the babies of a big black and white cat called Mini, who kept them warm and snug in a cupboard under the stairs.

Old Abe was clearly very fond of them too, and was pleased to see that Marcelle liked them so much. 'Don't let *him* see them,' he whispered hoarsely pointing at the ceiling. The grave expression on his face made it clear that he was deadly serious.

Marcelle was puzzled. Who on earth was up there? And why was Abe so afraid? Who or what could ever want to hurt his cats?

'He'll take them, he will,' muttered Abe. 'Torture them, he does. Look what he did to Mini.' Lifting up the cat, he showed Marcelle a scar and Mini's tail, which had a piece missing from it.

'Why does *he* want to hurt them?' enquired Marcelle, still wondering who *he* was.

'Can't help himself,' whispered Abe patting his head. 'He's not quite right.'

Marcelle would have liked to continue the conversation but at that moment the door opened and in stepped a man. With a sweeping bow, he took off his funny hat and said: 'I greet thee, little white faun from the forest.'

'Oh, Will's off,' grumbled Abe and bustled away to finish his chores.

Marcelle stared half shyly and half aggressively at Will. Was this the odd one who hurt animals? She was not one to like him if he was. But then she looked into his merry grey eyes, and at his foolish grin which she found quite contagious, she was sure that he could not hurt any animal ever. So he was not the one Abe had been afraid of.

Later that evening, they all sat down to supper – Marcelle, Annabelle, Abe, Will and the two girls who worked in the dairy. In the large warm kitchen with its low oak beams the conversation was merry and the food excellent. They sat up until very late, drinking home-brewed wine and swapping stories. After they had eaten, Marcelle sat on the floor near Annabelle's knee. Annabelle reached out and stroked the girl's shiny hair over and over again. There was warmth and love here and Marcelle knew she was going to be happy.

In the little room at the top of the stairs, a room which was to be her very own, Marcelle prepared for bed. Annabelle brought hot water for her to wash with and then plaited her hair before tucking her snugly into bed. 'How old are you, Marcelle?' she asked.

'I'll be fifteen in September,' replied Marcelle.

'You look younger, I suppose that's because you are so small and thin. You have a fragile beauty,' she remarked, looking intently into Marcelle's face. 'I would have had a daughter your age,' she said, a little sadly. 'But she died when she was only five years old.' The sad expression lingered for a moment, but then her quick smile was soon restored. 'We must fatten you up for Dour Thomas,' she joked. 'He has waited a long time to choose a bride. But he has chosen well. Goodnight, love, sleep well,' she said gently as she blew out the candle and tiptoed out of the room.

As Annabelle went along the long polished corridor to her own chamber, her thoughts were upon the new guest in her home. Why was it that this child reminded her so much of herself at that age? It must be because she had been fifteen when she married Abe. Her mind drifted back to her childhood and the lodge where she was born. She undressed and climbed into her lovely bed with its lavender silk hangings. It had been a wedding present from her mistress, the Duchess of Suffolk, mother of Frances Howard, now the Countess of Essex. But it was a lonely bed now, occupied only by Annabelle. Where Abe slept, she was not sure – probably in the communal guest room on the bottom floor. He no longer shared her bed and had not done so for many years. As she tossed restlessly in bed, she recalled her wedding night. How terrified she had been and how awkward and embarrassed Abe had been. He had been forty-five and she fifteen. It was a big age difference, and they did not choose each other. Abe never liked women much and Annabelle had seen few men in her young life as a lodge-keeper's daughter at the Howard country estate. The Duchess had thought it best for servants to marry, believing that they settled down and were more easily controlled, so every effort was made to get Abe the coachman, a wife. He was getting on a bit and his cottage was meant for two not one. So it was that little golden-haired Annabelle, the children's nursemaid, was chosen. Naturally, she rebelled but it made no difference; her father was too much under the influence of the great Howards.

It seemed a very long night to Annabelle as she continued to lie awake, with her thoughts going back down the road of her life. She pulled up the bed covers impatiently. What the hell was the matter with her? She was not usually one to get so moody. Perhaps she was a bit jealous of this youthful little girl, Marcelle. Had she fancied Dour Thomas herself so that seeing him with this young girl had been a shock to her? No, it could not be that. No, that was not the problem. Thomas was too humourless to interest her. A man must be gay and debonair to attract her, just as Donald had been. Her dearest, handsome, Donald . . . She had been seventeen when she had fallen in love with him. Little shivers ran up and down her spine as she remembered those lovely long hours they had spent making love under the tall pines in the woods near her home. She had already been married three years but had been starved of true sex, so her affair with Donald had been wonderful and unforgettable. All the happiness

and even the tragedy that followed, were worth it all –
that is, apart from losing the child. And the memory of
that would never go, particularly of that charming
Donald with his smart kilted outfit and his lovely smile.
But their love had brought with it so many tragedies
before she was even twenty-one. Her affair with
Donald had been discovered but she was already pregnant and had given birth to a daughter. Outraged, the
Duchess had Donald shut up in prison for daring to
interfere with the wife of her coachman. It was already
well known that there could be no children from that
union, so Annabelle was trapped. But over the years
the Duchess made fine use of Donald's clever brain
and his extraordinary knowledge of medical matters
and allowed him the means to experiment in her black
magic cults. Imprisoned thus, Donald's mental state
had deteriorated, and then Annabelle's little girl, the
love child, died of smallpox. When he heard of this
Donald collapsed and never recovered. And he
announced that he was only to be called Merlin from
then on. Soon the Duchess tired of him, and when
Abe and Annabelle moved away, they took Merlin
with them. Merlin now lived in the attic at Craig Alva,
where he was always busy experimenting with medicines and black magic. He was frequently made use of
by Annabelle and Frances Howard who had much
need of the poisons and evil potions which were relied
upon in those days before sophisticated medicines.

In her room, Marcelle slept peacefully, knowing
nothing of the sleepless fears of Annabelle. She awoke
the next morning to fresh spring sunshine and the

song of the birds. Suddenly she felt so different, light, free, gay and happy as she stood at the window in her long white bedgown and watched old Abe bringing in the cows from the meadow to be milked. It is lovely here, she told herself, looking over the long sweep of meadowland to the dark green forest in the distance. On the hill stood a church with a square tower. 'That is what I would like to do,' she said out loud. 'I would like to go to church and thank God for this haven of rest and sanctuary.'

She dressed and went downstairs. Abe was back in the kitchen washing his hands at the pump. He was a queer-looking old fellow, grey and bent, but full of vitality. With his bulbous nose and pink-lined face, he reminded Marcelle of a pet rabbit she had once owned, particularly when he hopped and jumped everywhere as he tended to do.

'Morning, darling,' Abe greeted her. 'There's porridge on the fireside.'

'Let me help you,' she offered. 'I am used to being busy.'

Abe's bright eyes gleamed under the bushy eyebrows. 'Aye, there's plenty to do, lass,' he said. 'What with the garden and the house, I would be mightily glad of some help.'

And so it was that Marcelle and Abe became very close friends. Between them they cooked the meat and picked and prepared the vegetables and carried trays of food to the guests who frequently stayed. Marcelle was quick, bright and always willing, and Abe grew very fond of her.

Annabelle usually appeared about lunchtime when all the chores had been done, only to disappear again to her pretty little parlour where several visitors would arrive, mostly in great springless coaches but some arrived in sedan chairs carried by uniformed lackies who, having delivered their burden, would proceed to the kitchen to await the laborious journey home.

It was always lively and interesting down in Abe's kitchen, with lively conversation, plenty of good food and gossip. Within a few weeks, Marcelle's cheeks had filled out and her skin had lost its yellow pallor.

'How do you like our pretty new lass?' Abe would ask of the young men who idled about his kitchen.

'She be sweet. Is there a chance for me?' one asked.

But Abe shook his head. 'Betrothed to Dour Thomas, she is, and a royal messenger, he is.'

Listening to this exchange, Marcelle wondered whose idea it was that she should marry Dour Thomas, for so far they had never discussed it, and she had certainly not been consulted.

A week later, Thomas paid them a short visit. He and Marcelle walked in the woods together and stopped by the stile, where he looked at her strangely, his dark eyes soft for a moment as the hardness around his mouth disappeared. Marcelle would have loved to put her arms around his neck but a strange shyness possessed her. Their eyes held that look just for a second, but then Thomas said: 'Come on lass, it is getting late,' taking her hand. They walked back together to the cheery warmth of Abe's fire. 'I am very glad to see that you are happy here,' Thomas said before he left. 'I'll not be coming this way for a while. The King takes a hunting trip soon, so I expect Robert Carr will command me to go along.'

'Will you be away long?' asked Marcelle, trying to hide the disappointment in her voice.

'Several months,' replied Thomas. 'But don't worry, you will be safe here, little one.' He spoke gently as he caressed her cheek. Then he mounted his horse and rode away.

Will rode with him and Marcelle was doubly sad. She was going to miss Will's lively company. It was Will who sang all day and kept everyone merry. And the previous week he had taken her to the village fair. It had been a wonderful, exciting event, with Morris dancers and bears and all sorts of performing people and beasts. Crowded stalls had sold gingerbread and brandy snaps, and the local people had had a wonderful time. Then at nightfall Will had sat in a big tent strumming on his viol and everyone had sung and danced together – old, young and even the children. For Marcelle it had been a grand thrill all day. And then when they came home on the back of an old donkey, Will was much the worse for drink and kept falling off, at which point the donkey would immediately turn around and head in the other direction. Marcelle, who had known only tears and sadness in the last year, giggled and laughed until she was quite exhausted.

But when Annabelle found out about this outing, she had been furious, lashing out with her tongue at both Will and Marcelle. 'Young ladies do not go to

fairs,' she said angrily. 'Whatever would I say to Dour
Thomas if anything should happen to you, Marcelle?'

Marcelle had no idea of what was likely to happen,
but she dropped her head meekly and said: 'I am sorry,
Annabelle but it was all so funny and after all, Will was
with me.'

After that, Annabelle clearly decided to keep a
closer eye on Marcelle, so every afternoon the girl was
taken up to the parlour to accompany Annabelle while
she gossiped and passed round drinks to her friends.
Marcelle was made to sit amongst them all and sew
pretty dresses for her trousseau.

In the recess behind a silk curtain in Annabelle's
room there were many dresses made from lovely
satins, brocades and fur. They were all mostly gifts,
cast-offs from Annabelle's more wealthy friends. 'I'll
never wear this lot out,' she had told Marcelle one day,
'I'll tell you what we will do. We will cut them to fit you
and make them fashionable, so that when Dour
Thomas gets quarters for you at court you will be
smart and pretty, and we will all be proud of you.'

Annabelle had a heart of gold, and was always so
generous with her love and possessions.

'Everybody loves Annabelle,' said Abe. 'She has not
a mean streak in her anywhere.'

But from her vantage point, Marcelle, often saw a
different side to Annabelle, a side hidden from the rest
of the household. As she sat quietly sewing in the
corner of that bright little parlour, Marcelle would
observe all the grand ladies with their high-pitched
cackles who discussed in whispers some choice

scandals and were entertained by a smart, alert, very hard and brittle Annabelle. And when all these smart ladies had all gone, Annabelle would put an arm around Marcelle's shoulders and say bitterly, 'Those bitches, they are damned stinking bitches. Come on, darling, let us go downstairs.'

There was one place in the house that Marcelle hated and that was on the top floor, where she seldom ever went. For she was terrified of old Merlin. Her first trip to his quarters had been a great shock. She had seen this tall thin man in a long smock down in the kitchen several times. He never spoke to her but would tilt her chin up and gaze directly into her eyes pinning her, she felt, like a trapped animal. It was enough to make anyone terrified. Then one day, she had been forced to see him upstairs.

'Merlin has not been down today,' said Annabelle. 'Take his food up, will you Marcelle, dear?'

With a heavily laden tray she climbed the gloomy stairs up to the big attic where Merlin lived. It was dark and dismal up there, dust and cobwebs were everywhere. By the time she had reached the heavy oak door to Merlin's room, she felt as if her heart was in her mouth. She gave a gentle tap on the door. No reply. With her foot she pushed open the door which swung open slowly with a protesting whine. Marcelle stood and stared open-mouthed at the sight which met her startled gaze. Before her was a great dingy room with lots of dark corners from which strange faces stared at her. In the middle of the room was a large table from which a very strange blue light came and there, holding a smoking glass bowl, stood Merlin. His hair was hanging over his face and he was muttering wildly as he stirred the smoking glass. Suddenly he became aware of her presence. 'Enter!' he called irritably. 'And shut the door. You are making a draught.'

Marcelle was dumbstruck. She grasped the tray tightly and then, on shaking legs, she crept towards the centre of the room looking for somewhere amongst all the debris to put down the tray. Then the next sight sickened her. For on the table were two young starlings. They were alive but pegged down by their wings as they gasped and struggled to release themselves. Behind them was a headless rat and next to that lying very still was one of Mini's black kittens. The tray crashed to the floor as Marcelle grabbed the kitten's lifeless body and fled screaming hysterically down to the kitchen and straight into the arms of Abe.

Having heard the crash and Marcelle's sudden descent Annabelle came running in and tried to comfort the girl. But no one could console Marcelle as she hugged the dead kitten to her breast. 'He killed it,' she sobbed. 'There are birds being hurt up there, too, it is terrible.'

'The kitten died in the night,' Annabelle explained, 'so I gave him to Merlin. He did not hurt it.'

'But why did you give it to him? What is he doing to those poor wild things?' cried Marcelle. She was still trembling.

Annabelle looked at Abe but he was flummoxed, too. 'She's a sensitive girl, all right. She ain't going to let no one fool her. She's too fond of animals,' he told Annabelle quietly.

Annabelle looked down at him disdainfully, and then turned back to Marcelle. 'Listen, Marcelle,' she said. 'Merlin is a clever man. He makes sick people well, just as Our Lord did.'

'Oh, do not say that!' begged Marcelle. 'It is evil what I saw up there,' she cried. 'Horrible faces looked at me. Demons live up there, I saw them.' Her sobs became relentless. 'My mother,' she cried. 'My poor mother, they killed her, poked her under the water with long sticks, they did, the evil ones.'

Abe and Annabelle looked at each other in puzzlement. What preyed on this child's mind? Whatever it was, Dour Thomas might have given them some warning.

Marcelle was still clinging on to the limp body of the kitten and sobbing as if her heart would break. Abe knelt down beside her. 'Come little one,' he said gently. 'Don't take on so.'

Annabelle swept out of the room and returned with Merlin behind her. In the light Marcelle could see that his straggly beard was dyed several colours and his hands stained with dye and blood. She took one look and started to scream again. But Merlin came over to her and placed those long fingers on her brow. She immediately went limp. 'Sleep, little one, sleep in peace,' Merlin said. He spoke the words slowly and distinctly and Marcelle lay down on the bench and closed her eyes. Her body was relaxed completely as she slept.

Annabelle took the kitten and gave it back to Merlin who looked at the sleeping girl with a strange love in his eyes. 'This child has been through a bad time,' he said softly. 'But it will not trouble her now. When she awakes she will have forgotten.' Then taking the dead cat, he turned and glided out of the room with his stained robe flowing out behind him.

Annabelle covered Marcelle with a rug. 'Look after her, Abe,' she said to her husband. 'We had better not let her go up there anymore.' With that, she returned to her boudoir upstairs.

5

Whitehall

Thomas Mayhew was at Whitehall, having spent many frustrating hours sitting in Robert Carr's apartment waiting for his master to dress for the evening's entertainment.

'Stay here, Mayhew,' Robert Carr had ordered. 'I will probably need you,' his voice was shrill and irritating.

So Thomas sat waiting bored almost to tears, while Robert pranced and paraded around his chamber trying on first one coat then another. In the dressing room an old fellow was busy curling and primping his master's blonde hair and a young lackey was sent chasing in and out for wine and the various potions and pills which his master mixed up and swallowed, fretting and fussing all the time.

'God, what an ass, what a damned silly fool,' said Dour Thomas to himself as he sat waiting. His patience was wearing thin.

At last the finished product appeared. Robert Carr the courtier, the King's favourite playboy, paraded up and down like a mannequin. 'What think you, Overbury? Does the coat set well at the back?' he asked his secretary, a well-spoken and unusually intelligent young man. Overbury ran his hand over the shoulders of Robert's plum-coloured velvet coat. ''Tis fine,' he said. 'The embroidery goes well with the vest.' He seemed to have a genuine fondness for Robert, having known him as a youth.

Robert had been a fair-haired page at the court in Scotland, a pawn for every vice in that court of James. For a long while he had enjoyed being the favourite but he seemed to have been on edge lately as though things were on his mind. And he certainly had not been the same since the bewitching Frances had come on the scene. Thomas wondered if Robert was jealous. That type of man did not like women much. 'They are all a funny lot, I will be glad to get away,' he thought darkly.

'All right, you can go, Mayhew,' Robert squeaked at last. 'But stay in your lodgings. It is a devil of a job to find you sometimes.'

Thomas left with a sigh of relief. Taking deep breaths of air, he walked back beside the river to those stuffy lodgings and all that scent which sickened him. His lodgings were in a tall three-storey house facing the Thames, and belonged to a shipping merchant. Thomas occupied the two big attic rooms on the top floor, sharing them with two other young men who were only at home when the debts mounted up on them. When that happened they would never leave the house for fear of creditors catching up with them. At the moment the two of them had joined a hunting party and so were away. They would probably return, Thomas thought, with plenty of money in their purses, made, no doubt, on wagers and card playing. Then they would settle down for a while.

Thomas rarely dined at home. He usually went out or was simply away on his travels. But it was difficult to obtain lodgings in the crowded streets of London, so having paid the lease on these humble dwellings, Thomas thought it wise to stay put. It was just the place to hang his hat but that was all, he told himself.

Taking off his boots, he lay flat on the bed thinking over the events of the last few months. Marcelle's shy little face swam before him. It was strange how close he felt to this young girl. He longed to make love to her but so rare was a sweet young virgin in this world of vice, he felt he could never dishonour her. He could marry her, he was free to do that, but would she want him? He was nearly thirty and she just fifteen. He thought of the weddings he had seen at court – forced marriages between young people who hated each other standing before the altar of God swearing to love honour and obey. He remembered the wedding of Frances Howard and Robert Devereux and remembered how they had fought and kicked each other only half an hour after the wedding ceremony had ended, how the great Howard family had taken Frances home and the Essex kin sent Robert overseas. The grand world outside had known nothing of these happenings; it was only the serving class to which Thomas belonged, that saw the true colours of these pampered darlings of the royal court of the King. And it had distressed him. No, if ever he married it would be for true love. He would just wait for Marcelle to make up her own mind.

He lay staring up at the rafters, going back to the day when he had been at Theobalds, the great home of the Cecil family. It was on that occasion when the King had come to England from Scotland and everyone had waited eagerly for a change for the better after the years of Elizabeth's tyrannical rule. Thomas recalled how he had stood bare headed with the rest of his master's retinue. The sight of the great house of Theobalds had greatly impressed him and to this day he was still awed by its splendour, and could conjure it up in his mind at will, the tall towers of the house each surmounted by a golden weather vane glinting in the bright sunlight, and the broad expanse of window with the tiny leaded panes shining in a myriad of colours. The sight of the rich red bricks against the green magnificent parkland was certainly one to see and remember. That first sight had been nine years ago, when he was nine years younger. Perhaps he would not be so easily impressed by the sight of such a magnificent display now. And it had partly been the circumstances, for he could remember how the Privy Council and all the great men of England had stood before the entrance to the house waiting to greet the new king. In the centre of them all was the white-faced figure of the hunch-backed Cecil, son of the brains behind the late Elizabethan court. The owner of this great mansion was such a small, insignificant man, with the white hands of an artist, Thomas had noticed. He had also noted the way the plumes of the noblemen's hats waved in the breeze and the jewels glittered on their elaborate dress. But most of all, he remembered their tense set faces as they wondered how they would fare with the funny-looking Scotsman who was to be their king.

Not many of those men were now left, he thought. For heads had soon begun to roll. The new king was no fool. Thomas had watched him that day dismount and walk with his shambling gait as he surveyed his new ministers. With the absurd-looking bonnet on his head and the lewd look in his eye, Thomas thought at the time that he had never seen anyone looking less like a king.

Later that night, while the feasting was in progress in the great hall, small fry like himself looked on. The centrepiece of the hall was a fountain which sprayed water into a huge bowl supported by four naked figures; it was the wonder of the age. All around the walls were magnificent portraits of generations of Cecils, and the ceiling was carved in the form of a star with the painted sun which seemed to move across it. Yes, it certainly had been an exciting day which, for Thomas had ended with a maid, whom he had long forgotten. She had been drunk and very willing when Thomas came across her in the corridor. Oh to be young again, he thought with a deep sigh. His thoughts continued on the same lines as he remembered how the next morning he had accompanied his elder brother and several others to inform their master, Sir Walter Raleigh, of the situation at Theobalds. For Raleigh had not been certain of his own welcome and had sent out his spies to assess the situation before arriving himself to greet the new king.

The family of Thomas Mayhew had been land-owning gentry on the estate of Sherbourne and Dorset, the home of Raleigh, the famous Elizabethan courtier. Raleigh's son Cary, was close to Thomas in age, and the two boys had been good friends, riding the moors together and fishing in the wide rivers of Dorset. Since his father's fall from favour and subsequent imprisonment in the Tower, Cary had taken to roaming the streets of London and getting into brawls with the new Scottish courtiers. The Mayhews' love and loyalty to their famous master had been deep and enduring and his downfall had been a bitter blow to Thomas' father and elder brothers. But at the time, Thomas, who had been very young and prepared only to live for each day, had not really noticed the significance of these goings-on. However, on the death of his father, he had suddenly decided that the sea would be his life, being quite tired by that time of royal processions and philandering. He made up his mind to travel to the New World and perhaps, if he got the chance, to settle in Virginia. Now that his father was dead, his brother was back on the farm; times had certainly changed since that night at Theobalds.

He stared ruefully up at the ceiling. Here he was in London in a world of intrigue and with a lecherous old king on the throne of England who changed his mind with his vests.

Swinging his legs to the floor, he stood up. He had better go to the tavern, there was no sense in getting depressed. And perhaps he would meet Cary and their friend Ben Jones. Those two would soon get rid of his doldrums. Leaving his lodgings, Thomas walked to the city tavern in search of company. He pushed his way through the crowded streets past St Paul's towards Cheapside. There had been a hanging that day and a very bloodthirsty crowd was still standing around. Some of them were very drunk, watching the victim's remains being drawn and quartered, just as a butcher does a pig. The smell of blood and the evil expressions on the spectators' faces made Thomas' stomach turn. 'There but for the grace of God go I . . .' he muttered, very aware that these words had a different meaning for him today than they used to. He wondered, not without anxiety, if Betsy had disposed of old Sam's body securely, and he hoped that she could be trusted. Then annoyed by his worries and morbid thoughts, he shook his head. 'Don't know what the hell is wrong with me. I must be getting an attack of something,' he told himself. Leaving the crowds behind, he turned down a narrow passageway, where men wearing white aprons stood at the corners and little boys called out: 'This way, sir, a fine roast, turkey and good wine!' They were all touting for the restaurants that were huddled together in the small alley, but Thomas passed them and made his way into the dark interior of the steak house at the end of the row. As he climbed down the narrow stairs he had the feeling that he would find the company he needed so badly today.

The air downstairs was thick with smoke and the smell of food and wine. Deep voices chattered at each other in the high-backed cubicles, and rushes were strewn on the floor so liberally that the waiters carrying heavy trays slithered across it. At a long bar at the end, young men dressed in all their finery quaffed ale from pewter tankards. On the walls were hunting scenes and scenes from the popular plays of Will Shakespeare and his Company of Players. There was not a woman in sight, for this was a male stronghold; no female ever crossed its threshold. It was Charlie Brown, the proprietor, who insisted on this. 'A man likes to relax when he's drinking,' he would pontificate. 'Wenches is all right once you have had your fill.'

Thomas ordered a meal and after he had eaten and drunk several tankards of ale, he began to feel much better and more light-hearted. Several young men he knew greeted him and offered to join him. Most of them, it seemed, had run out of credit with Charlie Brown. Thomas made it clear that he wanted to remain alone for the time being, but kept his eyes fixed on the door, as he looked out for Cary. When they had been lads, Thomas had taught Cary to fish in the rivers at their home in Dorset and Cary, a wild youth, had run with him happy and carefree over the moors. They had climbed the tall pine trees and pelted each other with the large cones that fell from them. Then Cary had gone to sea but in spite of the separation and the difference in their stations in life, Cary never passed Thomas. Whenever Thomas was feeling depressed, it was the sight of Cary that always gladdened his heart, and it was the jolly look in those strange wide eyes that he longed to see.

Now he had spotted him, and Thomas watched with affection as Cary gracefully descended the stairs into the room.

Tall and slim, with chestnut curls, Cary was wearing a smart green and white doublet with long white pantaloons. A short, fur-trimmed cape hung about his shoulders. Young Cary was a man of fashion but he was no fop; and he had been in more scrapes than the average young man of his day.

'Ye Gods, is that you, Dour Thomas?' he cried, when he saw his old friend.

''Tis me, not a ghost,' answered Thomas, jumping to his feet and slapping Cary on the back.

'You look worn to the skin and bone. Is thy mistress overworking thee?'

Thomas laughed, for he knew that the quip referred to his new master. The effeminate Carr was always the subject for his joke.

'Join me for dinner,' said Cary. 'Will you, Thomas? I have an invitation to dine with Robert Rich. You may join us.'

The two young men adjourned to the private dining room behind the back of the restaurant. There were other men in there, red faced and arguing amicably. In all it was a lively evening. After an eight-course meal, musicians were summoned and sang bawdy songs. They had wagers on drinking feats, which added to their consumption.

Robert Rich was a pleasant young man of about twenty-four. He had spent a long time out in Virginia, and his skin was tanned brown. His eyes were very bright, and shone as he told stories of a land of gold where untold treasures were to be found, of Indians, a race with a strong sense of honour even though they were savages, and he told of a certain captain who had brought home an Indian princess and introduced her to the Queen.

Thomas listened fascinated. Other young men had joined them in the room and there were now about twenty in the room all sitting in little groups. One thing they all had in common was that they were young men of good families, whose fathers and grandfathers had always had a place in the court of the English king. Now they were being elbowed out by the hordes of Scotsmen who came south with Jamie. There were no wars to fight or occupy their time, so they hung about the town spending their money and getting into fights with Jamie's followers. All these young men were interested in getting away, with youth's urgent need of adventure. So they listened to Robert Rich with fascination. Each one was determined to get a slice of the fabulous treasure he spoke of, probably more for the adventure it promised than the riches it would bring.

''Tis a pity the king will not free my father,' Cary said. 'I'd be off soon enough.'

'It is rumoured that Prince Henry is very interested in the sea,' another young man said.

'That is true. He spends long hours with my father learning the art of navigation,' Cary informed them.

'Well, here's to a new sailor King, God bless him,' said Rich, raising his glass.

All stood with glasses raised high to the Crown

Prince Henry, who would never live long enough to be king.

'I am off to sea again this year. Is there anyone here wishing to join my venture?' cried Robert Rich.

All hands went high and even Dour Thomas got carried away by the excitement of it all, and waved his hand in the air.

'Good, we will meet again to discuss details. Now I propose we continue to enjoy ourselves.'

In the early hours of the next morning, Robert Rich's servants threw Thomas into bed. At the time, Thomas was completely unconscious and much the worse for drink. But he had had a very enjoyable evening and his worries had been well forgotten.

Old Sam's body was safely disposed of. With bricks and flat irons attached to his limbs, he now lay snugly beneath the waters of the Thames. In the dead of the night Betsy and Rolly had wheeled a little cart with the lifeless body on it through the back streets, a big red cross painted on the cart to keep the watch from stopping them. Had they been stopped they could only say that Sam died of the plague and they were taking him to Moorfields to the communal burying pit. This manoeuvre passed off without a hitch and these last few months they had drowsed in luxury. For Betsy was now the owner of the Duke's Head Tavern which she immediately set out to make more popular. She encouraged the young gentlemen to drink there and provided entertainment for them with Rolly's feats of strength which he would perform outside on the cobbled courtyard, lifting heavy weights and challenging bystanders to bouts of wrestling.

And if Betsy had the time and the inclination she would perform with a nice young gentleman upstairs in bed. Betsy's ideas were changing. She no longer needed the money, so sex was just a biological urge. Betsy was becoming almost respectable.

One bright sunny morning, while Rolly raised many peals of laughter from the folks outside, Sir Fulke Greville from Brook House came riding by on his way from Epping with his hunting party of young gentlemen. They stopped their horses to watch Rolly's antics, and then they all dismounted and went into the inn to drink some ale. This was a special occasion which Betsy rose to. She spread a snow-white cloth on the table and provided plenty of food and hot spiced punch. Sir Fulke was a handsome man, now in his fifties, and was still very partial to a pretty woman. That morning inside the inn, he lounged by the large red brick fireplace, and observed the attractive Betsy. For her part, Betsy took him in, with his clear-cut aristocratic features and his smart attire. From then on all Betsy did was in aid of his Lordship, and Sir Fulke and his followers frequently dropped in for some extremely enjoyable evenings, when much of the entertainment was put on especially for the pleasure of the local lord who resided at Brook House.

For the first time in her nineteen years Betsy knew the meaning of prosperity. Her business thrived, and she often thought of her youth when she and Rolly had begged for money and food in the streets – she in her ragged dress with her bare feet all blue and frozen and, tagging along behind her, the muddy, bewildered little Rolly who was all of five years old. As the crowds had milled around them, no one looked or even cared as the little girl with a mop of fair curls held out her hand for pennies. Betsy once stole some oranges from a woman outside the playhouse at Shoreditch, but the woman caught her and beat her. Betsy could still hear her shrill voice now: 'Steal from a poor working gel, would yer? Plenty of damned pockets to pick off those who don't work so 'ard for it.' Then with a sudden change of heart the woman had taken them home, washed and fed them. Orange Molly introduced Betsy to prostitution while her brother Rolly was hired out to a local sweep master. Rolly's was a hard and dirty job climbing up those big chimneys to clean them, and his master was often brutal and unfeeling. All the young boys were bound to their masters so there was no way they could escape. So at such a tender age, Rolly was pulled away from the protection of his loving sister to be a small slave to a cruel sweep master.

Orange Molly had a heart of gold really, and Betsy grew to be very fond of her, so what else could she do except help Molly to entertain her gentlemen? And later, poor Molly died of the smallpox and left nothing but a basket or oranges. Meanwhile, poor Rolly had grown up daft from the bashings his sweep master had given him for running away. One day Betsy had found Rolly in a ditch where the sweep master had left him, black with soot and utterly naked. She bathed him and cared for him until he was able to breathe properly again, she clothed him and then they had fled deep into London town and got lost in the big city. But Rolly was never the bright little brother he had been. He grew up big and strong enough, but his brain remained like that of a child. But Betsy loved him deeply; he was all she had to care for.

That was the year the Black Death stalked London and people were dying like flies. It had been for Rolly's safety that Betsy tried to leave the town along with a great horde of other refugees. As they fled they came to the borders of Essex but the soldiers of the Earl had lined the roads and beaten them back. The aristocrats in their carriages had flown but the little people were trapped, driven back into the disease-ridden city to die like rats. It was old Sam who had befriended Betsy then, allowing her and her brother to hide in the stables until the way was clear.

Betsy felt a twinge of conscience now, for he had not been so bad to her, old Sam, even though he had been a rogue. But after all, she didn't kill him, and it was about time that she and Rolly had things a bit easier. Now Betsy had the great Lord of the Manor as her patron and things were really looking up.

His Lordship was very interested in inns and taverns, having just been granted the monopoly on the wines and spirits sold in these establishments. It was a nice little extra income, of the kind old Jamie always rewarded those who were useful to him. Although Sir Fulke Greville came from a Catholic family he was no stickler for religion and he knew which side his bread was buttered. The wily old king appreciated that.

'Where's that slovenly old swine who used to own this place?' Sir Fulke asked Betsy one day.

Betsy's face paled but her ready wit found an answer. 'Oh, you mean Sam, my poor husband. He passed on a short while ago, your Lordship,' she said, looking sad.

Sir Fulke gave her a shrewd look. 'I thought his wife was dead. He came to me whining about something like that last year.'

'That was his first wife,' said Betsy, very subdued.

'Good, so the tavern is yours, then. Pay your rent regularly and keep it fairly respectable, and don't bring those stiff-necked Puritans down on you, wench, and you and I will get on fine.' He pinched her cheek.

Looking coy, Betsy curtsied low. 'Thank you, sir,' she said.

To Rolly later, Betsy was loud in her praise of his Lordship. 'We've dropped in a bit of luck this time, love,' she told him.

'Why?' he asked like a small child.

Betsy had to explain. 'This ground underneath belongs to the great Sir Fulke Greville, so if he says we can stay no one can interfere with us.'

'He wants me to go running over the marsh on Sunday morning,' said Rolly, with a proud expression on his big face.

'Well, you do that, dear,' said Betsy. 'Run fast and he will make a wager on you and it will all be in our favour.'

Every Sunday morning, sporting events were held out on the Hackney Marshes, the flat green marsh that stretched from the banks of the Lea out to Epping Forest. There was usually a running contest and bull- or bear-baiting, cock-fighting and wrestling were the choice of sporting events. Many young gentlemen rode out from London town to place wagers on their favourite sport. This was the way in which Rolly spent most of his time now. His fine physique made him a popular figure amongst those who wanted to lay wagers on him. It didn't matter that he had such a childish mind; to please them he would run or wrestle his heart out.

6

Intrigue

There was an air of excitement at Annabelle's house for her friend and former mistress was paying her a visit, travelling to Craig Alva *in cognito*. All day long, Annabelle fussed and fidgeted.

'What is the matter with Annabelle?' Marcelle asked Abe.

'She gets like this sometimes,' replied Abe calmly. 'I expect the great one is coming.'

In the afternoon Marcelle was sewing in her usual corner, when a Madam Weston was announced. Frances Howard always insisted on having false names when she travelled in case there were spies about. A strong waft of perfume followed her in, and she seemed to fill the small parlour with the wide stiffened folds of her beautiful garments, a lovely fur-trimmed tan-coloured, velvet coat and dress, and a large hat from which a long white plume drooped.

Sitting quietly in her corner, Marcelle did not dare look up at Frances, but instead she kept her head down, rapidly pushing the needle in and out of her work. There was an air of tension in the room which made her feel extremely nervous. But every now and then she did quickly glance up to catch a glimpse of the elegant figure in the room, spotting the Countess' set little white face, her ash blonde hair which hung down in long curls on her shoulders. Annabelle ran to greet her and the two women embraced as if they were sisters.

'Oh, my dear!' burst out Frances. 'It is getting terrible. It is more than I can stand.'

Suddenly she realized that they were not alone. Her face went cold as she stared at Marcelle.

'It's all right,' said Annabelle, noticing her hostility to the girl, 'Marcelle is my companion.'

'Dismiss her!' ordered the Countess in a hard voice.

'Leave us for a while, dear,' said Annabelle kindly.

Marcelle got to her feet, inclined a quick curtsy towards the countess and obediently left the room. Outside she shuddered. For some reason the fair, beautifully-dressed gentlewoman gave her the cold shivers, as if a grey goose were walking on her grave.

Inside the parlour, Frances unburdened her unhappy soul to Annabelle whose china-blue eyes filled with tears as she listened sympathetically to this well-to-do madam, whose family was one of the most ill-starred of England. Their greed and ambition were always their downfall and every generation sent a lamb to the slaughter. Under Henry VIII, Anne Boleyn had gone to the block, followed by Katherine Howard. Now members of the younger generation were being thrown like dice around the political court in an effort to regain prestige and power behind the throne.

At first the target had been the Crown Prince, who had had eyes for no one but Frances ever since they had played together as children in the gardens of Greenwich, and then later became secret lovers. But the Protestant King James was no fool and he did not intend to be over-run by a Catholic family like the Howards. So his first step had been to lure the two rival families, the Essex and Howard families into a marriage settlement.

'They will be too busy doing battle with each other to worry over me,' the canny Scot had thought as he blessed the union between Robert, son of Lord Essex, and Frances Howard. Both were very young – Frances not yet thirteen and Robert not fourteen, and from the beginning the marriage had been disastrous. The newly-weds hated each other and fought like cats every time they met. So they parted, Robert to the war in France and his child bride to the fabulous home of the Howards at Audley End.

It was here earlier that Annabelle had become the first real friend and confidante of little Frances. Annabelle had been first maid to Frances, having been promoted from the nursery when the children had grown up. There were not many secrets in the great house that Annabelle did not know about, what with her husband in the coachhouse and Annabelle in her lady's chamber. She had helped dress Frances in her bridal clothes and had comforted her when Frances' irate parents brought her sobbing and screaming back from court. Once Frances was married, it was made very difficult for her to meet her lover, the Crown Prince. And young Henry was too proud to dishonour his royal house, now that his father's feelings were clear, so each young heart moped and pined for the other, Henry at Whitehall and Frances at her ancestral home.

Robert of Essex, a hulking, ill-mannered youth of nineteen, had returned from the wars in France and claimed his bride, but now rumour had it that the marriage had never been consummated and, after two years of a terrible married existence, his hard-faced child bride was asking to be divorced. She sat in Annabelle's little parlour with tears of misery streaming down her cheeks and Annabelle wiped them away gently, just as she did when Frances was a spoilt little girl in the nursery.

'It will all come right. Did not your uncle promise to see the Bishop this very month?'

'But it will be useless,' sniffed Frances, hanging her head. 'They will not allow a divorce. You know, Annabelle, that I have not been a virgin since I was twelve.'

Annabelle bit her lip. In some way she felt responsible for Frances' affair with young Henry; she always knew she should have informed Frances' parents, but her own life would have been worth nothing if she had.

'They will have me examined by those damned vile Bishops,' moaned Annabelle, 'and you know they thrive on things like that.'

'But surely Robert Carr will protect you,' Annabelle assured her.

'He will look after himself, as he always does,' Frances replied bitterly.

'This is all very dangerous for you, my dear, for me,

too,' said Annabelle. 'Would it not be better for you to settle to your married life? The wounds will heal; time erases many things.'

'No, I will get even with them all! I swear before God and my friend the Devil that they will not beat me!' Frances' voice was hard and cruel.

Annabelle looked shocked, 'Hush, my dear, don't do anything you will be sorry for.'

'It is all right, Annabelle, do not worry, but I will need your help.'

Annabelle sighed. 'My help is yours for the asking, my lady. I cannot help myself.'

When the guest had gone, Marcelle crept back into the parlour and sat quietly in her corner, her head bent over her yellow silk sewing. Without a word she watched Annabelle sitting with her head in her hands as though trying to find some relaxation from the worries and woes of the world. After a while she arose from her chair and came over to Marcelle to stroke the wisps of hair from the girl's eyes. 'I'll be so happy when you marry Thomas,' she said. 'At least it will be a match of your own choosing.'

Marcelle's eyes were inscrutable. She looked down her thin pointed nose and for a moment her lips pursed angrily, but she made no comment for in her mind she was not sure of the truth of Annabelle's words. On sleepless nights she often turned over the thoughts of a lover. Her French blood and the spring that was upon them made her dream strange dreams about the strong arms of a man about her, but in her dreams the face of Dour Thomas never appeared.

Whenever this happened, Marcelle would push these wicked thoughts from her mind, as does a nun in her little cell, and she would repeat Hail Marys until her body felt at peace again.

Now it had grown dusk and the light was getting bad. Annabelle pulled her up from the couch. 'Come my love, let's go down to the kitchen; it's time to prepare supper.' And so they went downstairs together, as sisters, Annabelle with her arm around Marcelle's shoulders, to the light and warmth of Abe's fire.

In the kitchen was Will. Already tired of the city, he had returned to Abe's fireside to strum and sing. Everyone was in a relaxed mood as they all sat around the big wooden table – master, mistress, maids and guests. There was no class distinction in Annabelle's kitchen. And Marcelle felt curiously content.

The summer came in with all its glory that year. The hedgerows were sweet with honeysuckle and late apple blossom still adorned some of the trees. On others the green buds were bursting into leaf and the tiny young apples were hidden in the shelter of the cool green foliage.

With a flowered sun-bonnet on her head Marcelle worked in the garden early every morning with Annabelle. Together they would weed and prune the bushes ready for the soft fruit, which, as soon as it was picked, went straight into special preserving pots. She did this important task every year. Last year's preserved fruit still lined the larder.

In the afternoon, Marcelle would sit under the big

oak tree while Annabelle sat stiffly in her stuffy parlour. The pattern of life ran very smoothly that summer at this cosy home in Essex. All was sweet and content. No one was ready for the black storm which lay ahead.

Sometimes Merlin's tall ragged shape would creep out of the back door and slope off over the fields behind the house, his long coat flying out behind him, his hair waving in the breeze.

'He's like a damned March hare the way he goes over that field,' Abe would comment as he watched Merlin disappear.

But Marcelle was too afraid to look. She knew he would return with some soft wild thing clutched close under his cloak – a rabbit, a field mouse, a starling or a bat and soon the poor animal would be stretched out in pain. She just could not bear to think of it. She would stick her nose back in the little prayer book that had belonged to her mother and put these evil things from her mind. Apart from old Merlin, life in Annabelle's was one long peaceful dream.

One warm afternoon Marcelle was sitting in her usual spot when she heard the sound of horses and wagons coming over the hill. It sounded as though there were many of them. Then in the sunlight she could see the glint of steel in the distance and then, coming along the road, a long line of armed horsemen, their coloured coats showing up vividly against the dark green background of the forest.

The maids ran excitedly out from the dairy down to the gate calling, as they ran, to the officer leading the troops. Marcelle then heard one of them run to tell

Annabelle that the king was passing this way on his way to Theobalds. A new road had been cut through the forest to shorten the trip and he was to pass by some time that day.

Once Annabelle had heard this news she was not content until all the maids had changed into freshly starched clean bonnets and snow-white aprons, and Marcelle had changed into a pretty, cool cotton dress. A table was placed near the gate with dishes of fresh strawberries and cream, and cool jugs of cider, in case some of the young lords wished to take refreshment.

Abe flatly refused to change his coat, so he was told sharply that he had to keep out of sight. 'Anyone would think old King Jamie was coming here,' he muttered. 'He's only passing by. He won't even look at us.' And having said his piece, he returned to his kitchen and cooking.

Annabelle was dressed in a new russet-coloured dress with primrose ruffs and sat at the window of her parlour with the casement window open. There is a strange story attached to this new dress. Merlin made all the starch and other useful things for the household, but one day he had got his colours mixed up and a blue ingredient was substituted by yellow. There had been much distress when Marcelle, whose job it was to starch the dress ruffs, had brought them out a bright yellow. Annabelle was not fussed by this and soon calmed her down and, with her inventive mind, washed the ruffs again and again until a nice pale primrose colour was produced. When attached to a russet brown dress, the ruffs achieved a very pleasing effect. So with her new fashion ruffs, Annabelle sat as still as a statue to watch the King pass. She was determined to be noticed, if not by his Majesty then at least by some gay young Lord who would see all her finery. For Annabelle was very vain and this streak of vanity in her otherwise pleasant personality was to be her downfall.

Will sat under the tree near Marcelle and kept everyone amused with his songs and lyrics as groups of men passed. Marcelle watched in fascination as the crowds passed – wagons of goods and troops of soldiers. Then the young lords came riding by, their steeds all gay with brass and embroidered leather trappings, the riders elegant in their dress even when riding. They were a lusty lot, waving gaily to the maids as they rode by in groups, surrounded by servants and armed men. Some stopped to partake of the refreshing fruit and cream or a jug of cider. One daring young man jumped the hedge on his white steed, scattering the maids, and then he grasped Ruth, the prettiest of the lot, and rested her up on his saddle before kissing her full on the lips and then putting her down again. Then he rode like the wind as the horse jumped back to the track again. The dust rose in the heat of the afternoon as the traffic began to abate, leaving a cloud of chalky white dust which settled over the garden. By now, everyone was tired of waiting. There was still no sign of his Majesty or his Royal Highness Prince Henry, who was a favourite with all his father's subjects.

It began to get cool as the sun went down. Annabelle left her post by the window and walked stiffly out into the garden, 'My, that was a disappointment. He never came,' she said to Marcelle, who was watching Abe's kitten and wondering if he was going to disturb the blue tits who were nestling in the honeysuckle. The royal procession held no interest for her.

'Better go down the village, Abe, and see what has happened to them,' Annabelle told her husband who had emerged from the kitchen.

Abe obediently went off and Will followed him in the hope that they might visit the village inn. The maids cleared away the trestle tables outside and Annabelle went with Marcelle into the parlour to continue the everlasting sewing.

It was getting dark when Abe and Will returned. Both were merry and full of porter.

Annabelle was looking angry as she asked them: 'Well, what happened to his Majesty?'

Will sidled off to the barn. He was afraid of Annabelle when she got into such a rage. Abe, however, between many hiccups explained that true to form, old Jamie had changed his mind. Halfway to Loughton he had seen one of the young white deer which dwelt in that part of the forest, and was not content till they had set chase to it. The little fawn had led them a merry dance as it skipped gaily in the path of the King and then disappeared. In its place there appeared a huge stag, his eyes glazed with fear. But as if to protect the little fawn he had led the chase through the forest paths over the green fields. King James on the hunting field was a very different person to the jaded neurotic man at court. He rode well, and once the prey was sighted, he was oblivious to all else. He had chased the stag, Abe explained, over the fields of Essex, and now he and the royal party were somewhere near Romford where they would stay until the morning.

'Stupid old fool,' muttered Annabelle. Abe was not sure whom she referred to and giggled nervously. Annabelle sniffed and swept from the room. She found Abe disgusting at times.

In the kitchen, Marcelle quietly prepared the supper. Her sympathy always lay with Abe; she felt Annabelle was so hard on him at times.

'Eat,' she ordered Abe. 'You will feel better.' She handed him some food.

Old Abe's blue eyes twinkled affectionately and his wrinkled hand stroked her hair, 'I don't know why she worries over them bloody Lords. The King will soon have the old chopping block out when he finds what they are up to,' he muttered.

After he had eaten, Marcelle put Abe's feet on a low stool and he dozed off to sleep. Then she began to clear the table and make ready for the morning. She often wondered about the relationship between Abe and Annabelle. They were so different and she seemed so very contemptuous of Abe. It was hard to believe that they were husband and wife. It was a funny way to live, she thought. Still, they were both so kind and good to her and she truly loved them. She was very happy here, and she loved the fresh countryside and all the little animals to care for. She hoped it would last forever. But in her heart she knew that she could not stay, she knew that Thomas would one day return and ask her to marry him and that she would not refuse him. Deep in her heart something stirred, and in her mind's eye she saw a loving young man on his knees and offering her his undying love. At sixteen, the world outside lay unexplored. In her mind lay memories of unhappiness and of the disturbed child she had been when Thomas had brought her here not so long ago from the outside world. But then there was something she could never remember, a deep dark mystery which was always in the background. However hard she tried she could not bring it to the fore, though she did know it was something connected with a cat and old Merlin upstairs. She would ask Thomas the next time he came; he would know what it was.

So with her mind thus preoccupied, Marcelle did Abe's chores for him while he sat snoring by the fire. Then she bathed and put on a cool white nightgown and crept quietly with lighted candle through the house to her room at the top of the stairs. Inside she knelt beside her lavender-scented bed to say the simple prayer she had learned as a child. As she slipped between the sheets, she heard a movement upstairs above her, a soft rustling sound and she knew it was Merlin. He never slept, but just shuffled about all night in his attic above her head. Marcelle sank down under the covers desperately trying to ward off the fear that Merlin's noise instilled in her.

The house was now silent. Only the hoot of an owl in the woods woke up the night as its black curtain descended on the land. Just over the hill, a few miles from Annabelle's house, the remains of the Royal procession set up camp in a haphazard fashion. No one was sure of what was going on or in which direction to proceed.

Young Lord Hay, the officer in charge, decided to wait until the morning for news. Just before dusk another troop of men arrived and with them his Royal Highness Prince Henry and David Murray, the Prince's aid and devoted servant. Immediately there was a noisy scene inside the hastily erected tent, as the huge Scotsman David Murray bellowed with rage, his red beard bristling. 'What tomfoolery is this?' he shouted at a worried-looking young officer.

The Prince was looking tired and weary and was crouching over a charcoal burner which warmed the tent.

'Gad, sir,' retorted the harassed Lord Hay. 'I, myself, do not relish the night on this draughty looking hill but we have been left high and dry, with no one knowing in which direction His Majesty went.'

David seemed concerned as he looked at the Prince's ashen face and sandy hair which seemed to increase the paleness of his skin.

'The laddie isna too weel. He should ne'er ha' come,' he relapsed into his broad dialect as he did in times of stress.

In a lower voice Lord Hay asked: 'Shall I send a messenger to Newly to say you will spend the night there?'

'It's ten miles away!' roared the angry Scotsman. 'His Royal Highness has had enough riding for one day.'

'There's a yeoman's house in the valley. It's clean and respectable and would certainly be better than this windy hill,' suggested Lord Hay.

David went slowly to his charge and spoke softly in the boy's ear. The only response he got from the young prince was a nod of the head. The boy seemed exhausted. Fetching a plain heavy riding cloak, David placed it gently on the young prince's shoulders and helped him to remount his horse. Then the three men rode off into the night, down the valley towards Annabelle's house.

Lord Hay was the young lord who had leapt the fence and had kissed Ruth earlier on in the day, so he knew exactly where to find the house tucked away in the trees.

The sound of heavy knocking on the door woke Abe as he slept before the fire. But the noise echoed through the still house and both Annabelle and Marcelle woke with a fright, for there was always an element of danger in any knocking at the dead of night.

A bleary-eyed Abe went to the door and two men pushed past him, escorting a third who was muffled in a big riding cloak.

'We crave your hospitality for the night.' The red-bearded man towered over Abe and spoke haughtily to him. 'You will be well paid. Our friend is fatigued with riding. We need hot food and clean beds.'

'Come inside, and you are welcome,' old Abe said, opening the door wide. His keen eye caught a glimpse of the auburn hair and the deathly pale face of the young prince. 'Go to the fire. I will soon rouse the house, and your wants will be attended to,' he said.

Soon the candles were alight and a huge fire was roaring in the guest chamber on the first floor. Annabelle was now up, and her lace gown fell gracefully about her shoulders as she served hot spiced drinks to the travellers.

Marcelle was called to put warming pans in the beds and fair rosy Ruth, the dairy maid, was hustled from her bed to help in the kitchen. In less than no time, hot soup and braised chicken in wine with various other delicacies were served.

Annabelle's eyes were very bright as she flitted and fluttered about. For she had recognized Prince Henry, the royal lover of her young mistress in those days at Audley House where both she and Abe had been servants. With his heavy lidded eyes and sunken cheeks, the young prince looked very ill, but Annabelle did not comment. She dared not let anyone else in the house know that they were entertaining the Crown Prince of England.

To Marcelle they were just another lot of guests who had come in late, not an uncommon occurrence at this inn, so she just went about her work helping Ruth in the kitchen. The other two male guests seemed to have cheered up a bit, now that the younger one was asleep. They had gently got their young master to bed and now they sat in the next room talking and drinking. The bearded one seemed to be quite upset and he drank some evil-smelling wine that he took from a flask he carried with him.

As Marcelle and Ruth cleared the dishes, the young Lord Hay looked at the golden-haired maid appreciatively as he remembered the sweetness of her lips earlier that afternoon.

With her eyes lowered modestly, Ruth demurely carried the tray from the room. She did not dare look at his lordship while Annabelle was present.

'Och mon, I am right tuckered oot maself. Been riding since this morning.' David Murray stretched and yawned.

'Get to your bed, then. I'll ride back to camp,' said Lord Hay, still eyeing Ruth.

'Mon, I daren't. He might wake in the night, and he'll be terribly scared.'

Lord Hay looked at him with disbelief.

'Aye,' returned David. 'It's these terrible nightmares he has. Goes walking off in his sleep. I have brought him in many times from the grounds in the middle of the night.'

'Poor devil, his mind must be going,' said Lord Hay, shaking his head sympathetically.

'Nay, it's his nerves. But it will go, all he needs is a mate.'

As David spoke it was obvious that he was exhausted. His head nodded and his eyes were almost closed.

'Come on David, old lad. Get off to bed. I'll guard your baby.' Lord Hay had a kindly way about him, so David Murray gave in and went to bed while the younger man sat by the fire to guard the royal guest. But as Lord Hay sat back in his seat, in his mind's eye was a vision of golden-haired Ruth with her pearl-like teeth and cheeks like rosy apples ready for picking. The more he stared into the fire, the more vivid this vision became. He fidgeted uncomfortably; it was going to be a long night. 'Oh, to hell with the royal baby,' he decided finally, when the temptation became too great for him.

Down in the kitchen Annabelle had just finished clearing up. 'Well, that's over,' she said. 'Now we can all retire for the night.'

Abe took a candle and lit up the path for Ruth to guide her to her sleeping quarters which she shared with the other dairy maids. The heavy front door closed with a click, and as Ruth skipped merrily through the orchard, a tall slim shape climbed down the ivy and a voice whispered: 'Don't go, darling, let me kiss you goodnight.'

Ruth was not afraid. She had half-expected his Lordship to be there, for she had a way with men and had had plenty of experience. So, with an attractive little giggle, she raced straight towards the barn with the young Lord Hay following her like a whippet.

Marcelle could not sleep. For hours she lay restless, tossing and turning from side to side. Unlike Ruth, whose instinct it was to give way to the urge of nature, Marcelle had no understanding of why the sight of the young men disturbed her sleep. The young visitor she had seen had been so pale, she felt quite sorry for him. As she thought over the events of the evening, a strange sound reached her ears. It sounded like a tiny cry for help, perhaps from an animal in distress. Almost immediately she thought of the kitten. Had Merlin come down in the night to steal yet another kitten? The thought horrified her but she was too terrified to move. Then again she heard it. It was a deep sob, something or someone was crying. Her soft heart had to know. Creeping from the bed, she opened her door silently. Her bedroom was at the top of a small flight of stairs and down below was a long corridor which ran alongside the guest chambers. As she stepped noiselessly down into the corridor she saw that the door to one of the guest rooms was open and through it emerged a slim figure walking, his hands stretched out in front of him. As he moved, violent sobs convulsed him. Even in the dim light, Marcelle caught a glimpse of the auburn hair. The young man was walking towards the blind end of the passage. When he reached it, he seemed to wake up, for now he was beating his fists on the wall.

Without a word, Marcelle ran silently up to him and gently turned him to face her. 'Come sir,' she said. 'This way. You have been walking in your sleep, I think.'

The man clutched at her convulsively. 'Franci!' he exclaimed. 'I knew you would come.' His words ended in a mutter.

Marcelle guided the man along the passage to his chamber and tried to coax him through the door. But he held on to her tight, his tears streaming down her bare arm. 'This way, sir, just a few more steps.' She piloted him along, humouring him as a nurse would a child. He went quietly holding tightly to her arm and every now and then pressed his burning lips to her bare flesh, now exposed since the bedgown had slipped down from her shoulders.

'Franci, my love,' he murmured. 'Don't leave me ever, not ever again.' He said these words over and over again.

Marcelle got him to the bed, but he would not go any further. Instead he knelt on the floor beside the bed and pulled her down with him. Marcelle felt overwhelmed with pity for this young boy; she felt strange flickerings of emotion as he held on to her. She opened her mouth to speak but he covered it quickly with his hand. 'Hush, my darling, they will hear you and kill you as they are going to me.' He pulled her closer, covering her with kisses, and Marcelle relaxed as they lay down on a rug of sheepskin beside the bed. Her gown came apart and he pressed his body against her, pouring words of love in her ear. The hot sensuous blood of the Stuarts consumed his body and Marcelle had no chance, not even for a protest. What was happening was wonderful; she could not resist. After a while she began to return his love with equal passion until they tired. Then they curled up and slept close together like two young puppies on a rug.

The crowing of the red rooster awoke Marcelle in the early hours as it did every morning. But this morning it was different. She had had a strange dream, and what was wrong with her arm? She could not lift it. Turning her head sleepily, she saw to her amazement, a young man's head with a wealth of red hair resting on her arm. Suddenly she was horrified. It was no dream; it was all true! She had forsaken her virginity for a strange young man. She shuddered and her eyes looked down at her bare white limbs stretched out before her. 'Oh, Holy Mother,' she whispered. 'Dear Virgin, don't let it be true.' She pulled out her arm from under his head and reached for her bedgown.

The young man stirred in his sleep. 'Don't go, Franci,' he whispered.

Tears trickled down Marcelle's cheeks as she bent over him and gently pressed her lips to his brow. Taking the rug from the bed, she covered him up and went silently from the room.

In her own chamber, she had just finished dressing when Annabelle rapped on her door. 'Come on, sleepyhead,' she called. 'There's work to do.'

Down in the kitchen, Annabelle was busy and brisk as usual. 'Come on, Marcelle,' she chided. 'The gentlemen need their breakfast. Abe is bringing the cows in for milking. Go down and see if the girls are up, and bring some fresh butter up from the dairy.'

Once outside the house, Marcelle stopped for a while. The morning air tasted like wine. The grass was a deep green and fresh with dew. Looking away over the fields towards the sun as it struggled through foamy pink clouds, Marcelle heaved a sigh of intense pleasure. What had happened? How wonderful she felt this morning. It must be love. Yes, she was sure that what happened last night was that she had fallen in love. She picked a rose petal from a nearby rose and pressed it to her lips. How lovely his soft lips had been, just like this petal, she thought as she danced towards the dairy. Yes, she did not care about anything. She was really terribly in love with that young man though she did not even know his name. When she reached the outbuilding where the dairy maids lived, there was a lot of noisy commotion going on. One of the maids was ranting and raving outside. Her face was pale and showed up the large brown freckles that adorned her otherwise fair skin, and she was waving her milking stool in a threatening manner at someone inside.

'Whatever is wrong Wanda?' asked Marcelle as she approached.

'It's her!' yelled Wanda bursting with temper her cap awry. 'The slut, that's what she is. I'll tell the mistress, I will.'

'Who? Ruth?'

'Yes, nice goings-on there have been. She's been in the barn with his lordship all night, and she won't get up now. The cows are bellowing to be milked and she is still in bed.'

'Shut your big mouth!' yelled Ruth from her bed. 'I said I was getting up, didn't I?'

'Whore!' screamed Wanda. 'I saw you in there.'

'Jealous bitch!' retorted Ruth. 'Didn't fancy you, did he?'

Marcelle stood open-mouthed as she listened to the lewd exchanges. Two spots of colour had appeared on her cheeks as she went towards the dairy.

'Done it now, you have,' Ruth shouted at Wanda, putting her ruffled head out of the window. 'She's gone to tell the mistress, that prim little miss has.'

'And a good job, too,' returned Wanda, marching

off to the cow shed. Her strong sturdy legs soon disappeared amid the herd of cows that Abe drove into the yard.

Marcelle quietly took some butter from the dairy and returned to Annabelle, who was looking a bit annoyed. 'Well, I need not have bothered myself, after all, they have gone.'

Through the window Marcelle saw the silhouettes of the three horsemen as they rode off over the hill. Her heart sank down, feeling so heavy, like a ton weight; he had never even said goodbye.

7

Home Sweet Home

A little man sat by the roadside staring down at his feet which were bound up in pieces of sacking and secured with yellow string criss-crossed half way up his legs. But Chalky was not looking down at his feet in admiration; he was worried. He had worn out his only pair of boots, his feet were very sore, and he still had many miles to go. Binding his feet with the remains of a flour sack was not really going to solve his problems nor take away the pain of the huge blisters on the soles. He was a scrawny little man who looked much older than his twenty-five years. His features were marred by the ravages of the sun, wind and cold of many countries. His nose was distorted by frost-bite and his skin had darkened to the colour of tree bark. There he sat, a pathetically round-shouldered creature with his few possessions in a small bag over his shoulder. He had walked many miles from Harwich and although he was exhausted, he was now just twenty miles from his destination and he did not intend giving up. He rubbed his legs ruefully as he wondered what sort of reception he would get when he got there. It was five years since he had been home. He did not expect to be given the fatted calf, that was certain, but perhaps old Sam had matured a bit now. Some people did as they grew older.

He began to think of the fights he and his old man used to have. He had always lost, for Sam had the advantage over him just by sheer weight and evil temper. Chalky was not sorry he had run off but the years in the fleet and months in that hellish Spanish prison had made him long for a home, a place where he belonged. Yes, by God he would stand up to Sam now. And if by chance his father had died, well then, the inn would be his, for he had no other kin. With a look of sullen determination on his face, Chalky braced himself as he got up and limped along the final stretch of road.

Ten minutes later a heavy wagon lumbered up behind him with its huge wooden wheels grinding in and out the deep grooves made by similar carts which had travelled the road before it.

Chalky stepped to one side and hailed the carter, 'Hi there! How far are you going?' he called.

The carter stared down at the ragged figure from under his straw hat 'What's that to you, vagabond?' He practically spat the words out.

'Thought you might let me ride a bit of the way,' replied Chalky. 'My poor feet have given in on me, they have.' He spoke in a cajoling manner, for he knew that the folk in the country were not too friendly to travellers.

The carter's round weather-beaten face continued to look down at him in an unfriendly manner. 'How do I know you won't attack me and pinch me cart?'

'Don't trouble, then,' said Chalky, his head hanging in woe. 'Might as well die by the roadside for all anyone cares. But it's no nice way to treat a soldier returning from the wars.'

'Get up then,' the carter said quickly. 'Only going to Waltham. What's all this about a war? I didn't know we was having one.' His moon face looked interested.

Once he was safely on the cart, and his back warmed by the large sacks of grain, Chalky told blood-thirsty stories of his adventures as a soldier of fortune. His tales were so vivid and full of interest that the carter listened as a boy to his tutor. Chalky possessed a fluent manner of speech which had got him out of many tight corners over the years.

In the next couple of hours Chalky enjoyed half of the carter's supper of bread and cheese and had a good sup from his jug of cider. When they reached Waltham, they had covered eighteen of Chalky's twenty miles, and on the edge of the forest, they parted with hearty farewells. Chalky was nearly home. Standing by the roadside again, he looked down the hill and, faintly in the distance, he could just see the tall tower of the church of St John. His mother was buried in that churchyard. Twenty-five years ago Chalky had been christened Frederick White in that very same church. It was odd to think that. Feeling a lot happier, he shuffled along on his uncomfortable feet getting nearer to his goal all the time. Soon he was crossing the familiar dilapidated wooden bridge which spanned the Lea and gazing at the little brook as it wound its way over the marsh. He was surprised by the feeling of nostalgia that swept over him, and he felt oddly content. Yes, he was glad to be home. Once back he would look for a clean homely wench; it would be nice to settle down, never to roam again. As the black-and-white towers of Brook House came into view, he wondered if old Sir Fulke Greville still owned it. He would never forget the whipping Sir Fulke had given him when he once caught him scrumping apples from the orchard . . . Chalky drew a deep breath; nearly there.

In the Duke's Head, Betsy was busy. It had been market day and it had been hot and busy, for the carts rolling towards London had been passing ever since sunrise with the thirsty carters pulling in for a cool foaming jug of ale. She had been on the go all day and her face was flushed red and her hair untidy. But she still had a bright sunny smile on her face as she bade the customers welcome. Or most of them at least. When a weary, dirty creature came into the inn, her sweet smile was quickly replaced by a frown. 'Go round the back door, beggar,' she said sharply. 'I will send you food and drink there.'

A sly grin was on Chalky's face as he gazed with some surprise at this buxom blonde glaring at him over the long carved oak bar. He had been sure that the first thing he would see would be the big hulk of his father, but instead, here was this full-blown beauty telling him to go to the back door and calling him a beggar. Caution was not something that Chalky lacked, and he showed it now. He touched his fore-lock with an ingratiating bow. 'Thank you, madam,' he said. 'You are very kind.' And went to the back door as Betsy had directed.

Betsy was as good as her word. Within a couple of minutes, a tall young man came out with half a cold beef pie and a jug of ale for Chalky.

Rolly sat on the bench beside Chalky while he made short work of the food. 'What's wrong with your feet?' he asked staring with the interest of a little boy at Chalky's bound-up feet.

Chalky looked up and grunted at this big hefty fellow who towered over him as he ate. The size of him made him nervous.

Suddenly Rolly went hopping off around the yard on one leg, and then returned with a broad smile on his face as though he had done something clever.

'He's a bit gorn,' though Chalky. 'Poor devil, but I bet he ain't half strong.'

Rolly began to pick up stones and hurl them at the road. 'I can do tricks,' he informed Chalky.

Within moments, Chalky's astute mind had Rolly in focus; he was a big strong chap with the mind of a child. Chalky had heard of people like this but had never actually seen one. For a while he forgot his mission and started to amuse Rolly. He showed the lad a fascinating game in which a pebble was seen in one hand only to disappear and reappear in Rolly's ear. To Rolly this was real magic. Then Chalky told him a long, highly coloured story of how he had once nearly been eaten by cannibals.

Rolly sat at Chalky's feet with his eyes glowing eagerly as he listened to these tales of adventure.

The light had begun to fade when Betsy's shrill voice rang from the entrance of the inn. 'What the hell are you up to, Rolly? It's closing time and you ain't done a thing.'

Rolly scrambled hastily to his feet and in a shame-faced manner darted inside. Betsy came out into the yard and, with her arms akimbo stood over Chalky. 'Ain't it time you was on your way?' she asked aggressively.

'Me feets is a bit sore,' replied Chalky softly. 'I couldn't bunk down in the stables tonight, could I?'

'All right, but you hop it in the morning,' said Betsy closing the door and making off towards her warm bed.

Chalky was soon huddled in the straw in the stable and wondering what to do next. What the devil had happened to old Sam? Now it seemed like the blonde was the mistress here. My, but she was a comely wench, and her brother daft but easily adaptable. He would hang around for a while, he decided. Someone would know where Sam was. So he pulled a sack over his head and settled down into the warm straw. 'Welcome home, Chalky old chap,' he muttered wryly to himself as he closed his eyes.

It was later as the night got cold and the dampness of the stable rose up around him that he realised he had company. A dappled old grey mare lay sleeping in the stall next door, scuffling and grunting in her sleep. He got up and found another sack to cover himself with and moved over nearer the wall. He did not fancy having his brains kicked out while he was asleep. Slightly warmer, he settled down until chinks of light came through the roof as dawn broke. The old mare rose and shook herself. It was only then that Chalky saw that he had another stable companion; sunk deep in the yellow straw behind the manger was an old man, with a long grey beard and long white locks. He was lying on his back with his mouth open, and he snored deeply. Chalky grinned. 'Well, darn me, if it ain't old Jem. I thought you'd be kicking up the daisies by now.'

The old man woke up with a start and looked very cross. 'What's to do?' he muttered, sitting up and staring bleary-eyed at the intruder.

'It's me, you silly old fool,' yelled Chalky. 'It's yer ol' mate Chalky, Sam's boy.'

The old man's jaw dropped and he gaped. 'Ain't you dead?' he asked uneasily.

'Course I ain't,' snapped Chalky. 'I'm still alive an' kickin', and so are you, by the looks of it.'

'Only just, boy, only just,' sighed old Jem. The pieces of straw sticking to his whiskers made him look like a scarecrow.

'How comes you sleep with the horse, then?' asked Chalky. 'What's wrong with the old shack what you lived in?'

'It's too cold for me old bones, lad, so I comes in here and snuggles up to old Nelly. She don't mind. Come to think of it, she's the only friend I've got left.'

'Gawd, you must be 'bout ninety,' Chalky's pointed teeth showed as he grinned.

The old man foraged in the straw and brought out

a leather bottle. He took a long swig at it, after which he seemed a bit brighter. ''Tis a wonder I ain't dead of starvation since old Sam went. No one bothers with me,' he muttered with a touch of pathetic self-pity. He beckoned Chalky to come closer, 'Murderers, they are,' he whispered. 'Done old Sam in, they did. I hide, cause I ain't goin' to let 'em do me in, too.'

Chalky looked at old Jem and wondered if he was rambling. He was indeed very old. He had been old even when Chalky had been a boy and had helped him tend the horses. Still, you never know, he thought, he might know something. He leaped over the stall and sat down in the straw beside Jem. 'Where did you say me old man's gorn?' he asked.

'Hell, I reckon,' Old Jem muttered. 'Never wus no good, he weren't. The devil's got 'im for sure.'

'You mean he's dead?'

'Dead as a doornail. Took 'im out in a barrow, they did. I was layin' in 'ere wi' old Nelly and I saw 'em, I did.'

'You mean the woman? Was she his wife?'

'Nope, she were a bloody streetwalker,' snarled old Jem.

'What about the big fellow? Who is he?'

'Supposed to be 'er brother. But I wonders about that, I do.' Jem nodded his old head up and down. 'Barmy, he is. Could kill yer wi' one blow, so yer won't catch me in there,' he muttered, taking hefty swigs from his leather bottle as he talked.

'Come on, old Jem, I'll help you get home,' said Chalky, pulling him to his feet. He did not know whether to believe the old devil or not. Jem always did have an evil tongue.

Together they walked down the alley, with Chalky helping old Jem who was a bit tottery on his legs and was mumbling and grumbling all the time. When they reached the door of the dilapidated little shack that Jem called home, Chalky let go of his arm and slapped him on the back. 'I'll come back and see you, Jem,' Chalky promised as he left.

He walked back towards the inn lost in thought. He was both alarmed and intrigued by what he had heard and his mean little eyes glistened under their bushy brows. If it was true that these people had done in his father then they were diddling him out of his rightful inheritance. And this put a completely different light on the matter. No one did old Chalky down and got away with it. This new information needed careful thinking about.

When he collected his bag from the stable it was getting brighter outside; daylight lit up the grey cobbled yard, in the centre of which was still the old pump. That pump! He remembered how his father had held him head down under the icy cold water as a form of punishment. And now, it seemed that Sam was dead. That fact did not matter to Chalky, there was no love lost there, but after all, he was Sam's legitimate son and heir, and what was Sam's should be his. He washed himself briskly under the pump and put on his remaining clean vest. Then, hoping that he looked nice, he went round to the back door of the inn and gave a gentle tap on the door.

Betsy appeared looking as though she had just tumbled out of bed. Her hair was in rag crackers and she was wearing a grubby nightgown bursting open at the neck.

Chalky's small eyes squinted straight down at the heavy white bosom which threatened to overflow the opening.

'What the hell do you want?' shouted Betsy, pulling her nightgown together.

'I wondered if I might repay you for your kindness by doing a few odd jobs before I go on my way,' Chalky suggested.

Betsy blinked and looked suspiciously at him. He did look a bit cleaner this morning, she had to admit. Well, he might as well help since that lazy fool Rolly was not up yet.

'All right,' she said. 'You can get some wood, light the fire and sweep the entrance. Then I'll give you some breakfast.'

Very humbly, Chalky did his chores with his ears and eyes busy all the time. Once the inn was clean and ready to open, and they had eaten, he picked up his little bag and said pleasantly: 'Well, I'll be on my way.'

The harassed Betsy was rolling a big barrel of ale about in the cellar, and she called to him: 'Here, give us a hand with this, will you? Now that damned boy has gone off to the river.'

Chalky had fashioned a little fishing net for Rolly from a piece of wire and bit of sacking, and now Rolly had gone off with it, galloping off over the fields like a child with a new toy. Chalky had watched him go out of sight and then went to find Betsy in the dimness of the beer cellar. Together they pushed the heavy barrel into its position, and then Betsy stood panting from the exertion, pushing her fair curls back from her face.

Chalky edged closer until his body was level with hers, and eyes glittered as he eyed her rounded curves. 'You're a fine strong woman,' he stated, placing his hand on her fat fair arm.

'Got to be, ain't I.' Betsy was panting for breath but looking with interest at this lithe little man.

'I've seen women work like horses where I've bin,' Chalky made conversation, as he crept even closer. 'But to me there's none like the fair English rose, in bed or in a cellar.' Now his lips were curled up in a fixed smile.

Betsy was like a rabbit in a trap. She drew in her breath sharply as Chalky's hand went up her skirt. 'Get away,' she giggled, 'the bar is open upstairs.'

But Chalky's small hard body pressed her over the huge barrel and, because she was what she was, Betsy gave in. Her tongue came out and her legs parted.

Then just before that moment of bliss, he released her. 'Oh dear!' he apologized. 'Forgive me, I was carried away by your beauty. I am truly sorry for what I nearly did.'

Tears of disappointment and frustration came to Betsy's blue eyes. Her cheeks glowed scarlet as she pulled down her skirt.

The customers had begun to knock impatiently on the counter upstairs. Their pewter pots needed filling. But Betsy was perspiring gently and trembling as she whispered to Chalky: 'Don't go, stay around. I'll close the bar early.'

Chalky watched her white-clad legs as she ran upstairs to the bar and with a very satisfied expression on his face, he sat in the spot where old Sam's body had rested. Taking up a piece of wood and his knife, he started to carve out a boat for Rolly.

It was one of the longest days in Betsy's young life. She had known many men but none had excited her quite as much as this virile young man. She thought of the pot-bellied old ones, the namby-pamby young ones and with every comparison she longed more to be with her latest conquest.

During the day, Chalky helped her in the bar and each time he passed Betsy he would caress her body, driving her wild and even more anxious to get the bar closed.

That evening while Rolly floated his new boat on the stream outside, in the bedroom upstairs Betsy had already dropped her dress to the ground and was holding out her hands to Chalky. Her hot young body was his for the taking and Chalky did not disappoint her. As far as Chalky was concerned, he had control of Betsy and the inn was now in the hands of its rightful landlord.

For her part, Betsy was convinced that at last she now had a man of her own who loved and courted her like a real woman and not just like a paid whore. She bloomed like an overripe fruit with her newly acquired love and Chalky strutted around in a manner he thought conveyed that he was master of the establishment. Nowadays he wore a stiffly starched apron and had his moustache well waxed.

There was one disagreement in this otherwise agreeable situation; it involved the rent money which Betsy saved diligently and placed in a tin box. Although Betsy was illiterate, she was numerate and knew every penny that came across the counter. Now lately it seemed that the takings were less and less, even though she worked as hard as ever. Then one day when Sir Fulke Greville's bailiff called to collect the rent money, she found the tin completely empty. At first she suspected Rolly who, after several heavy clouts, admitted that Chalky had given him lots of money for sweetmeats and that when they went out fishing together, which they did often, Chalky never stayed with him for the whole time. Instead he would disappear, leaving Rolly with plenty of goodies to keep him busy.

During these times, Chalky was in fact off for his own pleasure, a nice game of dice behind the gravestones in the local churchyard. Now dressed like a young dandy man, Chalky was popular with the local layabouts, and he loved to gamble. With a little crowd of unwashed men and boys, Chalky would strut around waving a coin about and calling out: 'Come on, me lucky lads. What's it to be? The King's 'ead or his ass'ole?' Then he would toss the coin in the air. He was very amusing and a good sport and never seemed to mind losing. As a matter of fact, it seemed he usually lost and that Lady Luck seldom smiled on him. Still, he had a compulsive urge to gamble, and Betsy's rent tin financed the habit.

Betsy soon got wise to him. One day while he was engrossed in helping himself to some money, a huge rolling pin descended as if from nowhere on his knuckles.

'Christ!' he screamed. 'You bloody bitch!' He hurled himself at Betsy with a cry of rage.

But Betsy quickly side-stepped him, lashing out again with the rolling pin and yelling; 'Rolly, Rolly!'

On hearing his sister's cries, Rolly dashed in from outside and caught hold of Chalky, landing him a blow which sent him spinning over the counter and clear into the cobbled yard.

When he had recovered from the blow, Chalky shook himself and retired to the stables to think out his next move. As usual old Jem was in the straw settled down for the night. 'Aye,' he muttered when he saw Chalky. 'You still 'ere, then? You ain't been murdered yet?'

'They nearly did,' replied Chalky, sucking his sore knuckles and rubbing his head.

'They will, you know, get you in the end.' Jem wheezed and grunted as he settled in the straw.

Chalky looked at Jem and wondered if he would be reliable as a witness. They could go to the law – that would tame them – but it was a bit risky getting involved with the law, because he had a few things to hide himself. No, that was no use and it was no use telling Betsy and Rolly to get out, of that he was sure, for that Rolly packed quite a wallop. No, he would have to find another way. He nudged old Jem. 'Give us yer bottle, old Jem, I'll get yer some wine in it. There's some good strong stuff down there in the cellar.'

Jem drained off the little that was in the bottle, and handed it to Chalky. 'Wish me old legs was good enough,' he muttered. 'I'd get down that there cellar meself. I knows where old Sam hid all his money, I do,' he whispered hoarsely.

Chalky's little eyes gleamed. This sounded too good to be true. But come to think of it, his father had always hidden his money and if it was still there it would mean that he was certainly dead, for he would never go away and leave his pile behind. 'Tell you what, old Jem, you tell me where it's hid and I'll give you half of it, and you can have your half in booze, if you like.'

The old boy's face assumed a nonchalant look. 'Well, now,' he said, 'I could do with a bit of extra comfort, and a little drop of wine won't hurt.'

'Well then, come on, speak up,' said Chalky anxiously. 'Where is the money hid?'

'Dahn in the cellar, behind yon pile of old harness and under a tub of elderberry what went sour.'

Chalky thought for a moment. Yes, everything was the same down there and he had definitely seen the harness old Jem described. 'Give us yer bottle, me old love,' Chalky said. 'I won't be long.'

Silently Chalky crept towards the cellar, his trusty knife between his teeth. When he reached the window, he soon had the latch released and his wiry little body dropped neatly inside. Then slowly he crept down the steps to the cool earth floor which struck cold to his bare feet. Even in the dark he knew exactly where to look. Under that old tub was a hole. It was all coming back to him now as he remembered seeing old Sam down here counting his gains. Chalky put his hand in the hole, fumbled about a bit, and finally felt an earthenware jar. Pulling it out, he took off the lid and even there in the darkness he could see a glint of gold. He licked his dry lips in anticipation. There had to be hundreds of gold coins! Where in heaven had the old man got all that? There were some papers which looked like letters, and a piece of jewellery, a round pendant, edged with stones which shone out in the moonlight. He squatted beside the hole dazzled by his good fortune. If old Sam left this treasure behind, then there was no doubt that he was dead and that now all this belonged to himself, as Sam's next-of-kin. However, Chalky was not quite sure of what to do about it at this moment so he hurriedly put it all back into the jar, pushed it back into the hole and rolled the tub back into position. It would continue to be safe there until he had made up his mind about what to do. He filled Jem's leather bottle with strong wine and quietly climbed out of the cellar again.

Old Jem had dozed off. Chalky nudged him hard. 'Here's yer bottle, mate,' he said. 'There's nothing down there, mate, I suppose them rogues had it.'

''Tis a pity, a great pity,' said old Jem, sucking the potent liquid from his leather bottle. Then he slumped back into the straw and was soon snoring.

Chalky decided to try a ruse. Brushing himself down, he put his hands in his pockets and strolled out into the yard. Under Betsy's window he whistled a love tune and called in a deep whisper. 'Goodbye, my love, my beautiful Betsy. I'll never forget you.' Then he stamped hard on the hard path as if he were walking away.

Suddenly the window opened and out came Betsy's tousled head. 'Oh, so you did come home, did you?' she said patiently.

'Only to say goodbye, darling,' replied Chalky in a sad tone.

'Don't be daft, just because I caught yer nicking, yer don't have to go.'

'You mean I'm forgiven?' Chalky stared up at her in such a forlorn manner that Betsy started to giggle. 'Don't be soft,' she said. 'I'll come down and let you in.'

'No need,' said Chalky, as he clambered up on to the sloping roof with great agility. He was quickly through the window and just as quickly he was tumbling Betsy on to the bed. Betsy was more than willing and clung to him. 'Oh! I know I am a bloody fool with you,' she whispered, 'but I suppose it's because I love yer.' Foolish blousy Betsy had given her heart and soul to this wily young man and little did she know that there were to be many storms ahead of her.

The next day Chalky swept the yard rather wearily. Every now and then he rested on the handle of the broom, his mind pre-occupied with thoughts of last night's find. That morning they had found old Jem dead, so his only witness to what had happened to his father was now gone. Poor old Jem, the good wine and the excitement at the thought of a fortune must have been too much for him. Chalky was worried. Betsy was a sexy bit of goods but the initial excitement was wearing off for him. She wanted it too much and too often, and Chalky was getting worn out and bored with this life of being at her beck and call. She now knew that he had been pinching a few shillings, so it was not going to be so easy to get any more in the future.

The night before she had said to him: 'You ain't married, are you, Chalky?'

Chalky had been unprepared and did not have his usual lie at the ready: 'Well, I'm sort of betrothed,' he said rather feebly.

'Well, let's get married, then,' Betsy had cried. 'I'm crazy about yer.'

'All right but keep that big brother orf me.'

'Rolly! why, he won't hurt you. He likes you and he won't start anything unless I says so.'

Now Chalky was undecided. He could handle Betsy all right but not that brother of hers, so he had to make a plan to get rid of Rolly somehow. It was a pity but it had to be done.

Rolly was stripped to the waist and humping huge barrels about inside. The muscles of his huge body rippled and shone with sweat.

'Fine strapping fella, that,' remarked the carter who helped to unload the barrels. 'Shame he is so dull-witted.'

Through Chalky's mind came the sight of the tough men on the dockside. That's it! The sea! He would get Rolly press-ganged to the sea.

A few days later after a love session, he said to Betsy: 'Can I take Rolly to see the players at Shoreditch?'

Betsy gave him a shrewd look, 'All right, but don't let him out of your sight,' she warned. 'Otherwise he will be off to the cock-pit. Then he just gets into fights and gets himself all chewed up.'

As always Rolly was very excited to be going somewhere all dressed up with his best tunic on, and his face scrubbed until it was clean and shiny. Eagerly he set off over the fields, with Chalky almost running at his side in an attempt to keep up with Rolly's big strides. Over the hedges, stiles and the little dykes they travelled across the flat green meadowland towards the city until they came to the little hamlet of Shoreditch. It was here that Will Shakespeare built the first playhouse called the Curtain, but he had now gone to live in Stratford-upon-Avon and there a bigger and better playhouse had been built on the opposite side of the river to his home. But the old Curtain still survived, though with second-rate players. Chalky and Rolly did not go through the gate of the playhouse – that was for the rich – but they stood away on top of the hill and looked down into the arena. Rolly sucked sweetmeats and pointed to the dressed-up figures, his huge mouth open with great guffaws of laughter. By now Chalky had lost interest in the play and was engrossed in the cock-fight that was going on down the other side of the hill.

After a while they left Shoreditch and walked by the Thames towards the Tower. The river flowed sluggishly with its variety of boats and the streets got narrower and darker. At last they came to an inn set back from the road and surrounded by small houses. The front of the inn had a paved yard and a wooden seat ran along one wall.

'I got a bit of business to do, me lad,' said Chalky. 'I won't be long. You sit there till I come back,' he pointed at the long seat.

Obediently Rolly sat down on the seat. Pulling an apple from his pocket, he started to munch it while Chalky's small shape disappeared into the gloomy interior of the inn.

What happened next was a great shock to Rolly as he sat peacefully eating his apple. Two men jumped over the wall and grabbed hold of him. 'Got yer!' one cried. 'Come on, me lucky lad, 'tis the rolling briny for yer.'

Rolly lashed out with all his might and the two men went spinning back over the wall. Then came two more and for the next half hour he fought them with all his strength until the yard was spattered with blood and the seat broken in two. With his huge body, Rolly threw them off one after another.

'Chalky,' yelled Rolly. 'Betsy! Betsy!' But no one came to his aid.

The men persisted over and over again and gradually poor Rolly started to get weaker. One enterprising man stood astride the wall with a rope which he sent spinning through the air. It looped down on Rolly and was pulled tight, pinning his arms firmly by his side and in no time at all he was trussed up like a prize carcase. Then they dragged him over the river wall down to a waiting boat and soon they were out to sea.

Chalky had heard all the rumpus as he crouched beside the river bank but did nothing to help. When he saw the boat with Rolly tied up in it, he watched for a time and then stood up to shout: 'Goodbye, mate, I hope you enjoy the trip.' And then hands in his pockets, he set off whistling to Dog Row where he was sure there would be a spot of gaming going on.

8

The Proposal

Marcelle's face was pale and her eyes dark ringed from lack of sleep. But every afternoon she sat in Annabelle's stuffy parlour sewing endlessly and listening to the foolish gossip of the ladies who called on Annabelle. They chattered and tore to pieces the characters of their absent friends. Today Marcelle was not feeling too well. The heat and the noise oppressed her, and she had seen no more of her lover since he had disappeared over the hill. Still, she managed to keep her secret locked safely in her heart, and one thought remained uppermost in her mind that he would one day return and tell her that he loved her. She hoped and prayed that the mysterious young man would remember their encounter as she did and come back to her. Five weeks had passed and each day was more boring than the one before. It was a hot dry summer and visitors brought stories of the return of the plague. Annabelle made no journeys to town and was quite content to busy herself with her garden and her social afternoons. This past week Marcelle had been worried, for she was convinced that something was happening inside her. She was sure of it, but whom could she ask? No one, without betraying the secret of her love. She sat quiet as a mouse, her head bent to her sewing while the idle gossipers chatted and whispered.

The fair young countess had paid them a visit that day and there was much debate between her and Annabelle. They whispered quickly to each other and Marcelle thought at one point that she could hear them talking of the three visitors who had ridden through and stayed the night. She wished she had the courage to ask who the men were, but whenever this fair beauty was visiting, Marcelle felt as if her tongue clung to her mouth. She could scarcely utter a word when this haughty countess was around. Today the countess had arrived in a flurry of excitement, wearing an emerald green gown with a new kind of collar made of Flemish lace.

'I have heard a strange story in London,' the countess told Annabelle, 'of a certain young man who stayed at a yeoman's house overnight.' As she spoke her eyes glowed like dark coals and flickered quickly at Marcelle. Marcelle promptly lowered her gaze, and then, at Annabelle's request, she dropped her sewing and hurriedly left the room.

The countess seemed to have shown an unusual interest in her and Marcelle had a strong feeling of apprehension. She felt as if the painted and perfumed woman knew of her cherished secret.

After Marcelle had left the room, Frances turned towards Annabelle, her face white with rage.

Annabelle was distressed even before the countess had spoken. 'What have I done, my lady?' she begged.

'Either you are becoming a fool or there is treachery

afoot. It seems you know very little of what goes on in your own home, Annabelle.'

Annabelle stared into that beautiful cold face. 'My lady,' she protested, 'I do not know what you mean. Did I not tell you of our overnight guests? Was I wrong to accept them as my guests?' she enquired tearfully.

'No, of course not. But listen to me and I'll tell you of a story that I heard from my cousin Elizabeth, who is a lady-in-waiting to the Queen. She told me that Lord Hay told her of how he had been left to guard his Royal Highness but instead of doing so, he got drunk and slept with the dairy maid in the barn. When he awoke he visited His Highness' bedchamber to find him lying on the floor. Thinking that His Highness had perhaps had one of his usual nightmares, Lord Hay picked him up to return him to his bed. And under His Highness' head, he found a little lace nightcap.' She hissed the words out through clenched teeth.

'Annabelle's brown eyes were wide with amazement. She looked at her Ladyship in bewilderment. 'But, what is that to me?' she pleaded.

'It all happened under your roof, Annabelle, that's what.' A grim smile crossed Frances' sculpted face and the threat was clear.

'But, my Lady, it is not possible,' burst out Annabelle. 'It's a pack of lies!'

'For your sake, dear Annabelle, I do hope so,' Frances remarked.

'But who could have been with his Highness?'

'Obviously not you, Annabelle, as I can see by your surprise. So it must have been that little mouselike companion of yours.' Frances' mouth twisted with hatred. 'So she's not quite so shy as she looks, eh?'

Annabelle rung her hands anxiously. 'I can't believe it, my Lady. It could have been Ruth, but she could not have dared to come back into the house, and it would seem she was satisfied with Lord Hay.'

'He has given her the pox,' returned Frances spitefully.

Annabelle's lips trembled. 'Ruth ran away last week,' she stuttered.

'Well, so we have only the silent little Marcelle. Thomas Mayhew will get a well-stuffed bride and maybe a pair of cuckold horns on his return,' continued Frances. 'And frankly, Annabelle, I am beginning to wonder whether I can trust you . . .' With a haughty look, she rose from her seat and swept out of the room leaving poor Annabelle in tears.

That night Marcelle was in her room sitting on the edge of the bed when Annabelle came in. The sight of Marcelle's tear-stained face and her worried expression told Annabelle that something was terribly wrong. She sat down facing the girl and said gently: 'Where is that nice little lace cap I made for you, dear?'

'I have mislaid it,' answered the listless Marcelle.

Annabelle's voice changed its tone and sounded quite brittle as she replied: 'No! You lost it, dear, and dare I ask where?' Frances had been right: Marcelle's secret was out.

Tears trickled down Marcelle's face. 'Please Annabelle, do not be angry, let me tell you about it.'

'I love you as my own daughter,' said Annabelle. 'I

want you to clear yourself of the terrible story I heard today.' She related what the countess had told her and of what she had hinted.

Marcelle shook her head. 'I cannot clear myself,' she cried, 'because it is true.'

Annabelle rushed at her and shook her hard. 'It isn't! It can't be!' she insisted. 'Don't tell me that I was wrong about you, my dear, it would grieve me terribly.'

Marcelle now opened up and told of her lover, of how he had walked in his sleep, how he had been so kind and gentle and how she had surrendered her virginity to him quite willingly. But that was not all, she said, she was sure now that within her was his child.

Annabelle had gone deathly pale. 'Oh my God, what a terrible thing to happen in my house. What am I going to do?' Her thoughts were now for her own skin. One word of any of this in the ear of the King and the whole lot of them would go to the chopping block. Old Jamie would have no hesitation about it. Her head was spinning; but she was sure the countess would not betray them, since she had too much to hide herself. Marcelle's sweet voice broke in on her thoughts.

'Perhaps if I knew the name of my lover he would return to me, knowing now I am with his child. I am sure he loved me, as I did him. We have not committed such a great sin, have we? Is it so wrong to love?'

Annabelle looked up into her woebegone face and clasped her tightly in her arms. 'You poor little darling,' she sobbed. 'You poor innocent little darling. You must think of your lover as dead and put all thoughts of him from your mind because if the devil was your lover you could not be in more danger.'

Marcelle's tears fell silently and fast. She looked astounded that Annabelle should say such a thing.

The golden summer had drifted into autumn as Thomas Mayhew rode at a leisurely pace through Epping Forest. He was in no hurry and he wanted to enjoy the peace and beauty all around him. He had been away a long time and was now returning from Dorset where he had been settling his affairs before going to sea again soon. As he rode along the shady woodland path, the leaves were falling and made a crisp sound under his horse's hooves. Bessy, the chestnut mare, snorted loudly. She was also enjoying the leisure, having ridden many miles these last few weeks. A little red squirrel, seeking a store of winter nuts scuttled up a tall oak tree. He stopped halfway, his tiny paw clinging to the wrinkled grey bark as his bright eyes surveyed Thomas with fear. But as Thomas rode by, he whispered, 'It's all right, little one, I won't hurt you.' As the squirrel scuttled back down the tree, Thomas thought how fine it would be to be as free as the woodland animals. Well, thought Thomas, thank God he was free of Robert Carr for the time being. Of late he had begun to loathe the man even more and felt sometimes that he wanted to run his sword through his soft podgy body. But with all the padding that Robert Carr wore Thomas doubted whether his sword would even contact his

rotten flesh. Thomas urged his horse on and galloped
for a while, telling himself that he must not let his
hatred for Robert Carr spoil this peaceful day. He
had also made a definite decision. He would ask
Marcelle to marry him. She was young and would
not have minded waiting for him.

And he had other plans for her. His elder brother
had promised to help him prepare a ship and sail away
next year and to take the entire family with them to the
new colony of Virginia, where he intended to buy land.
His brother had told him he was tired of the family
farm and of this sick country, and he wanted to sail off
to the land of freedom, where a man could bring up
his family without fear of persecution on any pretext.
Thomas was almost sure that Marcelle would join
them. His family had been very pleased when he told
them about his intentions regarding Marcelle, and he
could not see any obvious objections to his plans. She
was alone; he was unmarried. He whistled a little tune,
well pleased with his thoughts of the future, and rode
cheerfully through the forest until he came to the hill
and saw Annabelle's house lying ahead of him tucked
cosily into the hillside.

Old Abe came out as Thomas approached and took
hold of Bessy's bridle. Thomas thought that the house
seemed unusually quiet as they walked up the drive.

'I'm mighty glad to see you,' said Abe, but he did
not seem his usual jovial self. Perhaps he is just getting
on a bit, thought Thomas.

Now he could see Marcelle in the garden with a
basket on her arm which she was filling with late

summer blooms. The basket was a blaze of colour contrasting wonderfully with the white cap and apron she wore over her pale blue dress. As she came forward shyly to greet him, he thought how very bonny she looked. She seemed to have filled out and there was a serene look on her face which suited her to perfection. He kissed the hand she offered and together they walked to a seat under the drooping willow tree, the most sheltered spot in the garden.

'My, 'tis fine to see you looking so bonny,' Thomas squeezed Marcelle's hand and admired the chestnut glint in her hair, the aquiline nose and the thickness of her lashes. All the while Marcelle modestly kept her eyes averted from him.

'Many things have changed since we last met Marcelle, and I have so much to say to you.'

Still Marcelle made no reply; she just picked petals in an absent-minded way off the flowers in the basket.

Thomas decided to get it over with and took a deep breath. Soon the garden would no longer be empty. He slipped to the ground on one knee, and took one of her small hands in his. 'Will you marry me, my dear? I have loved you since I found you almost a year since. Please tell me that you will.'

Hot tears ran down Marcelle's cheeks as she pulled her hand away and held it to her face.

'Don't cry, my love,' said Thomas. 'There is nothing to be afraid of. If you do not love me I will go away and not bother you again but don't you want to marry me?' he asked. He was indeed surprised by her reaction to his question.

'Oh, I do!' cried Marcelle fervently, 'and it breaks my heart to have to refuse you,' she sobbed.

'There is no need to worry,' replied Thomas patiently. 'I will wait for your answer until I come back from sea. I will never marry anyone else, my dear, I can assure you. Only you, Marcelle, will bend this old bachelor to domesticity.' He smiled as if to console her.

Marcelle took her hands from her face and he dried her tears. But she had an intense look in her eyes as she spoke. 'I betrayed you, Thomas', she whispered. 'I took a lover and now I bear his child in my womb.'

Thomas felt as if he had been struck. He got to his feet, reeling slightly, and gripped her by the shoulders so tightly that his fingers dug into her flesh. 'What nonsense is this, child?' he demanded harshly.

'It is true! It is true!' Marcelle's sobs rang out across the garden as she broke from his hold and ran up the path.

Thomas watched her retreating figure in a daze. He knew that Marcelle was an emotional and highly strung girl but whatever had possessed her to say a thing like that? It was impossible, right here in the heart of the countryside with Annabelle as such a good chaperone. No, he did not believe what she had said, it was sheer nonsense, a shock reaction to his proposal, no doubt. He had better talk to Annabelle, he told himself.

Annabelle had watched this garden drama from behind the parlour window, and now she waited white-lipped and nervous for Thomas' knock on the door. What could she say? Was he to be trusted? Her mind was in a whirl. She would have to tell him the truth; he would never be content till he knew it. 'Oh God protect us,' she whispered.

There was a gentle tap on her door and Thomas entered, hat in hand. His dark eyes looked perplexed and his mouth set in that downward curve that had earned him the name of Dour Thomas. Annabelle was usually delighted to have any visit from Thomas but today she was nervous because she knew that he was furious. Her white hand hovered shakily over the silver tray as she poured wine into two crystal goblets and handed him one.

Once the ritual of hospitality was over, she sat silently in her chair waiting for him to begin the conversation.

He was certainly abrupt. 'It would probably be no surprise to you, Madam, that I wish to marry Marcelle.'

'It's as I expected,' Annabelle replied. 'And she has refused you.'

'But she tells me an impossible story, insisting that she has had a lover and is with child.' He half smiled as he repeated the story. He felt reassured, for it was all so improbable.

Annabelle clutched her hands nervously in her lap. 'I regret to tell you, Thomas, that it is quite true.'

He stared disbelievingly at her. 'You mean that someone has tampered with that young girl?' He rose, the veins in his forehead showed thick as the blood rose to his head. 'What soundrel did that?' he shouted. 'And whatever possessed you to allow it, Annabelle, while she was in your care?'

Annabelle stood up to calm him. 'Please, Thomas, listen to me,' she pleaded. 'I am at my wit's ends, it is such a strange story.'

Thomas' dark eyes glowed with temper as he sat listening to Annabelle's tale of her late-night guests, and of how she had recognized the prince and of how, without her knowledge, Marcelle had tried to help the prince and taken him back to his bed. That, she told him, must have been the time when this dreadful fate had befallen her.

'Oh my God!' Thomas held his hands to his head until Annabelle had come to the end of her story. 'They will crucify her, poor little Marcelle,' he burst out. 'Annabelle, swear to me that no one else knows the identity of her lover, not even Marcelle, I hope.'

'She does not know,' confirmed Annabelle. 'He left here without even a farewell wave in the early morning.'

Thomas stood up and then began to pace the room. 'Are you sure that the secret will remain with us?'

Annabelle immediately remembered Frances and hesitated. Thomas' dark eyes bore down on her but she remained calm.

'No one knows but us,' she replied hesitantly. 'Not even Abe.'

'Good! Then your next duty is to persuade Marcelle to marry me.'

'But Thomas,' Annabelle protested. 'Would you deliberately cuckold thyself?' Her mouth dropped open, she was well and truly shocked.

'I would go to any lengths to protect that girl,' he

replied. 'You know the fate of an unwedded woman who tries to take care of a child in this part of the country.'

'I do indeed,' Annabelle whispered, 'and a house of correction would kill her, poor child.'

'Well, do be sensible, Annabelle. Tell her that today I will go and set up the banns and in three Sundays we will be wed. In that way she will have the protection of my name and even if I do not return from this voyage, whatever I possess will then be hers.'

Annabelle was wiping away her tears. 'You are a great man, Thomas Mayhew,' she cried. 'There are very few who would be as noble and as generous as you in these circumstances.'

'Never mind,' he said curtly. 'Talk to the child. I'll wait downstairs for an answer.'

Annabelle departed upstairs to Marcelle's room, where she talked to her of the forthcoming baby, of how if it were to be born out of wedlock the stigma would last all its life, and how Thomas would give her and the baby protection if she married him. 'Please, darling. Thomas loves you and wants to look after you,' begged Annabelle.

Marcelle was a soft gentle person but weak and easily swayed. In no time she had consented.

When the women returned downstairs to Thomas, Marcelle placed her hand in his and said: 'I am sorry, dear Thomas, for what I have done, but if you take care of my baby I will be a good and devoted wife to you, this I promise with all my heart.'

There was a lump in Thomas' throat as he put his

arms protectingly about her. 'I will go to the New World and make a peaceful happy place for us and the child out there. But first of all I will return in three weeks, when we will be wed.'

'Farewell, my love,' he said, as he rode away.

The date for the wedding had been fixed. It was to be kept a secret, though in a small village it was not easy to do that.

The priest always gossiped with his parishioners about the births, deaths and marriages in his area and besides, Annabelle owned a fair-sized property and she was obliged to include her servants in the festivities. In no time, word was sent around the village that a wedding was to take place at Craig Alva in a couple of weeks. The maids retrimmed their best dresses, the Morris dancers rehearsed every day, and the old folk of the village eagerly looked forward to the extra food and drink.

Marcelle continued with her work taking little or no interest in all the preparations for her wedding, and Annabelle became quite impatient with her. After all, getting married was to be the girl's highest honour.

Only Abe showed kindness and came to see Marcelle with cool drinks after her bouts of early morning sickness. Thomas had sent her a pretty green gown to be married in, and Will, who had brought the gown from London, was full of good humour, for he was to join the King's Players.

Will had brought with him a friend, an actor and a fine musician named Ned. Ned had a strange-looking head, and his hair seemed to start way back from his forehead, but he had a pleasant, soft-speaking voice and was a restful sort of young man. At night they all sat around the fire in the inn while Ned read parts from the various plays he had acted in.

Soon the big day arrived. It was a clear, cool crisp October day and there was a light layer of frost on the rooftops which foretold the coming of winter. Marcelle looked from her bedroom window to the garden below. A late yellow rose bloomed still on an isolated bush, and she surveyed it with affection for she had grown very fond of Annabelle's garden. She had had strange dreams in the night. She had heard that young man sobbing again but this time so loud that she had gone to the dark, unlit guest chamber, and it almost seemed as though the slim, red-haired young man held out his arms to her. She grew afraid and, shivering and sweating, she ran back to her room. Perhaps it was the devil whom Annabelle had suggested had seduced her.

That same morning, in his lodgings, Thomas dressed for his wedding. The finished product certainly looked very dandy. He had discarded his messenger's uniform and replaced it with his best brown velvet knee-length coat with a smart white collar and slightly lighter tight pantaloons. He brushed his hair and trimmed his beard, while all the time receiving wry comments from his two very dissolute room-mates who had had a very late night.

'My, Thomas, do not tell us that you have at last found a lady to please you?' One mocked. 'I was beginning to think that a gentleman would be his choice.'

They nudged each other and went into fits of giggles like young girls.

Thomas, however, only scowled at them and continued with his toilet.

'So you have left dear Robert,' said one. 'I heard news that will surprise you.'

But Thomas paid no heed to their gossip.

'They do say his Royal Highness is very ill. He collapsed at a tennis match yesterday.'

This time Thomas stopped what he was doing and looked round at the youth who had spoken. He was lounging on the bed. This rumour had been around before, Thomas thought, and then pulling impatiently at his shirt cuffs, he swore out loud.

His friends looked at each other, for it was not like Thomas to be foul-mouthed.

Then in an even louder voice, Thomas said: 'Curse him! I hope he dies. And curses on the whole damned lot of them – old Jamie as well.'

The youths were too shocked even to answer.

Picking up his bag, Thomas said; 'The rent is paid till the end of the year. I will not be back and you two bastards can take the quickest road to hell as soon as you like.' The door slammed and Dour Thomas had left.

'God,' said one to the other, 'what is wrong? Maybe he got a dose of something.'

'It's just pre-nuptial nerves, I fear,' said the other.

Thomas made his way to the Temple, where he handed to his friend expert in legal affairs a file containing his will and advice on the family property he was likely to inherit in Dorset.

The white-haired lawyer shook hands with Thomas and wished him Godspeed. Thomas then went to the stables, collected his horses and set off for his own wedding which was to be at three o'clock that afternoon.

The little church was bright and gay with flowers and the parson in his new cassock peered short-sightedly at Marcelle and Thomas Mayhew as he joined them in holy matrimony. Indeed, he thought they were an unusual couple, and both seemed rather unhappy. But the parson knew that in these troubled times one did not ask too many questions. He himself was still a Baptist at heart and glanced furtively to one side as the bride, at the end of the ceremony, made the sign of the cross. The young maid did look very sweet, he thought, in a green dress with large slashed sleeves which revealed glimpses of yellow satin to match the hand-made flowers on her little cap.

Will gave the bride away and Annabelle was the only other witness to sign any legal papers.

As Marcelle held on to Thomas' arm, she thought how different she had once thought her wedding would be. She had once believed that it would be a great exciting day, a day to remember all her life. But instead she felt sick and depressed. Tears ran down her cheeks and fell in drops upon her dress.

Thomas held her hand tightly, and worried how she would manage while he was away. But go he must – partly for pride and partly for money. 'Please, God, take care of her,' he prayed as she swore to love, honour and obey him.

Outside the church, the village children, dressed in their Sunday best, threw rose petals in the path of the bride and groom and one woman called out good wishes to them. Marcelle and Thomas climbed up into a farm wagon and set off for their reception with all the villagers marching along behind singing and laughing, all ready and willing to join in the grand feast that had been prepared for them.

Several hours later Thomas stood surveying the scene at the end of the long garden. The rowdy villagers were still in full swing celebrating his wedding, while on a small hillock, under a tree, stood Will and his new companion. Will was plucking at his viol while his friend Ned scraped frantically on the fiddle. Young men and maids held each other about the waist and whirled round and round. In the centre near the lawn, the elderly guests sat in troupes, drinking from long jugs, their voices joining in the songs or telling lewd jokes. They were crouched together, their red caps on their heads all awry. Thomas looked at Will's friend more closely and thought how much he looked like Will Shakespeare with that same head of chestnut hair receding from his forehead.

Beside Thomas sat Abe very full of beer, and next to him was the stout form of the village innkeeper. Together they talked of simple pleasures – badger hunting and fishing in the land of hills and dales, where they had both come from. Their voices were loud and merry, such straightforward men, with no axes to grind, and free to live and work without caring for the world outside. It was the sort of life Thomas dreamed of for Marcelle and himself.

Annabelle had taken Marcelle to her room. The guests in their lusty way had wanted to bed the bride and groom themselves, taking them to the bridal chamber, undressing them both and putting them to bed together with many rude jests. But Annabelle would have none of this, and no one dare defy her. So the guests contented themselves with eating and drinking as much as possible, but not a few were heard to remark that being refused the honour of bedding the couple had spoilt the wedding, and they sat desolate over their beer.

It was beginning to get dark and soon the guests would depart. Thomas thought that he should go up to Marcelle but a strange shyness held him out in the garden watching the gambols of the villagers, and so he lingered on. Just before twilight, a breathless hush came over the countryside and the sky shone red just before the hovering sun disappeared. It was at this moment, under the tall eves of the house, that a small shuttered window was flung open, and there appeared a head with thin, untidy locks and a straggly beard. The musicians stopped playing, the dancers stopped and everyone looked up. Merlin put his strange thin face out of the window and looked down just as the church bell boomed out in the distance. All eyes turned in the direction of the tall steeple. Again and again the bell boomed out. It was not the gay call of wedding bells or even the calling to church; just the dull clang clang of the toll of death. The maids screamed and hid their faces and their escorts put an arm of protection about them while the old folk huddled close together.

Merlin let out a strange cackle, pulled back his shaggy head, and slammed the shutters.

The innkeeper sent a boy on horseback to see what the parson was up to, creating such a racket and upsetting everyone.

The old folk pulled their shawls tighter about them and began to drift home. The party was over for them.

Ten minutes later, the messenger returned to say that the noble Prince Henry had passed away. And the remaining guests at the wedding party wept and wailed.

Thomas listened to the noise of the chatter and the weeping in stunned disbelief. It could not be true. A black cloud of guilt seemed to pass through his brain. Oh God! He had cursed this young prince every day and had wished him dead. Surely it had nothing to do with him! No, by God, he was not going to let such nonsense sway him. He had heard of black magic, but he was not going to let himself be influenced by it. It was simply as God had willed. It had been time for the prince to die; he would have gone anyway, whether it had been battlefield or in bed. There was a time to die and a time to live. Thomas shook his head. He would go up to see his bride. At least she did not know that the father of the child she carried had left this earth and, please God, she never would, he thought.

In Annabelle's best guest-chamber, Marcelle lay sleeping, mentally and physically exhausted by the events of the long day. Thomas crept quietly into the room and knelt beside the bed, taking her hand, which lay on the coverlet, gently in his own. Strange emotions disturbed him, as he felt an over-whelming love for this young girl. It suffused his whole being, but was mixed with a hatred for the fate that had caused this to be such a futile wedding night.

As he gazed at the tiny hand, he remembered the words of a poem in a play he had recently seen: 'Her fair hand of perfect white, Lay as an April daisy on the grass.' As he gently toyed with the dainty fingers, he allowed his gaze to travel to her face. Long lashes lay upon her rosy cheeks, 'Like marigolds they sheathed the light, Canopied in darkness sweetly, Till they might open to adorn the day.'

Thomas pressed his head on the coverlet. His feel-ings had gone beyond the power of his will, and he wanted only to get close to her and press his lips on that sweet rosy mouth. Grim despair overcame him as he pressed his hot aching body against the frame of the bed. He knelt there, touching her hand with his hot lips, and his tears fell on the white daisy-patterned quilt. Like a sleeping flower Marcelle clenched her fingers tight. With a deep sigh, Thomas pulled away gently, picked up his bag and left the room. He went downstairs to the kitchen where he found Abe, snor-ing in his usual seat at the side of the fire. Outside, from the barn, he could still hear the sounds of music. It would seem that Will and his friend were still cavort-ing with a few young guests. With a pale set face, Thomas sat at the long kitchen table for a while, his head in his hands. Rising wearily, he went to the dresser where he found a quill pen and an ink horn. Then he sat at the table, and wrote a farewell to his young bride.

The letter was long and entirely personal and scraps of it Marcelle was to remember for the rest of her short young life.

He wrote:

> *I love you dearly. God's will that on my return we will sail for the New World where I will do my utmost to make you and the child happy. Take care, and do not, if you can help it, leave the shelter of this pleasant home until I come back for you, my love. 'Tis better I leave now before you wake to spare you the anguish of parting.*
>
> *Money is available if you have need. The address is enclosed. Do not go alone. Take Annabelle to the Inns of Court with you, and take the marriage certificate. Goodbye, my love, I have waited a long time for you. A year will soon pass, take care.*
>
> *Your affectionate husband.*
> *Thomas Mayhew*

Then sealing the letter with wax and his heavy signet ring, he placed it on the dresser and silently went out to collect his horse from the stable. Before the dawn light streaked the sky, he was on the road to Harwich to join the company of the seafaring young men who were to sail to the New World with Robert Rich. It would be several years before Essex or Marcelle saw Thomas Mayhew again and much water would have flowed under the bridge in that time.

On that eventful day when the Crown Prince of England met his death, as the bewildered Marcelle married Thomas, some miles across country in the great manor at Audley End, the young Frances Howard sat hunched up in a window seat, staring out at the magnificent park land and over the undulating Essex weald. The huge cedars in the park stood as solidly as they had done for centuries, growing more broadly and stronger as each year passed since the Howard ancestors had brought them back as saplings from Lebanon on their way home from the Crusades. Their roots, like live snakes, seemed to rise above the ground as Frances stared listlessly at them, through the tiny leaded window panes.

She had been there for several hours, hunched up in a crouching position as though waiting for something, just as a cat waits patiently for a mouse. Dressed in a dark sombre dress and wearing no jewellery, her ash-blonde hair hung down straight to her waist. In her hand she clutched a little lace night cap. Her green eyes were flashing with hate, and her face was so white that the only splash of colour came from her scarlet lips as she bit them in tormented anguish.

'Goodbye, Frances,' her cousin Elizabeth called up to her from the bottom of the stairs. 'I must take my leave, but I must say that you show little gratitude for the favour I did you. And how much longer are you going to sit up there?'

But Frances merely gave her a languid wave of the hand and continued her vigil, with the little cap screwed up in her hand. Soon her husband would be leaving, and to hell with him. She would be well rid of him for a while. Why, the audacity of that stupid boyish husband, to think that she might return to that gloomy dark castle again! Nobody was going to get her to move from her father's home until she got her own way. She would mope and pine and then perhaps old Uncle Thomas might interfere and help her to divorce that oaf they had tied her to.

Her mind throbbed a tune of hate, and twisted and turned in the direction of her lover Henry. 'He is dying,' she murmured. 'I know he will die,' miserably she tried to blot out the image of that noble face and the curling auburn hair. They had been so young and gay, but what went wrong? Henry had been so weak and had gone cold on her when Robert returned to claim her. And now her sweet lover was about to die, she was sure of that. To think that she might have been Queen if they had not forced her into marrying Essex. Her nails dug into the lace cap, tearing it slowly to shreds. Well, it was no good now, but at least no one else was going to get him. And there was still dear Robert Carr. A strange smile crossed her lips as she began to think of the night when she had seduced Robert in order to make Henry jealous. It had been a most pleasant shock when Robert had gone to pieces in her embrace. Poor Robert. He had been a little page at the Scottish court, and sexually abused by those wanton earls. But now he was a favourite of the King and could ask for anything he wanted as long as he let old Jamie fuss and pet him. Frances' smile became more pronounced as her thoughts dwelt on him. After all, everyone had thought that Robert didn't like women until Frances convinced him that he did, and now, having become aware of his heterosexual feelings, he longed for Frances and wrote her love letters in which he swore that he could not live without her. Well, if she could get rid of her damned ugly lout of a husband, Robert could have the pleasure of her company for life. And, looking on the bright side, if Henry died, Robert would be on the way up. And Frances intended to share in his glory. After all, they shared too many guilty secrets to be parted now. So the complicated world of the fair countess revolved about her as she sat by the window. At dusk when the doom-laden bell boomed out, Frances relaxed. While the servants and villagers ran out into the night to hear the sad tidings, Frances rose with stiff limbs, and climbed the rest of the grand stairway to her room to sleep. Tomorrow the Howards would be riding for London, for the court mourning and to make a grand display at the young prince's funeral.

In the morning, as the Howard retinue rode in, King James rode out, in an effort to get as far away as possible from the sight and smell of death. A nervous man with a morbid fear of death, not even feelings for his own son could make him stay to face the funeral.

Before the Lying-in-State, the noble Henry was stretched out on a cold marble slab, his body cut up and probed while learned doctors endeavoured to find out the cause of his death. But in vain: the cause of his death remained a mystery.

The court was in mourning and the prince lay in state until December, when with great pomp and ceremony, the beloved Crown Prince was escorted to his final resting place in Westminster Abbey.

London buzzed with excitement, and many flocked to the city to the funeral of the young prince. The four-hour procession was watched sadly by rich and poor alike for this young prince had been very popular. The people wept at the sight of the black plumed carriage and the wax effigy of Henry on top of the coffin dressed in the state robes. Even his horse was draped in black, as were the drums of the drummers and they beat the slow mournful beat all the way there.

From the window of Holborn House, Frances Howard sat and watched the banners held by the heralds go by and saw the young Prince Charles on his thin wobbly legs being escorted by her uncle as Chief Mourner, followed by Frances' brother. There was no sign of Robert Carr, for he was with the timid King at Theobalds. All the other great ladies, dressed up in their black mourning gowns, sat near to Frances and glanced sympathetically at her, for many of them had known about her love affair with young Henry.

Frances, in fact, did not feel too bad, just a little remote and sad that Henry should die so young, when there was so much to be gained from life if you knew how to face up to it. Sentiment had never been for her. She looked over at her stepmother, Catherine, who looked sad and demure with her head bent and her face covered with clouds of black veiling. 'Bawdy bitch,' Frances muttered under her breath. Her step-mother was as treacherous as the rest of them; they were like rats scraping and chewing, all with the same purpose – their own survival. Frances' lips were set in a grim line. Thank God by tomorrow this weary period of sitting mourning would be over, she thought, and the gay court life would soon begin again. She would ask Annabelle to come up to live in town. She was a person she could trust. Annabelle would help her to get divorced. Her thoughts settled on an unpleasant matter. 'I wonder how that lily-livered girl who lives with Annabelle is. It would be a strange trick of fate if Henry had left her pregnant,' she thought. She ought to find out what the situation was, she decided. Slowly and gracefully she rose and went out of the long dark chamber as the order was given to retire. 'Thank God that is over,' said the noble but insincere Frances.

Out in the Channel the sea was calm and a huge four-masted sailing ship was riding at anchor, her white sails hanging loose waiting for the wind to fill them out and to carry her out past the coast of England towards the great Atlantic Ocean. Thomas Mayhew leaned over the rail and sighed. He could see the dim line of chalk cliffs in the distance. That was Dover. It was nearly three months since his wedding and still he had made very little progress. The ship had waited at Flushing in the Low Country for stores but a fever had raged in the port and many young sailors had died. So Sir John Smith, the Captain, now roamed the

South Downs searching for more men to replenish his crew, while at the same time waiting for the wind.

The inactivity bored Thomas. He had no time for gambling and steered clear of the fencing bouts which always ended in real battles. He had no taste for any of these things. The fresh salt breeze blew over his head causing his black plaited hair to blow out from his neck. He held up his hand. The wind was rising, thank God. At last they would be off, away before daybreak. A longboat drew alongside, and someone hailed the skipper. Thomas turned to watch as the pressed men were driven aboard. Poor devils, he thought, so cold and shivering. Some were cursing and swearing, but they all looked dejected. There were even small boys, half tipsy with wine. The last victim on aboard was trussed like a sucking pig ready for roasting. He was a huge fellow and although well trussed and gagged he still struggled hard. Thomas watched with interest as they removed the fellow's gag and a roaring voice yelled: 'Betsy! Betsy! Help me!' Thomas started. That voice, he knew it! Into his mind flashed the image of a blonde woman and a man dying on the floor of an inn. Surely it was not that woman's brother Rolly? Thomas went forward and looked down into the scarred and battered face of Rolly who lay there blubbering like a baby and calling out for Betsy as loud as he could.

'Stand back, Sir!' said the bosun, standing ready with a rope end. 'He's vicious, that one. Look what he done to the men . . .' He pointed towards a row of men who stood looking shame-faced, their noses still bleeding as their eyes gradually became puffed up and discoloured. They certainly looked a sorry sight.

But Thomas only wanted to comfort this poor boy, this childlike man, whose body was badly bruised by the kicks and blows of his captors. He knelt beside him and loosened the rope that held Rolly's hands. Rolly immediately started to struggle again.

'Stand back, sir!' urged the bosun. 'He is as strong as an ox.'

Thomas looked down at the youth and said: 'Hullo, do you remember, me?'

Rolly's eyes rolled with fright and he did not seem to recognize Thomas. Thomas helped him sit up. 'Don't worry Rolly,' he said. 'You are with friends.'

For a moment Rolly understood. 'I want to go home,' he wailed.

Thomas turned to the men who had gathered around. 'This man is an old servant of mine,' he said. 'Take him to my cabin, I will be responsible for him.'

Thomas took off the bonds from Rolly's ankles and wrists, and fed Rolly in his cabin. There they talked of Betsy and the Duke's Head, until at last Rolly calmed down and he was once more back to being the docile boy who listened in wonder to the tales of adventure of others.

The crew grew to like this strong, willing man and Rolly asked no more to go home but adapted himself to the life on board ship. During the time that they spent at sea Rolly was always close to Thomas and many times during running battles with the odd Spanish ship Rolly had saved Thomas from many a sharp blade. The rotten food never upset Rolly nor did the bloodshed. Times of pestilence passed over him for he had already survived both the plague and smallpox when he was young. Rolly enjoyed the task of throwing the dead crew overboard and with a good will he meted out punishment to the offenders tied to the mast. When necessary, the whip was put into Rolly's hand and he beat them whole-heartedly perversely, enjoying the excitement of it.

'That fellow is the most adaptable member of the crew,' the captain remarked to Thomas.

To Thomas Mayhew, Rolly was like a pet dog – always on hand to be kicked, cursed or fondled. It was all the same to Rolly. While to Rolly, Thomas was his saviour; he was devoted to him and he was never very far away. When weary of the endless expanse of sea, and homesick for England, Thomas found it comforting to have Rolly squatting near by, bronze skinned and glowing with health. And it gave him a boost to hear Rolly talking of Betsy for it brought Marcelle closer to him in his heart during these lonely months.

So there we have to leave them for a while to their adventures in the New World, where there was so much gold for the taking, the big, childish Rolly and the morose Thomas thrown together in a world as yet unexplored.

9

The Birth

In the quiet rural surroundings in Essex, the year came in and slowly passed. The winter transgressed into spring and dark nights and cosy fires gave way to longer evenings sitting out in the garden and rising early to plant and sow, in a happy anticipation of a warm summer.

At Annabelle's house the cows were still brought in at sunrise and the milkmaids sang as they worked. The blackbird repaired his nest and searched for a new mate, his throat bursting with song. And Marcelle, looking up from her chores in the dairy, sang too, in a soft, gentle voice because she felt so happy. Her figure was full and round, and her cheeks glowed with good health. She was nearly nine months pregnant and had never felt so well and content in her life. Whenever the healthy babe kicked and writhed inside her, she smiled and put her hand on the spot on her belly. It was a wonderful feeling: she would never be alone again. In her womb was part of her who would grow and talk and be with her always. It made her feel so exhilarated that in spite of the extra weight of her body she wanted to run, jump, dance and sing.

Old Abe whistled sharply from the doorway to let

Marcelle know that breakfast was ready. With loving care he had prepared a bowl of oatmeal for her, topped with the best of the cream. Now he watched her affectionately as she ate. 'That's right, love, nothing like a good bowl of oats to settle the tummy,' he said.

Abe had grown very attached to Marcelle and all winter long they had kept each other company. Abe taught the girl to play crib and shuffle penny, and in the evenings as they were seated by the crackling fire, he would tell her strange stories of the lonely Yorkshire moors that had been his home as a boy. Marcelle also learned the secret of Merlin, the crazy healing man, who lived in the attic, and she had been amazed to learn that Abe was Annabelle's husband and that old Merlin had once been her lover but had lost his wits while working on experiments years ago. She learned that when witches were no longer burned and more humanitarian forms of punishment were sought, apothecaries, of which Merlin was one, were called upon to experiment with different kinds of torture. And they experimented on human beings themselves. It did not take long for Merlin to be badly affected by the horrendous tortures he was expected to inflict on people all in the name of progress. He went quite mad, running amok and killing several people. He spent some time locked in a cage but then Annabelle and Abe had rescued him and brought him to this house strapped to a board, by then a raving lunatic.

'Did you not mind Annabelle having a lover?' Marcelle asked Abe, her soft eyes looking sad and bewildered.

'Aye, 'tis hard to understand, my dear,' he replied. 'But circumstances alters many cases,' he puffed the little black pipe that he had recently taken to smoking. 'I am more than a score years older than she,' he said. 'So when this flighty Scotsman came hanging around, I went back to the coachhouse and left them the freedom of the cottage. Annabelle was mad about him, and a nice-looking chap he was, too, and very clever. He was assistant to that Harvey chap, the one the King knighted. Well, to cut a long story short, they had a bonny bairn, a baby girl, but she died of the smallpox – I reckon that was the real beginning of him losing his wits. He tried to cure the baby with this new idea they got, all to do with the blood but it didn't work. I don't know what it was about, it was beyond me.'

Tears of sympathy for Annabelle trickled down Marcelle's cheeks. 'How terrible,' she whispered, 'to have a child and then lose it.'

'Here! don't you go fretting yourself.' Abe reached out and patted her cheek with his wrinkled hand. 'It was the will of God and Annabelle has been happy here in this house and so have I. Even that poor devil upstairs is all right now. No one bothers him now. Shut him up in a bloody cage, they did. You should have seen the state of him when we helped him to escape, and it could never have been managed without the help of Frances Howard. She was always fond of Annabelle, would do anything for her, she would.'

'I am happy here too,' said Marcelle, 'and I do hope

Annabelle will be back in time – when the baby is born, I mean.'

'She will,' Abe assured her, 'do not worry. It is this damned wedding that is keeping her in London. Waste of money, all them dances and masques. But it is all they think about. She would do better to stay here, it only makes her discontented, all that high society.'

So Abe grumbled away and Marcelle smiled fondly at him. He was such a nice old man, she had never known anyone so kind. She certainly missed Annabelle, but life was a bit more peaceful without her, for she was always chasing them all about.

The wedding that Annabelle was attending was that of King James' eldest daughter Elizabeth. The wedding was a grand affair with the sixteen-year-old bride in a gown of silver tissue studded with many fabulous jewels and her hair hanging loose about her shoulders to signify her maiden state. The country could ill afford this magnificent display but all the court had been preparing for the wedding for some time. The King himself was still in a depressed state since the death of his son Henry, and the day of the wedding did not help the King's feelings. In fact, he made a quiet journey through Westminster Abbey where young Henry's effigy was still on view.

A few weeks later Annabelle arrived home, very smart and full of chatter about the wedding and her stay at Holborn House as lady-in-waiting to her beloved Frances.

To Marcelle she seemed changed, there was a

certain tiredness in her eyes and she did not seem quite so responsive to the members of the household. Everything seemed to agitate her – the house, the farm, the servants and she nagged poor Abe from morning till night.

'I wonder what is eating her ladyship?' muttered Abe one day as Marcelle sat in the kitchen. 'She has got something on her mind, you mark my words.' He nodded his shaggy head and looked so worried that Marcelle put a comforting arm about him. 'It is the change after living in that fine house,' she said. 'Do not get upset, it will pass.'

Once again the great local ladies began to gather in Annabelle's parlour and the regular pattern of life settled on them all. One afternoon even Frances Howard came visiting again but her face was frozen and her green eyes stared insolently at Marcelle, her gaze coming to rest on the bulge of the girl's stomach.

Marcelle lowered her gaze and asked to be excused from the parlour. Then she stood a while in the corridor to regain her composure. The cat-like eyes of Frances Howard had disconcerted her. Inside the room she heard voices raised in temper. Annabelle and her beloved Frances were quarrelling. She could hear their shrill voices through the closed door, terror held her very still, and she crouched in a corner of the corridor trying in vain not to listen.

Annabelle's voice came wailing and tearful. 'Do not ask me to leave this house, Frances, I have become so attached to it,' she was saying.

'Nonsense!' came the acid tone of Frances. 'I have bought another house and I need you there, as well as Abe and Merlin.'

'Oh God! How will I tell them?' wept Annabelle.

'Whatever is wrong with you?' demanded Frances. 'Have you forgotten how much you owe me? Do not try to back out now or I swear you will regret it dearly,' her voice trembled with threats.

'Oh, I am sorry, dear, I do not mean to be selfish, but it is a responsibility that I have to the rest of the household,' pleaded Annabelle.

'Well, take them with you, then,' replied Frances. 'The house is out of town, so Merlin will be safe there. But that bitch of a girl is not my responsibility. Let that husband she cuckolded so well take care of her. Now, Annabelle, my patience is exhausted. Stop this whining and I will send for you in several weeks.'

As Frances left, she passed so close to Marcelle that the girl could smell her perfume. She almost fainted in terror. And even when Frances had climbed into her carriage and disappeared, she remained in the corner, stunned, her thoughts filled with confusion. So Frances knew her secret; had Annabelle told her? She wanted to run away, to go somewhere, away from everybody, to find a place to have her baby where no unkind voices recalled her crime of being seduced by an unknown man. With her hands hot and clammy, and her body shaking violently, she stood propped against the wall until Annabelle found her.

'What are you doing out there, Marcelle?'

Annabelle asked. 'And what is the matter with you? Are you not well?'

Marcelle could not answer. She just stared back at Annabelle, her wide eyes looking tragically at her. 'Come, my love, I will get you to bed,' said Annabelle, forgetting her own troubles. She guided Marcelle tenderly to her room and helped her undress.

'Is it three weeks yet till you are due?' she asked. But Marcelle did not answer, her face was buried deep in the pillow.

The next day Annabelle sent for the mother of one of the milkmaids. The old crone was experienced in midwifery. 'She may have the child soon,' the old lady said, 'It is very low. I will stay on, just in case, because she seems a funny girl and I do not think she will help herself, that one.'

Annabelle bit her lip. She was not sure what to do. There was an apothecary in town but he might not come all this way out for a childbirth. She took another look at Marcelle who was lying quite still. Oh dear, it had been a trying week . . . Then she decided to take a chance and send to town for the apothecary, in the morning. Then she closed Marcelle's bedroom door quietly and went off to her own flowery boudoir to rest.

It was a clear cold night and a full moon hung heavy in the sky. The silver light filled the room as Annabelle restlessly watched white fluffy clouds sail past. This was her home and she loved it; it was going to be very hard to leave it, as Frances wished. Then the air was suddenly rent by terrible shrieks – dreadful bloodcurdling screams which came tearing through the night. It was Marcelle! Annabelle leapt from her bed and ran along the corridor to where she found Marcelle lying at the bottom of the short flight of stairs that led from her room. The girl was doubled up in pain, her hands on her stomach, and she was screeching like one possessed. 'Oh! save my baby!' she screamed. 'Oh God! please help me! Send the devil away, do not let him touch my baby!' Her eyes were dilated and saliva frothed on her lips as though she were in a fit.

'Abe, come and help!' called Annabelle as she ran to aid Marcelle who was lying on the floor, her arms thrashing and her head twisting and turning.

'Oh God, she is demented!' gasped Annabelle, holding her close to her.

Abe picked Marcelle up gently, soothing her with kind words.

'I saw him,' sobbed Marcelle. The tears began to fall as she slowly recovered. 'He was there, the devil, that young man with the red hair.'

'Hush,' said Abe. 'Remember the little babe inside you. You do not want to frighten him, do you?'

By now Merlin had appeared, a nightcap upon his untidy locks. 'Get water, hot water,' he commanded.

Marcelle was gripping her stomach. 'He will be born soon, I know he will,' she gasped, and she soon began to scream again as the labour pains started.

Several hours later, strong and gentle hands brought forth Marcelle's premature child, a little boy with red hair in tight little curls and an odd-shaped mole on his buttock. By that time Marcelle had given up and had lapsed into unconsciousness.

Merlin breathed life into the child's tiny body, then wrapping it up gently, he handed it to Annabelle. 'Take care of his Royal Highness,' he said and went towards his attic.

'But Marcelle?' Annabelle called after him. 'Is she all right?'

'She will sleep for a while,' Merlin replied. 'No harm will come to her.' With that he was gone again.

The sun shone down on the weeping willow turning its leaves to a golden yellow. The lower branches trailed in the cool green water of the pond as if trying to reach out and touch the cream velvet petals of the huge water lilies floating majestically on the surface. This was Marcelle's favourite spot in the secluded garden of Craig Alva and on this bright summer morning she knelt trailing her fingers in the water and feeling at peace with all the world. Not far away, in the little crib hanging from the oak tree was her son, a quiet contented baby who had brought great peace of mind to his troubled mother. Marcelle was no longer a young girl and during the last three months she matured in many ways. Her figure was fuller, her hips were shapely and now her mind was as agile as her body was supple. When Annabelle and Abe left for Frances' new house, Marcelle watched sadly from the window as they loaded the wagon with all of Merlin's possessions. For he had refused to move without every one of his beloved maps, boxes and mysterious masks.

It had been amusing to watch as Merlin kept darting back inside, his long wispy hair flying back over his shoulders in the wind and gesticulating wildly with his arms as Annabelle tried to hurry him. And all the while, Abe sat quietly and sadly in the front seat with the driver, taking a last look at his beloved home and farm animals. He was such a good and kind man. Tears streamed down Marcelle's cheeks. She just could not believe that they were leaving. She had felt so alone and desolate.

Her baby had been only six weeks old when Annabelle had given her the sad news.

'Listen to me, darling,' she had said, hold Marcelle's hand. 'We have to go, all of us, I cannot explain why and I am just as unhappy as you over this move. I have made arrangements with your husband's solicitors for you to rent the house. Everything is in order and you have nothing to worry about. Thomas has provided well for you and it will be a home for you and your son until he returns. The farm is let to a tenant, so it is no concern of yours. Wanda has offered to leave the dairy and live in to help you take care of you and your lovely baby.' Annabelle was devoted to the baby, as was Abe. And even Merlin would poke a finger at him and say: 'How is His Highness this morning?'

It was very hard to see them go and Marcelle knew it had something to do with the fair countess but she could not think what it was exactly. But why were Annabelle and Abe so unhappy about the move? And why did they not refuse to go? Such questions frightened her and made her head ache.

Wanda came up behind her and placed an arm over her shoulder. Her strong hand gripped hers. 'Now, my love, don't 'ee oopset 'eeself. Think on thy babe.'

'I just do not understand it,' Marcelle sobbed. 'I love them like my own parents. I would have gone with them.'

'Now doan't 'ee be daft, gel, they be goin' up London. The plague and ev'rthin' is oop there, gor 'a think on little Roger.'

Marcelle nodded and smiled gratefully. She knew that Wanda had good sense.

Wanda was a big girl with a big moon face full of freckles and sturdy legs. Her personality was pleasant and she had a ready wit and good temper. Marcelle had found her a great boon in helping her to settle down at Craig Alva without Annabelle. Now it was August and the garden was a riot of colour, full of tall hollybocks, blue larkspur, golden marigolds and red rambler roses. Marcelle spent most days in the garden sitting under the oak tree with her baby while Wanda cleaned the house and got most of the meals ready. In the evenings they both sat in the porch until it grew dark. During these evenings Wanda would give a running commentary on the business of the folks in the village. Wanda visited her mother in the village twice a week, and it was she who was the weekly news-letter. It was on one of these cool evenings that Wanda mentioned that their old milkmaid Ruth, who had returned to the village with a child the same age as Roger. Wanda's mouth moved in all directions as she poured scorn on the misdeeds of Ruth. 'Our Mum ses that 'er husband's bin drowned at sea. "Do't 'ee be daft," ses I, "she slept all night wi' that Lord in the barn." "Still," ses me Ma, "she could be married." '

Marcelle glanced up at Wanda and then down again. Her face was flushed and she felt embarrassed by all this gossip. 'Oh, do not be unkind, Wanda,' she pleaded.

'Well, a'right, my love, but 'ee be too soft. She were a slut, that girl,' Wanda added unsympathetically.

Marcelle had gone very pale and quiet. 'Let us go up to bed,' she said, putting down her sewing and collecting her baby.

Nowadays Wanda slept downstairs where Abe used to sleep, while Marcelle and her baby still occupied the little room at the top of the stairs.

Wanda's head had hardly touched her pillow that night when she heard Marcelle screaming. Dashing upstairs in her large flannel nightgown which flapped like a ship's sail, she found Marcelle crouched on the floor looking very disturbed and crying out that he had come for the baby.

'Oh, God, forgive me! Do not let him take my baby,' she raved.

Wanda grabbed hold of Marcelle roughly as though she were a bag of beans, and dumped her back on the bed saying in a loud whisper: 'Shut up! You will wake Roger.'

Marcelle suddenly sat up wide-eyed and scared. 'What is the matter, Wanda?' she whispered.

'Matter!' grumbled Wanda. 'You was 'avin' a nightmare and shoutin' your head off. It was 'nuff to wake the dead.'

Marcelle shivered as she suddenly recalled her dream. 'Light the candles, Wanda,' she said, 'and do not go yet. Stay with me a while.'

'Tut! Tut!' Wanda was feeling tired but she lighted the candles and sat on Marcelle's bed. 'Now what is wrong with thee? You've got no worries, and you've got plenty money. It should be me what's getting nightmares – I ain't even got a man.'

'It is the man I see that frightens me,' said Marcelle, looking from side to side.

'Well, thee send 'im downstairs, then, I could fair do wi' 'im,' retorted the truculent Wanda.

Marcelle stared at the servant sitting there in her absurd-looking nightcap and enormous red flannel nightgown, with those queer blue eyes that some-times looked green. Then she looked over towards Roger sleeping in his little cot, his curls just peeping over the top of his covers. Wanda was right, she had nothing to be afraid of, so why could she not forget the red-haired young man she kept thinking of as the devil? 'Wanda?' she asked timorously, 'do you remember those three men who came late one night last summer?'

'Course I do. Weren't one out in the barn all night wi' Ruth?'

'But did you see the other two?' queried Marcelle.

'No, I never did. I were never allowed indoors them days, but Ruth do say that one o' them was a royal prince, but then she were a bit of a storyteller and a liar as well,' she added scornfully.

'It is one of those men I see all the time,' said

Marcelle 'and it frightens me. I keep thinking it is the devil.'

'There be no such one,' scoffed Wanda. 'Wouldn't catch me believin' in ghosts and suchlike.'

'But he walked in his sleep. I saw him then and I still do,' insisted Marcelle.

'Nonsense!' exclaimed Wanda. 'He be flesh and blood, I warrant you, if he be here. Move over, I'll stay with thee, and perhaps he might fancy me.'

Wanda's witty talk made Marcelle giggle and she felt comforted as the warm heavy body got into the bed beside her. How foolish she was! Wanda was right, she had this house, a husband and a baby. What was there to be afraid of?

From that time onward her nerves improved and she was no longer afraid to be alone. As Roger grew and he held out his little arms to her, his soft fingers clutching handfuls of hair, she would say to herself: 'Now you have enough courage for two – until Roger grows up, at least.'

In the peace and beauty of the Essex countryside, amid the flowers in the lovely garden, Marcelle bloomed and blossomed, her worries and concerns disappeared. Until, that is, when one lovely morning she saw a stranger coming down the path, a middle-aged man dressed in grey. He swept his large hat off with a courtly gesture. 'Excuse me, ma'am, have I the pleasure of addressing Mistress Mayhew?'

Marcelle blushed. No one had ever addressed her as a married lady before and she had been that for more than a year now.

'I carry a letter from your husband, from the New World. My name is Mr Spencer, assistant to your husband's lawyer at the Inns of Court.'

Marcelle flushed with pleasure. Thomas had written her a letter at last! Her heart beat fast with excitement as she invited the lawyer into the house.

In the small sitting room, which now looked quite bare without Annabelle's little treasures, Marcelle entertained Mr Spencer. Wanda bustled in and out bringing them food to eat and wine to drink. Each time she came in, she flicked her sandy eye lashes and cast coy glances at the gentleman, while Marcelle sat quietly reading Thomas' letter:

> *My dearest one.*
>
> *I do hope this letter finds you well and happy. It is a strange life out here, but it is a very pleasant and fertile country with space for all to enjoy. It is my dearest wish to show this land to you, God willing, and all going well, it will happen. I will not distress you with the hazards of the voyage out here. It took almost a year, but as time passes the voyages out here must improve. This letter I am giving to the captain of a ship returning to England in the fervent hope it will reach you to find that you have had a bonny child and may God protect you both till I return.*
>
> *By a strange coincidence I have made the acquaintance of a person whom you may recall. His name is Rolly, the strange child-like man who lived at the inn in Hackney where I found you, my love. Poor Rolly was press-ganged aboard but has settled*

down well. I have grown quite attached to him and have sent a letter to his sister at the inn to assure her that he is well.

Give my regards to Abe and Annabelle as well as to Will the minstrel. Take care of yourself, my love. I have enclosed the address of my brother so that you may write and tell him I am well. Goodbye for a while. Time will soon pass.

Your husband,
Thomas

10

Abduction

Rolly had been missing sometime now and an atmosphere of gloom had descended upon the Duke's Head Inn. Betsy sat pale with weariness and anxiety. Beside her was a large bottle of strong sweet wine from which she repeatedly filled her wooden cup, commiserating with herself in between each long drink.

'He's never been gone this long before,' she muttered morosely. 'Something's happened to him, I'm sure of it.'

Chalky stood with his hands in his pockets of the blue striped apron he wore, looking slyly down at the sawdust on the floor. 'He could be in the fleet,' he murmured softly.

Betsy turned her tousled head in Chalky's direction and sniffed scornfully. 'Well, he ain't. I've been to all them stinking bleeding prisons. I've walked all day and there was no sign of him anywhere.'

'I meant the navy,' said Chalky.

'Don't be such a bloody fool!' screamed Betsy, losing her temper. 'You know how childish he is. He'd never think that one up on his own.'

'Don't have to think about it,' replied Chalky gloomily. 'They just grab you from behind. That's how they got me,' he added.

'What do you mean, the press gang?' Betsy demanded. But after a moment's thought, she shrieked. 'That's it! They got him! Where else could he go? Because if he was still alive he would have come home by now.'

'It won't kill him,' said Chalky nonchalantly. 'He will come home when the ship docks.' In a good few years, he thought, but did not say so to Betsy, who was crying. Big tears like raindrops ran down her cheeks.

Betsy had a constant love in her heart for that foolish brother of hers, and the thought that she might never see him again was too much for her to bear.

'Never mind, love,' Chalky seemed to be kindness itself, and he could never stand to see a woman cry. A very mixed character was Chalky. He filled up Betsy's cup of wine. 'There, now,' he said kindly, 'you go up and have a nice rest and I'll keep the bar open. Then later, I'll come up and we'll have a nice bit of you know what . . .' He laughed coarsely, tickling her under the chin.

'You are a good chap, Chalky,' said Betsy. 'I don't know what I'd do without you.' She hoisted her tired body from the low stool and, still clutching the bottle in one hand and the wooden cup in the other, slowly climbed the steep flight of stairs to her bed.

Chalky's sharp yellow teeth showed in an almost crafty grin as he watched Betsy's plump thighs as she passed. When she had disappeared, he took off his striped apron, carefully dampened his hair and parted it on one side, and drew his hands across his neat waxed moustache. Then he crept out of the house, closing the front door quietly behind him, and made off towards the fields at the back of the inn.

Down where the little brook gurgled merrily over the stones, its clear water showing up a myriad of colours, sat Katy, Chalky's new love. Pink bare feet dangled in the water, and beside her on the bank was a basket of fish which she had brought down to the brook to wash in the cool water before arranging them on the stall her father owned in the market. Katy's hair hung down her back in dark plaits and the low neck of her red dress exposed most of her snow-white bosom. As Chalky hurried towards her, he licked his lips. Here was Katy, beautiful Katy, a peach, fresh and ripe for the plucking. He slid down beside her. 'Hallo,' he said pleasantly. 'Washed your fish, I see.'

Katy's dark brown eyes stared lazily at him and, pouting her red lips, she stretched out towards him. As she did so, one white bosom peeped through her blouse, the little nipple like a tiny red rose bud waiting to be kissed.

Chalky stared in fascination and shivered with passion, not daring to raise a hand. The previous morning when he had moved too fast with Katy, he had ended up in the brook with a cockle basket on his head. He had no intention of allowing that to happen again. So now he was back in his stride with his old cautious approach to seduction.

Little did Chalky know that he had met his match. The beautiful, six-foot-tall Katy was twenty, still a virgin, and hell bent on staying that way. She strongly believed in self-preservation until someone placed a golden band of security on her left hand. Nevertheless, she was an expert in love play.

'Don't want no help with the fish, then?' Chalky enquired, staring at her enticing bare flesh.

'No, thanks, 'tis done,' said Katy, but her hand was creeping nearer to him, passed his knee until it reached his thigh.

'Oh, gawd,' moaned Chalky, 'don't do that.' He pressed closer to her. 'Oh, give us a kiss, Katy,' he begged.

Katy pouted her lips in his direction and her hand reached the right spot.

Suddenly Chalky lost control and tried to jump on top of her, only to be thrown off like a leaf in the breeze.

As he rolled over Katy stood up, and loomed indignantly over him. In a voice that grated like sand, she said: 'I told you not to do that, didn't I?'

'But Katy, I love you,' Chalky almost wept. His face pressed to the damp soft grass for cool comfort.

'No man's getting me till he weds me,' said Katy haughtily, swinging the basket of fish on to her shoulder. She hitched up her skirt to reveal the whole of her sturdy white leg and marched back over the fields to the Broadway Market, where her father would be waiting patiently for the basket of fish.

Cold and shivering but with an inner fire, Chalky crept back to the warm bed of the blousy Betsy. Sleepy and comfortable, she cuddled him close. Now that Rolly had gone there was only Chalky to cling to.

As the weeks and months passed, this strange

courtship with Katy made very little progress. Each morning Chalky came timidly to the brook, and just as the male spider taps his feet for fear of the female mate gobbling him up, so did Chalky tap and fidget in an alarming fashion. In fact his nerves were going to pieces he became so harassed. He lost all interest in Betsy, who felt quite neglected and drank more and more sweet wine. She stayed in bed later each day and became very untidy in her dress. The fight had left her completely, and now that Rolly was gone, she had no one to protect her.

Chalky's vicious temper began to show itself more and more and no matter how hard Betsy tried to persuade him, he would not marry her. So Betsy got fatter and lazier and drank more. Something had to be done; these extreme tensions must come to a head.

Poor old Chalky itched and scratched and walked about feeling very sorry for himself. He was of two minds – one to wait for Katy in a lonely spot, rape her and then disappear with the haul of money he had stashed away, or to stay put and ask for Katy's hand in marriage from that red-faced fellow of a father. But then there was Betsy. She might turn nasty if he wed another; it was all very worrying.

But it was fate that took a hand in Chalky's problems. One day Betsy got very drunk and fell down the stairs, breaking both her legs. No matter how hard she tried to stand up, she could not keep her balance and the pain was blinding. She was forced to lie in bed and leave everything in the hands of Chalky who made her very comfortable with a bottle of sweet wine beside her.

Now Chalky could begin his campaign of love with a vengeance. Going down to the cellar he took a few of the gold coins from the jar in its hiding place. Smartening himself up, he went off to visit Katy in her little house in the Broadway. In the little room behind the shop Chalky proposed to Katy in the appropriate manner and although she was smelling of fish, she remained just as desirable to him as ever. Then rattling the gold coins in his pocket, and in the presence of Katy's three brawny brothers, Chalky asked her father for Katy's hand in holy wedlock.

Katy's father wore a dirty fishy apron stretched tight over his fat stomach and a battered straw hat on the back of his head. He surveyed Chalky with a careful scrutiny as if the younger man were one of those boiled lobsters he sold. 'Who is that woman at the Duke's Head, then?' he demanded. Silvery fish scales bounced off his chin as he stuck it out aggressively in Chalky's direction.

Chalky began to wish he had never come to the house but he stood his ground. 'She's my stepmother,' he said. 'Me old man got drowned at sea. He left the business to me, he did, so I ain't short of a few shillings.' He rattled the gold nobles and pulled out a handful so that the men all got a glimpse of the gold.

The old man pursed his fat lips speculatively. 'Got a good dowry going with that girl, and ain't letting her go until the chap not only matches it but doubles it.'

His piggy eyes squinted at Chalky. 'What's your offer?' he demanded.

'I thought to start off with a nice little partnership – a stall outside the inn with a bit of lobster, crab and shellfish for the late-night customers.'

A beaming smile crossed the fishmonger's fat features. 'Well, now, you've got your head screwed on the right way, all right. You're a boy after me own heart.' He put an enormous arm about Chalky's shoulder. 'That's a good idea. We'll do a bit of eel in jelly, and Katy could run the inn until you got wed. Shake hands, boy, we're in business.' He held out a big, fishy hand and grasped Chalky's. 'Katy!' he yelled. 'Come in here and get your future husband a drink.'

In her best dress and her long hair in a silver snood, Katy sat coyly next to Chalky on the horse-hair sofa. Chalky sat unusually quietly but secretly he was undressing Katy with his eyes. Katy was aware of this and enjoyed it.

'Wait till I get you up in the inn, my girl,' he whispered, and Katy fluttered her dark lashes in anticipation.

The day's courting was over. Chalky walked back to the inn whistling a tune. Well, that was not a bad day's work, he thought, especially since there is an extra bit of cash with Katy thrown in, he thought shamelessly as he let himself in to the dark deserted inn. He heard a plaintive voice calling from upstairs. 'Is that you, Chalky? Where have you been? Me bottle's empty.'

Chalky grimaced and his face hardened in a cruel look. He would have to sort this out somehow . . .

★　★　★

Frances Howard's new house was on the estate of her uncle, the Earl of Nottingham who lay very ill with the gout and the ailments of old age at his country house in Halling, near Croydon. All his life Henry Howard had kept away from the court intrigues and loyally served his king and country to the best of his ability. This policy had fortunately been to the advantage of his great family. But new stars had been rising – for James had many favourites – and the old courtiers of Elizabeth's time were gradually being pushed into the background. So when Henry Howard's favourite niece wanted to marry the king's main favourite, Robert Carr, it was a great boost for the Howards, and it would also bring Robert Carr over to their side. Therefore all strings were pulled to help Frances, who was determined to get her marriage with Essex annulled, insisting that it had never been consummated. And there began the weaving of a great web of intrigue to prove that Frances was still a virgin.

With Abe, Annabelle and Merlin installed in her new house on her uncle's estate, Frances spent most of her time at court accompanied by Annabelle, trying to strengthen her position as the betrothed of the king's favourite, and Robert Carr seemed to gain more favour from foolish old Jamie every day.

Abe did not like his new home, one bit. In fact he hated it. One afternoon, he leaned over the garden wall to watch the long line of carriages coming out of the city – heavy wagons loaded with goods, mounted men in all their finery and the grand retinue that rode with them dressed all in a blaze of coloured coats and gold braid. Travelling along that winding road sloped out of London towards the west country, they reminded Abe of an army of ants. What a dreary place this is, he thought, with its neglected gardens. Abe shook his grey head gloomily as he surveyed the battered cupids and the sad-looking one-armed goddesses perched in the centre of the lawn. What a contrast to the beloved garden he had left behind. He thought of the neat rows of carrots and onions. 'I'll never get used to it here,' he muttered to himself. 'Why there's no room to swing a cat round in.' He stared moodily towards the distant city, with its row of church spires and haze of black smoke that hung over it. 'I wonder what that bitch of a countess is up to,' he pondered. 'It fair worries me the way she monopolises Annabelle, always out dressed up to kill.' Once again he shook his old head like an old donkey. 'Don't like it one bit, I don't. We should never have come to this dull house.'

Frances was for once at home, and she was preoccupied as she sat in the long elaborately furnished drawing room with its wall tapestries and luxurious couches, deep in conversation with Annabelle and a young girl. This was a poor Howard cousin and she was almost identical to Frances. To look at her you would be convinced that she was Frances' twin, since she had the same ash-blonde hair, classic features and same protruding eyes. But the expressions on their faces were totally different: the young girl looked sweet and gentle, while Frances' full heavy lips only turned down disdainfully at the corners. Frances leaned forward to talk to this young girl, forming each word carefully and making signs with her hands. The young girl touched her lips and with her hands indicated that she understood. For she had no power of speech. She was totally dumb but her hearing was not impaired.

'Listen, my dear,' Frances said, looking earnestly at her. 'Do you think you can manage to do as I ask? Remember, it is very important for me to get my marriage annulled. Do you understand?'

The girl nodded her head.

'Good,' replied Frances, looking satisfied. 'Now we are on the way to success. Come my love, we will rehearse again.'

The little Howard cousin was dressed by Annabelle in a plain dress and a long veil. Over and over the two women explained to her what the matrons of the court would do and say when they examined her to see if she was a virgin. They would ask if her name was Frances Howard, and then she must only nod her head. This young girl whose tongue gave no sound was the child of a Howard who had married a poor village girl in Ireland. The rebels had burned their house and her parents but the little girl had escaped. But she had never uttered a word since. She had been taken into the Howard family and brought up with the rest but very few knew of her existence. Now a good use had been found for the poor young child by her own scheming family.

The fact that this preposterous plot succeeded highlights the formidable power of the Howard family. The matrons who examined Frances Howard proclaimed her still a virgin after two years of being married and there was much gossip and many jokes. The great committee of Bishops granted her divorce on the grounds of her husband's impotency. When the news leaked out, there was much gossip and many jokes. Most of the court knew of Frances' many little indiscretions, not the least of which was with Robert Carr's secretary, Thomas Overbury. And he was not slow to talk of this. Thomas was a writer of poetry and he was reported to be the author of a scurrilous poem that had been read out at the Mermaid Inn in Fleet Street, a place patronised by the leading literary lights of the day.

The news of her annulment made Frances extraordinarily happy. Now the only cloud over her bright horizon was the fear that Robert's secretary would go too far with his indiscreet talk.

Several weeks later, Frances stared at her white-faced reflection in the new Venetian mirror which had been a gift from great Uncle Henry. Behind her Annabelle brushed her mistress' long blonde hair. Frances' greeny grey eyes gloated as she looked at herself. 'I fooled them,' she said. 'Fat old hypocrites, those Bishops. And I'll get him too, that Thomas. I'll teach him to revile me,' she threatened.

'Are you talking to yourself, Madam?' asked Annabelle as she pulled the jewelled comb through the long strands of fine light hair.

'Well, what if I am?' Frances retorted harshly. 'Really, Annabelle, you do say the silliest things.'

Annabelle's pale face betrayed the fact that she was not very well. The late nights and the temptations of the town did not seem to be agreeing with her.

'I need something from Merlin,' said Frances. 'How is he these days? I intend to silence that snake Overbury and I will need your help.'

'But my lady,' pleaded Annabelle, 'why not leave well alone? Soon you will be a great lady when you marry Robert. Surely it is not wise to cause trouble.'

'Don't be a fool!' sneered Frances. 'I will do as I please. Who is to stop me now?'

Annabelle sighed, her brow wrinkled in a perplexed expression. Where was it all going to end? How gladly she would give up this life for the peaceful scene of Essex and Craig Alva again, but Frances was a Howard and greed and ambition were two very important ingredients of her make-up. Annabelle knew that she had no choice.

That afternoon Frances rode through the city streets in her new carriage which bore a coat of arms and was carved and gilded. Beside her sat Annabelle who pressed a posy of rosemary close to her nose because she was afraid of the plague which still hung about the city. Frances wore a velvet outfit which was bedecked with jewels. She was travelling to Holborn House to meet great Uncle Henry the oldest and the wiliest member of the Howard family.

Annabelle waited below while Frances visited the duke in his chambers.

Henry Howard was very pleased to see Frances; he had always been fond of her. But today he was not well. His gout had become very bad and he was not in a very good mood.

'Ah,' he snarled as she came in. 'Calling for your

wedding present, are you? I suppose you are expecting me to die and that you might not get it.'

Frances smiled that rare smile that lighted up her cold countenance in a most charming manner. 'Now, Uncle, I have come to cheer you up,' she said, ignoring his tone. 'I heard you had a touch of the gout so I have brought some balm for you.'

'Take it away!' he snarled. 'I do not want any quack experimenting on me.'

But Frances clung to him coyly, putting her arm about his neck. 'Oh, don't be such an old grouse,' she cooed.

Uncle Henry's stern thin face immediately relaxed as he relented. He had a soft spot for women. 'Well, poppet, what is it you want of me?' he asked. 'Since you have got rid of young Essex and are about to marry the King's favourite boy, I should have thought that you had obtained all your desires.'

'It is that man Overbury,' said Frances pettishly. 'Do you know what he called me?' She repeated Overbury's slander.

A grim smile played around the old man's lips. Whatever the truth, Frances was a Howard and no one had any business saying things like that, he thought. 'Oh, he did, did he?' His eyebrows went up. 'And you want me to defend you, eh?'

'Please, Uncle. Did you know that he has written a dreadful poem about me?'

'Looks like the fellow's causing trouble,' pondered Uncle Henry. 'I will see what can be done for you.'

'I will tell you a secret, if you promise,' she persisted.

'All right, I promise,' said Henry, always eager for gossip. 'What is the secret?'

'His late Royal Highness left a bastard behind.' Frances delivered this message quickly and dramatically.

Uncle Henry stared at her with amusement. 'Well, well, little Frances, don't tell me that you have been hiding the heir to the throne all this time?'

'No, not me, silly,' giggled Frances. 'It's a young girl in Essex.'

'Sounds interesting. Tell me more.'

Frances then told him of Marcelle's secret.

'Can I rely on this information?' Henry asked Frances.

'Oh, yes, I have witnesses – Annabelle, my waiting maid, and also a girl called Ruth, who lives in the village and spent the night in the barn with Lord Hay who was supposed to be guarding His Highness.'

'Well, 'tis certainly worth investigating,' the old man murmured, stroking his pointed beard which was streaked with grey.

'I will have to go now, Uncle Henry. You will do what you can for me, won't you?'

'You know I will, you little minx.'

Smiling sweetly, Frances left the large stuffy room. She felt well satisfied by her visit.

Annabelle was still waiting patiently for her downstairs and when she saw Frances' triumphant look as she gracefully descended the wide oak stairs, she knew her mistress had got whatever it was she had come for.

What she did not know of course, was that little Marcelle was to be sacrificed.

At Craig Alva, the lovely summer had come and was almost gone. Marcelle was very proud of Roger, her baby son, who sat up and cooed and laughed all that long summer as he swung in his homemade crib from the big oak tree. The baby thrived, the apples grew heavy on the boughs and the soft currants, black and shiny, were ready to be picked. While the sturdy Wanda cleaned the house, Marcelle dressed in a blue sun bonnet, picked the fruit and kept an eye on Roger's curly head as he lay kicking and gurgling beneath the leafy green branches.

One afternoon, a carriage travelling along the narrow road outside, slowed down and then halted outside the gate. A servant came in and asked if the gentleman in the carriage could come into the shady garden to rest awhile. When Marcelle gave her permission, a tall distinguished old man climbed down from the carriage and walked slowly down the path with the aid of a stick. He was a cautious-looking gentleman in a dark velvet suit with a stiff white lace ruff around his neck.

Marcelle came forward and showed him to the old oak bench where he could sit in the shade to rest. The old man stayed for a while, drinking the cool ale that Wanda brought to him and frequently gazing at Roger who was enjoying all the extra attention.

'He is a fine boy,' he told Marcelle. 'Such fine colouring. Only once in my life did I know of a family with such deep red hair and such bonny brown eyes. You must be very proud of him, my dear.'

Marcelle blushed shyly.

The gentleman did not stay long, and after thanking Marcelle and Wanda for their hospitality, he limped away down the path to the waiting carriage.

The weeks passed and when autumn gave way to winter, the frost lay like a silver blanket on the lawn. Each evening Marcelle would sit in front of the log fire knitting or working on a large tapestry – a country scene – which was to hang on the wall of the sitting room. One evening at about dusk as the needles clicked and the shadows leaped around the walls and the candles flickered, there was suddenly a tap at the front door. Marcelle and Wanda lifted their eyes from their work and then looked at each other, wondering who it could be at this time of day between dark and light. Visitors did not come calling at dusk; the road from the village was too dangerous at night.

Wanda rose and went to open the door. A little boy stood out there. His nose was red and he wore ragged trousers. 'Yer muvver wants ter see yer,' he told Wanda.

Wanda's big moon face turned deathly white. 'Why, what's the matter?' she asked.

'I dunno,' the boy replied with a shrug, 'but they told me to say it's a matter of life or death.'

And before Wanda had time to reply, the boy had turned and disappeared into the grey mist.

'Oh dear!' Wanda stood with her hands over her big wide mouth in shock. 'What am I going to do? Something's wrong with me ma.'

'You had better go before it gets too dark,' said Marcelle, standing beside her and trying to console her.

'I can't leave you alone all night. How am I going to get back?' wailed Wanda.

'Now please go,' pleaded Marcelle. 'I do not mind being alone. I am not nervous any more, not since Roger was born.' She place a cloak around Wanda's shoulders urging her towards the door. 'Now take the lantern, dear, and mind how you go. Even if you don't come back until the morning I will be all right.'

Fussing and clucking like an old hen, Wanda departed with the lantern swinging in the breeze and her dark cloak flapping like the wings of a bat.

After Wanda had disappeard, Marcelle closed and locked the door and retired to bed. She slept peacefully with her little babe asleep in his cot in the corner of the room. Soon after midnight, a pale wintry moon appeared from behind the clouds and the long dark shadows of two men threw eerie shapes over the garden path as they crept stealthily towards the house. They crouched down low and stopped just below a window. Then one man mounted on the other's shoulders and, with the aid of a knife, he severed open the window and jumped through, dropping lightly inside the room. He then reached out of the window to assist his companion.

In the silence of the night, an owl screeched. A dog barked in the distance and Marcelle turned restlessly in bed. There was a hoarse whisper as one man indicated to the other the cot in the corner containing the sleeping babe. He reached out and swiftly picked up the little bundle. The baby let out a plaintive cry and Marcelle awoke immediately. As her terrified gaze caught sight of an evil face looking down at her, she opened her mouth to scream but a pillow descended on her face. In wild panic, she kicked and fought hard; she saw stars, then a blinding flash, and then knew no more.

A hoarse voice in the dark said: ''Ere, take it easy. We ain't supposed to kill the woman, only snatch the nipper.'

Then out of the window they went, off into the night taking Roger, Marcelle's son, away out of her life. And all the while little Roger was calling out for his mother as he was roughly thrust into a smelly cloak.

The horsemen were joined by another man who had been acting as a look-out on the road, and the three men, ruffians who did the dirty work for the Howard family, went speeding away through the silent village.

Down in the village, Wanda sat on a low rocking stool in the shack where her old mother lived and she heard the rattle of the horses' hooves echoing in the quiet of the night. Mounted men! What could be happening? They could only be highwaymen, she thought, since they were travelling towards London.

Wanda's old mother, wheezed and coughed from her bed in the corner of the shack. 'I don't know what made ye think something was wrong wi me,' she grumbled. 'Spoilt me night's rest, ye have, dropping in on me sudden like that.'

'I told you once, Mother, a boy brought me a message,' replied Wanda irritably. 'Don't think I fancy sitting up here all night.'

'Having a game, some boy was,' argued the old lady. 'What did he look like?'

'Got a feeling it was Ruth's little brother,' replied Wanda.

'Well then, there you goes,' said the old lady. 'Don't like you, does she? Gettin' her own back, she was.' The old lady cackled and coughed. 'Always a bit soft, you was.'

Wanda hunched her big shoulders. 'Hurry up, morning,' she cried. 'I am worried over Marcelle and the baby; there seems some strange goings-on this night.' But gradually her large head nodded and she dozed off. She awoke with a start some time later, just as the dawn washed the old wooden walls of the shack with a rosy glow. The fire had sunk low so Wanda threw on a few logs and watched as the sparks started to fly up the chimney. Taking a quick look at her mother, who was still snoring loudly, Wanda left the shack and started on her way back to her little mistress. She took the short cut over the fields tripping occasionally on some frozen ruts filled with ice. The sun was not yet warm enough to thaw the ground properly. She squelched and puffed her way sturdily towards the house. It was all very silent, and there was a strange feeling in the air, like the stillness before a storm.

The tenant farmer and his son were shovelling manure as Wanda tore past. The elder man looked round in bewilderment to see Wanda at this time of the morning rushing along, puffing like a pair of bellows and besplattered with mud. He was still gazing towards the house she had disappeared into when she suddenly reappeared screaming.

'Help!' she shouted, the range of her strident voice loud and clear in the still morning air. 'My lady has been murdered and the baby stolen. Fetch a priest and the doctor.'

The farmer rushed over to Wanda and followed her into the house. In no time, Marcelle's room was full of gawping people all jabbering excitedly as they looked at Marcelle's scrumpled body on the bed, still and white as death, her head twisted to one side. And in the corner their eyes gazed at the empty cot as if expecting a miracle to take place and the missing baby to reappear.

The farmer's wife calmed the hysterical Wanda, and then sent her son on horseback to the church on the hill to fetch the priest.

The new young parson came immediately, riding behind the farmer's son. On arriving at the house he quickly dispersed the crowd of boys that had gathered outside. Then he shooed the neighbours out of Marcelle's room and set about reviving Marcelle as best he could. He bent down and listened to her shallow breathing. 'Thank God,' he whispered to himself; she had not quite left this earth yet. The farmer's wife sponged Marcelle's body, and got herbs from the garden and held them under her nose. In the meantime the farmer was riding hell for leather to the town to get the apothecary.

Wanda began to recover from her shock and sat close to the bed watching her little mistress for real signs of life. To her immense relief, Marcelle's heavy eye-lids started to flutter as slowly but surely life came back into the shattered body. Marcelle tried to struggle feebly and then dreadful chilling screams came from her trembling lips.

Wanda held her close, knowing that she was trying to tell them what had happened to the baby but then Marcelle had drifted back into unconsciousness.

The doctor had arrived and stated that there was no doubt that Marcelle had suffered an extensive shock and there were signs that her neck had been dislocated. She would require great care for quite a while, he told them.

'But who could have taken the child?' sobbed Wanda. 'Someone has taken the baby!'

The doctor was very sympathetic. It would be reported of course, but so far no one knew what had happened.

'But I heard them!' cried Wanda. 'I heard them riding towards London, I did!'

'But, my dear, that is not proof, just because you heard riders in the night,' he said kindly. 'I will get in touch with her husband if it is at all possible.'

With tears of desperation running down her face, Wanda was insistent. 'Find Ruth!' she cried. 'She used to be dairymaid here. She sent her brother to get me to leave the house. Something strange has definitely gone on.'

The elders of the village had sent for Ruth but they

were informed that she had left in a grand carriage, or so the village gossips said. And her little brother only stared open-mouthed when they questioned him. All sorts of rumours spread like wildfire, and a constant little knot of people stood outside the house to stare, while there was plenty of talk of vampires and other evil things that swooped down in the night

Wanda, now fully recovered, drove the inquisitive ones off with a big knobbly stick. The word 'witch' had been mentioned and there were plenty of people who remembered the strange figure of Merlin, who used to live there in the house. But Wanda charged down the path waving her stick and yelling: 'Get away, you superstitious lot! Don't come hanging about here or I will beat the daylights out of you!'

The noisy crowd would drift off still whispering and nodding to each other.

Wanda sat beside Marcelle. 'I will look after you, my love,' she murmured reassuringly, 'and when you are better we will go and look for Roger. Whoever has taken him must have had a good reason, I'll be bound.'

As the days passed, Marcelle got better but her mind was very disturbed. She would sit staring into space, her eyes glazed, and calling out: 'Go away,' or 'Give me back my baby. Oh please, devil, if you want me, take me, I am no good without my child.'

Wanda would stare at her in puzzlement. Who was this devil she thought had taken the baby? 'Tell me, Marci, darling,' she begged, 'Who took Roger?'

'He did,' whispered Marcelle. 'It was his and he

came back and took him. I am a very wicked woman.'

'Marci, dear, don't say such things,' begged Wanda, looking about her nervously.

Marcelle's health gradually improved, but her obsession still did not leave her. She looked such a pathetic little creature with a slight twist in her neck which kept her head always tilted to one side, her beaky nose and bright little eyes, she had the appearance of a frightened bird.

The loyal Wanda remained close to her side. She never left her and was always on the ready with a heavy stick in her hand in case of any further intruders.

The winter passed and spring came in all its sweet-smelling glory. But the red hawthorn blossom had no interest for Marcelle now as she still sat all day in a chair by the fire nursing a little bundle, which was only a towel tied in a knot which Wanda had given her to cuddle in her moments of undue stress.

The night the three horsemen had ridden through the village with Marcelle's baby tucked inside the riding cloak of one of them, the men had ridden like the wind, without stopping and barely uttering a word to each other. With a final protesting whimper, Roger went back to sleep, as babies are apt to do even in moments of danger. They rode swiftly through the Hundreds of Becontree, passed the village of Waltham and down into the Lea Valley. As they crested the hill they saw a strange light in the sky. A comet had appeared and hung down low over the city, giving out an eerie blue glow.

One of the riders pointed upwards to it. 'What's that?' he asked.

The other two pulled up their horses and stared skywards. They were three brothers – in flesh and in crime – and they drew close together in fear as they stared up at the comet hanging so low in the heavens. ''Tis a sign,' said one, crossing himself. 'We did devil's work this night.'

'Hold your tongue,' said the ugliest and the oldest brother. ''Tis not only us who sees that star hanging low but the rest of the world can see it.'

The younger and the smallest of the men opened his mouth to speak but no words came – he was paralysed with fear.

'Oh, get going!' said the elder with impatience. 'Let's deliver the child and return to Flanders. I will feel a damned sight safer there.'

Picking up speed again they galloped off into the city where hundreds of people stood out in the streets just looking up at the sky. Beneath the tall columns of Holborn House, the trio halted. One carried the sleeping child up the steps while another pulled the massive chain of the door bell which could be heard clanging and echoing through the house.

A footman answered their call and on opening the door held up his hand in dismay. 'You cannot call here tonight,' he said. 'His lordship is very ill.'

But the brothers pushed the servant aside and strode into the marble-tiled hall. 'Tell his Lordship that the business is done. We have brought the child,' one said gruffly, holding the sleeping Roger towards the footman.

The old man backed away. 'Come tomorrow,' he urged looking a little panic-stricken.

Down the carved oak stairs swept the Duchess of Suffolk, Henry Howard's sister-in-law. 'Hush, hush,' she commanded. 'What is going on down here? Be quiet, there is death in the house.' Her voice was loud and imperious.

'Sorry, my lady,' apologised the elder brother. 'We did our job, and now we wish to be paid and get on our way.' He laid the sleeping babe gently down on an oak chest which stood beside the huge doors.

'What job?' demanded the Duchess. 'And whose child is that? Take it away. Lord Howard has just left this world. Have you no respect?'

'No, madam,' he replied. 'That's not our business. We want the money we are owed, and then we will leave.'

The Duchess hesitated for a moment. God only knew what devilment old Henry had been up to. She had better settle with these men amicably, she decided. Drawing from the finger of her right hand a magnificent ring, she handed it to the man. 'Now go! And don't let me ever see you again.'

A thin, claw-like hand grasped the ring and held it to the light. 'This will do for now,' he said. 'I can't promise that it is enough – there are three of us to share, but be sure I will be back.' He said this in a threatening manner and then swiftly turning on his heel, he went out of the door with his brothers following behind him.

The aged footman came forward and looked down

at the tiny bundle which had begun to stir. His tiny legs were kicking vigorously.

'Go and get the maids,' the Duchess snapped, looking down at Roger disdainfully. By now the baby had opened his large brown eyes, seeing that he was among strangers, he let out a terrific yell.

A maid came buzzing in, picked up the baby and took him to the servants' quarters, where they changed this cold wet little babe and fed him, fussing over this little mite who had so recently been taken from the comfort and love of his mother's arms.

For the next few days, the Duchess received hundreds of relatives and visitors who came to pay their respects to old Henry Howard. And all thoughts of the strange babe she had taken in were forgotten. What with the excitement of the comet in the sky and the superstitious ones foretelling bad tidings, it was a time of great turmoil. For the Howards, the death of the head of their great family was devastating, even though Henry had been of a great age. But once the clamour had died down and life returned to normal a little, the Duchess remembered the babe at last. She broke into a cold sweat at the thought of him. Oh God, who were those evil-looking men who had threatened her in that fashion and the child they had brought into the house just as Henry's spirit had departed? What did it mean? She had to get rid of that baby – he could only bring bad lack. Almost quaking in her shoes, she consulted her cousin Elizabeth.

'What do you think, Elizabeth? Whose child could it

be? From whence did it come? It is all so very strange, what with the comet appearing at the same time!'

Elizabeth Brook was only married into the Howard family and scoffed at the idea of evil coming into the house. She had also taken to little Roger. 'He is a dear little soul,' she said as she patted his curly head. 'I will take him out to Uncle Fulke. There are several children out there, and he does love children so. Mrs Powell, his housekeeper, has brought up his little girl well. She is so marvellous with children.'

So little Roger was washed and wrapped up warmly, and sent off in a carriage with cousin Elizabeth and her maid to Hackney to stay with Sir Fulke Greville in the warm hospitable Brook House.

It was true that Sir Fulke Greville loved children. When he was not in his study writing or reading the works of his best friend, the famous Philip Sidney, he was playing in the garden with his 'family' – his adopted nephew Robert and illegitimate daughter Elizabeth. He would sit with them telling them stories or teaching blind little Elizabeth how to feel the beauty of the great books of coloured paintings, works in gold on parchment drawn by the old priest who lived at Brook House. Elizabeth's tiny dainty hand would pass gently over the page, and she would tell him the number of the page and the name of the picture.

He would kiss her gently on the top of her fair head and say, 'My dear, if only I could leave you my eyes so that you could see the great beauty of these pages.'

As a young man, Sir Fulke had been a bit of a gay courtesan but now as an old man he was kind and studious, only ever leaving Brook House to attend parliament, where he was known as a wise and elegant speaker. To the family he was the well-loved Uncle Fulke but to the world outside he was very proud, vain and slightly parsimonious.

So to this home came Roger, Marcelle's baby, as a new little brother to the other children. No one knew where he came from, for none knew or cared. Sir Fulke would look after him. But by some great twist of fate, the baby had in fact come to the home of a great ancestor. His father's grandmother, the Duchess of Lennox, had lived and died mysteriously in this house, while dining with the Earl of Leicester. Her ghost was supposed to be seen often, trailing about the corridors. So to the warm cosy nursery went little Roger and there the spirits of his Tudor ancestors smiled down on him.

Wanda stood in the doorway watching the black stormy clouds roll over the weald. Her eyes focused on the distant skyline, and the setting sun threw a replica of her wide figure on the cobbles. She screwed up her eyes to get a better view of the black-and-silver lined clouds as they drifted overhead.

''Tis a fine night, Marci,' she called. 'Come and look.'

Marcelle crept timidly beside her and Wanda put a protective arm about her. 'That's right, my love, some nice fresh air will do you good.'

Lately Marcelle's health had improved a great deal. She no longer sat cuddling the towel but wandered across the meadow picking little daisies to make a daisy chain, her lips moving as she talked to herself. Wanda still watched her very carefully. Of late, she had not uttered a word about the baby she had lost or of that strange devil that used to haunt her. She just smiled constantly, a secret little smile, with her head to one side, giving herself an odd appearance. The village folk would cross themselves when they passed by her and the little boys on the farm would run past her with their fingers crossed as if their behinds were on fire.

It had been very quiet down at the farm cottage, that day. It was Whitsuntide and the farmer had taken his wife to Waltham Fair, leaving their two young boys in charge of the farm. In the distance Wanda could hear Daisy the cow lowing frantically in the barn. Wanda knew that the cow was in calf and hoped it would not give birth before the farmer came back.

Suddenly the storm broke and a torrent of rain came pouring down.

'Let's go in. There's no sense in getting wet,' Wanda said to Marcelle. 'Close the front door,' she called and went back to the unfinished business of making the bread. She was up to her elbows in a bowl of flour when a cry was heard, rising above the noise of the thunder.

'Did you hear that?' Wanda glanced at Marcelle.

'It's the boys from the calling,' Marcelle replied.

Wanda went to the window and saw the two boys standing on the path. The rain was beating down on them but they were too scared to come any nearer the house.

'Drat the buggers!' swore Wanda. 'What the hell is the matter with them?' She ran quickly out down the path towards them.

'It's Daisy,' they blustered. 'Come quick!'

Wanda plodded along beside them to the barn where the brown-and-white Daisy lay in the straw. The calf was half born, and wedged partly out of her body. Wanda rolled up her sleeves and knelt down beside the animal. With kind coaxing words and her gentle hands, she manipulated the calf out into the world. It stood up on spindly legs, and toppled over once or twice, its soft wet body and great doe-like eyes seeking its mother. Wanda helped the cow to rise and placed the young one near to her. Soon the mother was licking her calf and the young one had found the udder and was sucking healthily.

For a while Wanda completely forgot everything else and stood there wondering at the miracle and the wonderful spectacle of a new life coming into the world which she had witnessed and taken part in, but suddenly she remembered that she had left Marcelle alone and that in her haste she had left the front door open. Frantically she ran all the way back to the house. The door was still open. She called out, but got no reply. The kitchen was empty and the black shawl which usually hung behind the kitchen door was missing, as was a pair of clogs. She ran out into the grounds calling out Marcelle's name. The wind whistled around her and the rain drenched her clothes. There was no sign of Marcelle anywhere; she had disappeared into the wide open countryside.

Wanda walked to the village and then to the church where she saw some people sheltering in the porchway, but they said they had not seen anyone go by. By nightfall Wanda was back in the house, wearily waiting for Marcelle to return.

Marcelle's small elf-like figure was almost five miles away by now. Even as darkness descended, Marcelle walked on, her eyes turned towards the towers of London which she had seen in the setting of the sun. In her deranged mind, the fair Countess lived in that big town. It was she who had taken her friend Annabelle away, and so now Marcelle must go to find Annabelle who would know where her baby Roger was hidden.

She staggered through muddy fields, and climbed hedges, and stiles. There was no stopping Marcelle; she had to get to London.

In the cold light of dawn, Marcelle's rain-soaked body lay huddled in the hedge. The black shawl was bedraggled, and the wooden clogs caked with mud. She felt cold and hungry but inside her was an inner glow. 'Almost there. More than half way,' she talked to herself. Getting up with renewed energy, she trotted on. Soon she came to a rickety old bridge which crossed the river Lea. Beside this was the little brook. It left the river and with gay little trickles wended over the fields. Here Marcelle bathed her sore feet and drank the cool water. There was something about this stream that jogged her memory, a vague shadow in the back of her mind as she stared into the clear water and the well-washed stones beneath. There had once been kind hands that had lifted her up and words of comfort spoken in her ear. But, no, it was only a daydream . . . She got up and walked on, following the path of the brook, walking beside it as if some hidden force drew her to the spot where the Duke's Head Inn stood.

The inn's tall chimneys and white-washed walls stood outlined by the morning sun. Marcelle hesitated. She was looking cautiously at it when a tousled fair head appeared out of an upstairs window. A shrill voice screeched and a hand waved in her direction.

The shock of hearing Betsy's voice was just too much for Marcelle's bewildered mind. She wildly panicked, turned and ran towards the city, away from the brook and the woman who had shouted at her.

As she got into the city, the streets became very narrow and people walking past pushed and jostled her. But scarcely knowing what she was doing, Marcelle walked on and on deep into the heart of London. Then the road widened a little as it wound its way up a hill to where, at the top, were tall stone towers. 'At last!' Marcelle thought, 'the King's castle. Now to find Annabelle.'

There were many groups of people thronging the hillside and Marcelle could hear snatches of conversation as they talked mostly about a hanging that was to take place later that day. Hangings were always popular. Just outside the castle gates, groups of people stood, held back by soldiers in scarlet uniforms who held burnished pikes. They seemed to be guarding something that the people were staring and jeering at.

Marcelle crept closer to see what it was. To her horror she saw that it was a man who was naked but for a strip of cloth across his loins. He was stretched out and his arms and legs tied to pegs in the ground. Huge weights rested on top of him, his face was distorted with pain, and as he writhed in agony, his bloodshot eyes stared straight at Marcelle. It was Abe! Abe, her poor kind old friend from Craig Alva. She dropped on her knees beside him to pray. Abe's dry cracked lips moved as if to speak but only a murmer of 'water' issued from his mouth as he tried to plead with Marcelle for help. Running to a nearby horse trough, she filled her cupped hands with water and ran back to place them to Abe's dry lips. As she did so a rough hand grasped her shoulder and dragged her away.

'Hi!' said the angry guard. 'What's your game? He ain't supposed to 'ave any food or drink. Hoppit!' He gave her a hard push. 'That is, unless you want to join 'im.'

Marcelle fell to the roadside and there she remained, her tears falling thick and fast. Now her mind had become clearer. Oh, poor Abe, whatever are they doing to him? I must find Annabelle, she thought. She will save him. Marcelle stood for a moment looking at the still figure of Abe who seemed to have become unconscious.

A tall young soldier came over to Marcelle. 'You still here?' he asked. 'What's up? Is he your father?'

'No.' Marcelle shook her head. 'He is my dearest friend.'

'That poor devil has been there eight days and I reckon he has stuck it well,' said the soldier callously. 'And he's still alive, you know.'

'What will happen to him?' whispered Marcelle.

'Oh, he'll be hanged. They did his missus this mornin' .' The young soldier spoke as if it were just an ordinary conversation.

Annabelle hung? Oh, dear God! Marcelle held her head; she could not believe what she had heard.

The soldier continued. 'He told me to say you're to go away. He thinks it might be dangerous. He rambled on about some other thing, the poor old devil – about a brook and a baby.'

To Marcelle's shocked mind the words came clearly. The brook! It was all connected with the brook. She had to return. She got to her feet and tottered off on her thin legs, with her head to one side.

'Funny little body,' the guard said to his mate. 'She knew that old fellow. How is he now?'

'Still alive,' said the other. 'It's ten o'clock. We might as well take him in. I expect they'll do him tomorrow.'

II

The Fall

But what happened to cause the fall of Annabelle and her husband, the harmless old Abe?

Only a few weeks before Marcelle saw Abe stretched out on the hill, he had been at the new home he had grown to dislike so much. Still, he consoled himself, it was a lot better than the Tower of London, that gloomy prison on the hill near the river. It certainly had not been his choice to take on the job of looking after poor old Thomas Overbury. Abe, now a very old man, shivered as he remembered those last days when Overbury's body had turned black and swollen. And it stank horribly. God, what a death! But how they had managed it, he did not know. On instructions from Annabelle he had destroyed every bit of food the countess had sent in. They had poisoned him all right, but how? That was what puzzled Abe. But there was no sense dwelling on it. He was not going to live for ever so he had better forget the whole sordid affair. He would like to go back to the country but Annabelle had said that he was to stay here. He wondered how Marcelle was and her dear little baby. How nice it would be to see them. He got up from his seat. It was getting cold, for the evenings were beginning to draw in. Poor Abe was beginning to feel his age; the pace of life in these last months had begun to tell on him.

Merlin still pottered about. He had a sort of glass observatory upstairs but came down often to tell Abe of the amazing happenings going on in the heavens. But Abe scarcely listened. Both of them were missing Annabelle. Her gay bright serene presence had ruled them for so long that they were lost without her. At the moment she was on a tour of the royal houses of the kingdom with the Duchess Frances and her weak mamby pamby husband, the Duke of Somerset, the King's favourite. They had been away for several weeks now.

This very cold evening as Abe coughed over the fire, Merlin left his cold attic and crept down to crouch beside him at the fireside. The veins on his long thin hands stood out like little blue hillocks, and he rubbed his hands together as he stared thoughtfully into the fire.

Watching him, Abe wondered, as he often did, what he did to his hands. The backs of them had a score or more of small pia pricks as though he plunged needles into himself. He could have been such a clever doctor, Abe thought, he had been given the education. It was such a pity that Merlin had lost his wits when he did. Abe's thoughts went back to those ten years he and Merlin had shared. He supposed he should be jealous of Merlin, really, since he had been originally his wife's lover. It was strange how time heals everything. Annabelle loved neither of them now. Many lovers had replaced them, though the chief one was her passion for her mistress Frances. Now, as the only two lonely inhabitants of this gloomy empty house, Abe and Merlin seemed to grow closer. Tonight it seemed that Merlin wanted to confide in Abe about something.

Merlin's hair hung untidily over his head. It was stained in many colours, as he was forever absent-mindedly wiping his hands over his head after some experiment. His eyes were very bright, as usual, as he looked at Abe, and in a jerky tone of voice he announced: 'I've discovered the reason for it.'

Abe, had recently acquired a taste for smoking, a new habit that was all the rage, though rather expensive. He now puffed on the clay pipe which was almost his one interest these days.

'That will kill you,' said Merlin, gazing at Abe reflectively.

'A pleasant way to die,' replied Abe, puffing more vigorously.

'Rots the lungs,' said Merlin, then he went very silent again. He scratched his long hair and put his hands on his thin ankles. He always liked to sit in this awkward position like a monkey.

'Want some ale?' asked Abe.

Merlin shook his head. 'No, I want to go out into the city. You will come with me, Abe. My memory fails me and I might not remember the way.'

Abe stared at him aghast. 'You know I can't do that, Merlin, I promised Annabelle to look after you.'

'We will return. It is important to find Mr Harvey. He is at St Bartholomew's Hospital.'

Abe shook his head. 'No chance, sorry, mate.' He

was adamant. He could not let Merlin loose in the streets.

When they had first come to London, Merlin had escaped and pinched a little puppy. He had run back to the house with angry Londoners chasing after him. Those same citizens had lingered outside the house for days, throwing stones and calling for the mad man to come out. No thanks! Abe was not going to let Merlin out of his sight any more until Annabelle came home.

Merlin came closer, his hot breath fanning Abe's face. He seemed very excited tonight. Abe looked at him with a worried expression in his eyes. He hoped that Merlin would not get violent, as he used to, because he was sure that he had not the strength to manage him now.

'Listen, Abe, it's nearly over for us,' said Merlin. 'A planet is travelling to earth. It will soon be over. The world will end.'

'Well, what you worrying over?' said Abe stoically. 'If it ends, it ends.'

'No, it must be written down, the knowledge I have. There may still be time. I want to see Harvey.'

Realising how earnest Merlin was, Abe relented. 'All right, I'll go to the hospital for you in the morning. I don't promise that Harvey will come. He might have forgotten you by now, you know.'

Merlin immediately relaxed. 'Good,' he said. 'I'll go and write a letter.'

Abe sat up late, still puffing his pipe and thinking of what Merlin had been talking about. He could not make head or tail of it, but he would take the letter to Dr Harvey at St Bartholomews's Hospital in the morning. It was a terrible place, that hospital, where all the sick and needy gathered. But this poor creature Merlin, as mad as he was now, had once been one of its most brilliant medical students and Dr Harvey had been his mentor. He puffed at his pipe thinking of Merlin's words. 'It's all in a circle. It goes round and round, just like the world.'

Abe was confused. Whatever had he meant?

True to his word, Abe took the letter, which was written in Latin, to the hospital to be given to Dr Harvey. Within days, three very distinguished looking men were secreted upstairs by Merlin. Then towards evening they emerged looking rather pleased with themselves. They took with them a large sheaf of parchment and talked together earnestly as they entered their carriage.

Abe went upstairs to see if Merlin was all right, and found him fast asleep on his little trestle bed, flat on his back like a contented baby.

Merlin had handed over the information about the circulation of the blood, the greatest discovery of the age, to his old master.

12

The Predicament of Chalky

Chalky was in his element, and very pleased with his latest accomplishments. Out in the courtyard under two glowing candle lamps and the silvery moonlight, Katy served the satisfied customers with wooden bowls filled with jellied eels or some other tasty fish. All the while Chalky was trotting in and out. 'Nice plate of lobster with your ale, sir?' he would enquire. 'It goes down lovely, it does.' And so he touted for more trade, with one eye on Katy and the amorous gentlemen who hung about the stall half-drunk. A real businessman was Chalky.

Katy's hair was piled high and held in place with jewelled combs. She sold the fishy goods laughing and giggling as the male customers reached forward trying to catch a look down the low neck of her blouse.

Then every night shortly after closing, Chalky and Katy would go off to the day bed in the sitting room to make love before Katy's big brother came to collect her and find them at it.

It was a very profitable, exciting life for Chalky, and he was thoroughly enjoying himself. There was only one faint shadow on his horizon, and that was poor old Betsy upstairs. So far her legs had not improved, and the apothecary was not too hopeful about her overall condition. The apothecary was a dried-up little man who was much better at attending horses than humans. He had taken off the heavy splints from Betsy's legs and found that she was still in great pain and her legs still quite stiff. In fact, she could not move her knees at all.

'Made a fine bloody mess of her legs,' complained Chalky to the apothecary. 'I've a good mind not to pay you.'

'It will take a bit of time, these jobs always do,' replied the apothecary.

'She can't stay in bed for bloody ever,' moaned Chalky. 'She can't even get downstairs, and we've got a business to run.'

'Don't let her eat and drink so much,' returned the apothecary. 'She might be able to keep her balance if she were not so fat.'

'Get out!' said Chalky, putting his money back into his pocket. 'Get back to them poor bloody horses. Starve the poor cow? Blimey, even horses have to have their oats.' So with his homespun philosophy, Chalky chased the apothecary out of his house and saved himself a lot of expense. From then on he tended Betsy himself.

Chalky was genuinely sorry for Betsy, and was most sympathetic and kind. 'Poor cow,' he would say as he helped her on and off the commode. Betsy had really become very fat during her illness. The rich food she ate and the sweet wine she was so fond of, all helped to increase her weight. Under her tousled mass of blonde hair, her face was as white as death. She reminded Chalky of a big white cabbage slug when she tried with desperate slowness to get around her room on her two very stiff legs.

Occasionally, Betsy lifted her stained nightdress, smelling of wine and body odour, and said, 'Come and cuddle me like you used to, Chalky.'

Chalky would look at her horrified but then he would say in a kind voice: 'All right, won't be a tick. Just got a job to do first.' Then he would dart, like a rabbit to its burrow, downstairs to mix up a drink of poppy seeds and wine which would put Betsy out like a light.

It certainly was not much of an existence for poor Betsy, but what could he do about it? After all, he thought, she would have done the dirty on him if he had allowed it and besides, they did knock off his old man, she and that daft brother of hers. So Chalky went on his busy way consoling his conscience and planning his wedding which, according to Katy, was to be a rather big affair.

'Can't we just pop over to the parson and get signed up, Katy?' Chalky pleaded.

'Not on your sweet life,' replied Katy. 'We always have a big do. I've got a big family, I have.'

'Gor blimey!' exclaimed Chalky, but then shrugged his shoulders. It was not worth arguing about, and anything for a quiet life. Besides, she was a smashing bit of goods, was his Katy.

The days passed and soon it was springtime. The

evenings got longer and Betsy managed to pull herself to the window and disconsolately look down the road. The first time Betsy saw Katy at the stall she was so incensed that she nearly toppled out of the window. 'Chalky!' she screamed and banged on the floor with a stick.

Chalky came running from the cellar, red faced and perspiring. 'Gawd, what's up, Betsy? I thought you'd done it in the bed.'

Betsy pointed out of the window at Katy down at the stall. 'Who's that?' she demanded.

'It's the new barmaid. I got to have a girl about, you know. The gentlemen come in when they see a pretty girl; it's good for business.'

Betsy stared out of the window suspiciously. 'I don't like the look of her. She looks like a whore to me.'

Chalky breathed a sigh and looked sorry for himself. 'All right,' he muttered. 'I'll send her away. Here I am, slaving me fingers to the bone to keep this bloody place running and what thanks do I get?'

Betsy looked affectionately at him and then relented. 'Let her alone, then,' she said. 'I'll watch her and see what she gets up to.'

So it was that part of Betsy's day was spent sitting at the window keeping an eye on Katy and occasionally shouting out at her. Sometimes Katy and Betsy would hiss and spit at each other much to the amusement of the gentlemen customers who loved to see two women fighting.

It was on one of these afternoons when Betsy was stationed in her usual spot at the window that she saw

Marcelle. She spied the little figure walking slowly towards the inn, her head bent, a black shawl about her shoulders, and she could hear the clip-clop of the little wooden clogs as she walked. The sight of Marcelle's tired-looking figure, brought back memories of the day she and Rolly had walked out of London to avoid the plague. The little figure drew near the inn and just stood looking so forlorn and bewildered at the window from where Betsy watched. The nut-brown hair shone in the sun, the head hung a little to one side. But Betsy recognised her. 'Marci! It's little Marci!' Her shrill voice rang out. 'Marci, look up! It's me, Betsy!'

But the sound of Betsy's voice had terrified the little figure so much that she turned and trotted off in the direction of London.

Betsy was astounded. She yelled and rattled at the window, shouting for Chalky, to come up as she watched Marcelle disappear into the distance.

Exhausted, Betsy plonked herself into a chair. 'Damn me, if that wasn't little Marcelle,' she said to herself. 'I'm sure of it, and she looked so sad. Blast these bloody legs of mine. Why could I not go down to her?' Then she started to cry, blubbering like a child and all the while pouring herself drinks until she dropped into a befuddled sleep.

Returning from a visit to his future father-in-law that evening, Chalky helped Betsy into bed. 'There's a bloke down in the bar asked for you, Betsy,' he said. 'He won't tell me his business and it's the second time he's been here.'

'What'd he look like?' Betsy felt scared, for you never knew when your past might creep up on you.

'He looks like a toff. He's a sort of a parson in a dark grey suit with an old-fashioned ruff.'

'Better let him come up,' said Betsy. 'It might be the bailiff from Brook House. They own all the land around here.'

'No, it ain't him. I knows him,' argued Chalky.

'Well, for Christ's sake, send him up,' retorted Betsy. 'If I am going to see him at all, I'd rather get it over with.'

The neat tidy little man sniffed and coughed a bit as he entered Betsy's bedroom. He was the rather fastidious Mr Spenser the Clerk from the Inns of Court. He had been to the inn many times to try and deliver this letter from his client, Thomas Mayhew, who was currently in the New Colony. 'To Miss Betsy, surname unknown, who resides at the Duke's Head Inn in Hackney.' At last he had accomplished his task. The sight of this poor creature who was obviously bedridden and slightly drunk was very disturbing, but he was fairly used to handling these unhappy matters, and he just had to get it over quickly. The smell in the room was vile, but with a brisk little bow he handed the big parchment to Betsy.

She sat in bed looking at the misive, her eyes wide with astonishment. After a moment, she looked away. 'I can't read,' she whispered in embarrassment.

'In that case, madam, it will be my pleasure to read it for you,' Mr Spenser said kindly. He closed the door so that Chalky, hiding in the corridor, had to move forward and press his ear to the key hole in order to hear.

Taking up a dramatic pose that might have done credit to Will Shakespeare's players, Mr Spenser started to read aloud:

> *Dear Madam,*
> *You will no doubt recall the night I called at the Duke's Head more than two years ago, and took Marcelle away with me. She has since done me the honour to be my wife.*
> *However, it is of more intimate things I write to you. I bring you good news of your brother Rolly whom, no doubt, you have given up for dead. He is alive and well and serves me in the most devoted manner, having been pressed to sea and being fortunate enough to end up on board my ship sailing for the New World. He sends his regards and tells me he will bring home rich presents.*
> *When, and if, you get my letter it will be a long time ahead, as news is hard to transfer, but he will return safe, I do assure you.*
> *Best wishes.*
> *From Thomas Mayhew and*
> *your loving brother, Rolly*

Betsy's pallid face glowed red for a minute and she was too overcome to speak. Out in the corridor Chalky was feeling shocked too, but felt better when he heard the bit about the New World. Not many returned from there, he thought.

Betsy called out to him: 'Come in, Chalky, something wonderful has happened. Rolly is alive! Oh, thank God, my little Rolly's coming home again.'

Chalky came in and made the appropriate delighted noises while he buzzed about getting a chair and a glass of ale for Mr Spenser.

Betsy stared at Thomas' letter in wonder. All those lovely signs, strange signs which had brought her such happiness.

'I can't write back, but can I send a message . . .' Betsy looked hopefully at Mr Spenser.

'I will call tomorrow when you have had time to think what you want to say, and then write a return letter for you,' Mr Spenser promised. He left hurriedly without finishing his drink. The smell in Betsy's room had become too overpowering.

After he had gone, Betsy lay back and dreamed of Rolly as a swashbuckling hero coming home from the sea and bringing caskets of gold and jewels to lay at her feet. Poor Betsy was happier than she had been for a long time.

As she lay there, her thoughts settled on Marcelle. Did not Thomas say that she was his wife? If so, then it could not have been Marcelle she had seen, after all. She would not have been tramping the road if she were married to Thomas. He was a squire to royalty. No, it could not have been Marci, even though that woman had looked much like her. She would not bother to mention the incident in her return letter. But what could she mention? She lay turning over in her mind what she would say. It was an important event to send a letter, and Betsy had never done anything like that before.

When Mr Spenser came the next day, the whole afternoon disappeared while Betsy chopped and changed her mind about what news to send Rolly and Thomas. However, by the evening the letter had been written and a very fatigued Mr Spenser was eager to go home to his dinner. Betsy, however, wanted Chalky to see this important manuscript and asked if she could hold on to it for one night.

Anxious to get going, Mr Spenser suggested that he leave the letter behind and that Chalky bring it to his office the next day.

A beautiful smile crossed Betsy's bloated features. 'You don't mind?' she said gratefully. 'I'd like him to read it; he can read, you know,' she said proudly.

The busy clerk left at last, pleased to get out in the cool fresh air after the stench of Betsy's bedroom.

The next morning Betsy seemed very subdued. Chalky noticed how quiet she was as he helped her wash and made up her bed for her. He never minded these little chores, for they eased his conscience slightly. Betsy's face had not a trace of colour in it, and her eyelids drooped as though she were tired.

'What's up, love?' Chalky asked kindly.

'Oh, I'm all right,' said Betsy. 'In fact, I've not felt so happy for a long time, now I know that Rolly is safe.'

'Good,' said Chalky. 'That's what I like to hear.'

His cheerful countenance belied the furious thoughts that spun around his head. All I need is for that great oaf to come back, he thought, what with

Katy screaming her head off to get married quick now that she is sure she is pregnant. Chalky sighed a deep sigh. 'I'll fill your bottle up, love,' he said, as he tucked Betsy up in bed. 'Stay there today, if you are not feeling so well.'

Betsy held her letter and looked at it wistfully. 'I wish I could write,' she murmured.

'It's only to be taken to the office. I'll do that later,' Chalky consoled her.

'You can write, Chalky,' Betsy said. 'I wanted to say something else. You can write on the bottom of the letter for me.'

'Later on, love, I got a lot to do.' Chalky was trying hard to avoid this task, for he was not sure that he remembered how to write.

'Oh, please, do it now,' she pleaded.

'All right,' Chalky relented and went to get the ink and a long quill pen that was used by the more important of the customers. 'What do you want to say?'

On the bottom of the parchment, in a funny unpractised scrawl of letters, she got Chalky to write: 'I saw Marci. She was by the brook.'

'What's that mean?' Chalky asked in surprise. 'Who's Marci?'

But Betsy seemed tired. 'Thanks, Chalky,' she said. 'Get us a drink, mate.'

Chalky looked bothered but he sealed up the letter. 'I'll take it to the parson,' he said. 'He will be going up to London sometime this week.'

Taking Betsy's precious letter, Chalky went over to the church and knocked at the manse door. The parson did not often see Chalky but he welcomed him in now and gave him a nice heavy jug of wine. Then Chalky gave the letter into the parson's hands who then agreed he would deliver it to the Inns of Court.

That was quite a day, for Chalky, for he had been given constant threats from Katy as to what her brothers would do to him if he did not marry her before her father found out she was a month overdue.

'All right, love,' Chalky had replied nervously. He had given in to her pressure at last. 'Tomorrow we can put up the banns.'

Katy's eyes lit up at that but she added: 'By the way, I ain't living here with that old stepmother of yours up there.'

'She ain't so bad, old Betsy,' replied Chalky. 'It's just that her legs got broke.' Chalky loyally defended poor Betsy. 'I'm getting her a little cottage to live in as soon as I see one,' he consoled Katy.

Katy then put her arms cajolingly around him and made it obvious that she wanted to make love. So a passionate session on the day bed, before the inn opened, was just about the end of Chalky. Afterwards he trailed back and forth serving jugs of ale to his customers and feeling devoid of all sense and feeling.

The bar was very busy and lots of people were outside in the street, all staring up at a strange star in the sky. It made them quite thirsty as they popped in and out of the inn all talking and explaining his own theory as to what the omen was.

The night was hot and close, and there was a stillness in the air as just before a storm breaks. Wiping the sweat from his brow on his apron, Chalky was really beginning to face the strain. I've a good mind to scarper and leave the whole lot, he told himself repeatedly. Then he thought of the tiny baby inside Katy's strong body. He had never been a father before. I'll bet he'll be a strong boy, thought Chalky, and good looking. He had always dreamed of having a son. That settled it. No, he could not go. He would stay. The evening was so busy Chalky never got a chance to see how Betsy was upstairs. At midnight, the inn closed and a noisy throng still hung about outside. The heat of the night had become worse. And when Katy came in, glowing with exertion of handing out bowls of fish to the attentive male customers who paid her many compliments, she was hot and eager for more love.

Chalky, however, was anxious to get the day over and go up to Betsy. 'No, not now, Katy,' he said.

'You don't want me,' Katy sobbed, throwing herself down on the bed. 'You don't want me now. Like all the men, you had what you wanted, and now I have to take the consequences.'

'No, Katy, darling,' Chalky knelt down beside her. 'Don't cry, you might upset his Lordship.' He fondly rubbed her tummy, and Katy threw her arms around him, catching him was like a rat in a trap. He wanted to leave but was quite unable to do so. Half an hour later he had just dozed off to sleep in the arms of his passionate Katy, when a loud bump from upstairs aroused him.

'Gawd, it's Betsy. I'd better go.' Chalky tried to

disengage himself from Katy's embrace but she held him tight.

'Let the old cow wait,' she said. 'We are busy.'

And because he could not help it, Chalky stayed and slept the sleep of pure exhaustion for a while, only to be awakened once more but this time by the banging on the back door. It was Katy's irate brother who had come to collect her.

'What's up with you two?' he demanded. 'I've been knocking for ages.'

It has been quite a session, Chalky thought, as he climbed the stairs wearily to his bedroom. I'd better take a look at Betsy. As he opened the door he saw poor Betsy lying on the floor, a huddled mass by the bed. Her head was bent backwards, vomit had filled her throat, and blood came from her nose. Poor Betsy had left this world and no one knew or cared. She had obviously tried to reach the chamber pot and fallen head-first from the bed.

Chalky knelt beside her for a while. Poor old Betsy, he did feel sorry. He ought to have come up when he had heard that thump. Then a terrible thought struck him. They might think he had done her in! Oh dear! Chalky ran to the window shouting out as loud as he could to the linkman who patrolled after dark. 'Help! Come quick! Someone is dead!'

Soon the linkman brought the watch and the doctor who all certified that Betsy had died an accidental death. Chalky breathed a sigh of relief. He would give her a slap-up funeral with a nice big headstone: 'Here lies Elizabeth White,' it would read, 'Wife of Samuel White who was drowned at sea.'

None of it was true but it didn't matter. And at least she had died respectably. Chalky then went straight round to the church from the churchyard to put up the banns for his wedding to Katy. Nothing could stop him now. She had not been so bad, old Betsy.

13

The Waning Star

At the grand funeral of Henry Howard, the Londoners had come to stand and stare at the display of riches and grandeur of this wicked old man on his last ride. There had been many murmurs of discontent among the poor. Times were bad. Taxes were very high and even the middle-class merchants complained of the greediness of the Royal Treasury and of the King's servant, that evil agent Topcliffe. It was he who still ordered the hangings and torture of those who held on so dearly and persistently to their old religious beliefs. The climate was so bad that many great families were planning to leave England – either to the placid Low Countries or to the New World, but there were many poor little birds who would not fly and could only stand in the street and talk and grumble about the hard times and watch their previously more fortunate fellows being dragged on hurdles to their deaths.

When the strange comet hung low in the evening sky, they all stood looking and wondering what there was in store for them. 'The Queen will die,' some said. Others claimed that the king would be assassinated. Rumours like these spread like a forest fire until the population became tense with fear and blamed any strange happening on the comet.

The crowds parted as the carriage of the grand Duchess Frances rolled by. There was no sign of her husband, Robert Carr, who still stuck vainly to the rôle of King's favourite, always at the beck and call of King James. But alas, his power was waning, for King James had found a new boy to be his favourite, a beautiful blond vivacious lad, as ambitious and unscrupulous as any at the court. This was the famous George Villers, who was to become the great Duke of Buckingham and hold England in the palm of his hand. While the old king simpered and fussed over this new boy, Robert Carr was eaten up with jealousy, blaming Frances for trapping him into a marriage for which he had no taste.

The beautiful Duchess rode alone to the funeral of her Uncle Henry, her pale face set in an angry mask, as the dirty common people stared into the coach and shouted rude rhymes: 'The Queen of Hearts made the tarts . . .'

Frances was beginning to get worried. Strange things were happening everywhere. Was her secret safe? Had she been as discreet as she could? The mind of this rich and beautiful woman was seething like a volcano as she watched and waited for the blow to fall. It had to come, there was no doubt. Robert Carr's star was falling just as the Villers' star was rising and shining as bright as the comet in the sky. And on top of all this, her beloved uncle had died. The world was a nasty, bewildering place.

After the funeral, the guests called at her house in Croydon but Frances wanted to be alone to consult Merlin. With Annabelle at her side, very silent and smartly dressed, the two women drove up the long drive flanked by green-and-yellow spotted laurels. To Annabelle's surprise, by the silvery moonlight she could see Merlin looking out of the window in the direction of the road. A small crowd stood there looking up at him with his straggly hair blowing in the breeze while he gazed through his long telescope examining the heavens. The crowds were shouting and jeering while Merlin jeered and shouted back at them.

'Scum!' called Merlin. 'Rotten, dirty scum! The end is near. Tomorrow we will all die, and disappear into flames, the whole dirty pack of you. Yaah!' he yelled, waving his hands more and more erratically. 'The end of the world is coming. I warned you – see, it's getting nearer.' He pointed up to the comet.

The people stared up into the sky. Some looked afraid and while others only laughed and egged Merlin on more for a bit of fun.

Annabelle dashed panic-stricken into the house. 'God in heaven, Abe,' she called. 'What is Merlin up to?'

Abe sat staring wearily at the fire and puffed his pipe. 'So, you're back, then,' he said quietly.

'For God's sake, go and get Merlin. The countess is here.'

'He won't come for me,' said Abe. 'He's gone berserk, he has. It's that comet what's excited him.'

Annabelle dashed upstairs. Merlin was so pleased

to see her that he came away from the window peacefully and went quietly back into his attic.

After her consultation with Merlin, Frances came downstairs and gazed disdainfully at the dust and disorder of the house. 'I shall return to Holborn,' she said. 'You stay here, Annabelle, and get things straight.' She picked her dainty way through the dirt towards the door where she stood in the porch, outlined by the silvery moonlight, her gown glittering with jewels, her hair shining with dusty silver and her profile clear, cold and hard.

The harassed Annabelle looked at her for a moment and a strange sense of foreboding crept over her. Something dreadful was going to happen. And after Frances had gone and there was only the empty doorway, Annabelle knew in her heart that it was the beginning of the end.

As she closed the door on her mistress, Annabelle's face looked worried, showing that she had much on her mind. With her hair dyed and frizzed in the latest fashion and her face painted, Annabelle no longer looked like the fresh-faced wench who had lived in Essex at Craig Alva.

Abe sat surveying Annabelle's tense expression as she bustled about cleaning up the kitchen. A chicken was cooking on the big open spit and Abe helped by preparing the vegetables. Annabelle's face was hard, he thought, and she seemed pretty worried about something. It would not be long before he found out.

An hour later, they sat eating their supper. Merlin

was thoroughly enjoying the chicken and onions but Annabelle ate very little.

'I have something to tell you, Abe,' she said quietly.

Abe looked up enquiringly, his brow wrinkled as if to ask what was wrong.

Annabelle came straight to the point. 'There is to be an inquiry into the Thomas Overbury case. It seems that a young man has confessed to murdering him.'

'I knew it,' said Abe. 'Someone done him in, but how they got at him beats me.'

'But you will be questioned, Abe,' said Annabelle. 'So you must be very careful not to involve anyone.'

'I can keep my mouth shut if I want to,' muttered Abe.

Annabelle glanced at Merlin who was busy shovelling up the last remains of his meal. 'I am seriously thinking of sending you and Merlin back to Essex,' she said thoughtfully.

'Good,' said Abe. 'It will be nice to see Marcelle again, and the boy. He must be more than a year old now, and I bet he is bonny.'

Annabelle's face became pathetic and her brown eyes filled with tears. 'Marcelle is not there anymore,' she whispered.

'Not there? Well, where is she?' demanded Abe in surprise.

'She ran away. No one knows where she is.'

'Ran away!' Abe was shocked. 'Where could she run to?'

'No one knows. Her child was stolen during the winter and several weeks ago, Marcelle ran away to look for him half-witted with grief.'

'Good God! Whatever has been going on? Tell me, please Annabelle. You were not implicated in this terrible crime, surely!'

'No.' Annabelle shook her head woefully. 'I did not know of it until today.'

'Dear me,' Abe wagged his old grey head. 'What a terrible thing to happen.'

'Listen, Abe, I do know where the child is. He is with a relation of the Howards and is well cared for.'

'I thought they were in it,' muttered Abe with disgust.

'That is why I want you to go to the lawyer's tomorrow and try to trace Marcelle. You must also get a message to Thomas Mayhew. That is the best I can do. Believe me, Abe, I would not have hurt Marcelle for all the money in the world.' Annabelle began to sob quietly.

Abe patted her head. 'Don't cry,' he said. 'Things may brighten up by the morning.'

But when morning dawned things were decidedly worse. At six o'clock a long line of mounted men arrived at the house. They were manhandled roughly outside while the sergeant-at-arms read the charge: 'All three persons are to be arrested for being accessories to the murder of one Thomas Overbury by name.'

Later in a little cart, they were taken away. They sat huddled together, Annabelle covering her face with her hands, Abe sitting motionless with a grim face and Merlin protesting and waving his arms and calling out that the end of the world was nigh.

They had already been charged and were on their

way to prison, followed by a jeering mob calling out insults and throwing filth. One hefty fellow with a cudgel in his hand tried to take a swipe at them as they swung along in the dirty old cart. Annabelle and Abe crouched down but Merlin sat bolt upright and returned their jeers. Suddenly he reached out and caught hold of the big fellow by the beard. Yelling out loud, Merlin stood up and pulled the beard hard, wedging its owner's face against the tailboard. Then Merlin lost his balance and fell over the side of the cart, falling down under the wheels. With a wild cry, the mob pounced. Like a pack of wild animals they tore off Merlin's clothes. The big bearded ruffian had recovered. Picking up his cudgel, he swung it high, and with one terrible blow, he shattered the side of Merlin's head as he lay helpless on the ground. The wonderful clever brains of Merlin lay like a quivering bloody mass of jelly on the muddy road. Merlin's body gave one convulsive jerk, and then lay still. The crowds drew back as the soldiers came to drive them away.

Annabelle had fainted and Abe's face was covered by his hands as he gave way to tears. He had been useless to Merlin at this tragic moment, after guarding him so carefully all these years. Later that morning, the prison doors clanged shut on the heartbroken pair as they awaited their trial in the terrible Marshalsea Prison.

The trial was a farce and Frances, Annabelle's mistress, did nothing to save the lives of the two she had used for her own ends. Abe was taken off to the Tower to be tortured in the vain hope that they would get the truth out of him, and Annabelle was hanged by the neck until she was dead.

Several people died over this terrible affair of Thomas Overbury – eight, all told, and every one a fairly innocent little bird who could not escape, while the real culprits, Frances and her husband, Robert Carr, remained free, for the time being.

Just as Annabelle was parted from Abe, dragged away by the soldiers, she whispered urgently to him: 'The baby is at Brook House. Tell Marcelle.'

This message stuck in Abe's mind, and during the terrible days when he was racked and pegged out naked on Tower Hill with no food or water, the words 'Brook House', tumbled around his brain, he repeated them over and over like a chant to pass the long hours away.

'Tell all you know,' his torturers had urged him, but Abe knew nothing, being only a cat's paw for the great Duchess who was still free.

Frances' trial had been postponed because she announced she was pregnant, but the postponement was only for a little while. Before long, they came for her as well.

The dreadful heat which had been hanging over London suddenly burst one day into a terrible storm. Long blue flashes lit up the sky and with sharp crackles the forked lightning split the thunderous clouds. There would be a breath of silence before the return of that long roll of thunder which began loudly and then rolled gradually away over the town to the open country, rebuilding its store of electric energy in order to return with equal violence. This continued all day and far into the night. In the morning, the streets were clean and fresh with the downpour of rain that had come with the storm, and there was a soft calm breeze. The Londoners emerged into the streets in cheery anticipation of a new lot of hangings and executions that they might have to brighten their day.

'Surely the big trial will end soon,' they muttered to one another, and gossiped fervently about the scandal of the King's boyfriend who had married a whore and poisoned his best friend.

Down in the Strand Frances was under close arrest. She had spent the stormy night like a caged animal, walking back and forth along the gallery of her uncle's house. Dressed in a heavy house coat of purple velvet trimmed with white ermine she paced the shiny marble floor. The portraits of her long dead ancestors looked down at her and seemed to her to sneer.

'Your time has come,' some seemed to be saying. Frances shivered. The beautiful young duchess wanted very much to live. Inside her she could feel the next Howard kicking. Biting her full lower lip, she gave vent to her misery, continuously twisting the golden girdle of her house coat. Not one word did she utter or cry but paced back and forth like a tawny-haired cat. 'There must be a way,' she muttered to herself. 'Surely James will not convict Robert – there would be too much at stake if he tells all. James will not risk that.' She was trying hard to convince herself. Today they would bring her husband from the Tower to the Star Chamber and tomorrow it would be her turn to appear before that great Judge Coke on a murder charge.

Frances hoped that the sentimental old fool, King James, would not allow her to be put in prison because of her pregnancy. She was pretty sure of the old King, and very sure of the support of the Howards. But would Robert betray her? His attitude had changed towards her since she had become pregnant; perhaps he doubted his ability to become a father. A twisted smile crossed her lips and she tossed her head defiantly. She would beat them all in the end. No – she would not die the way her cousins Ann and Katherine had done. There had to be a way out, there had to be.

Later that morning two visitors were shown into the hallway. Peering from the balcony, Frances recognised them as the King's men, Lord Fenton and the Earl of Montgomery. Perhaps it was good news. She hurried downstairs. The men greeted her with low sweeping bows with hats in their hands. Dressed in their flowing capes of bright glowing colours, the King's courtiers were certainly a magnificent sight. But Frances only had to look at their faces to know that things were not going well with Robert.

'We do not bring you good news, Frances,' said the young Lord Fenton.

'Did he plead guilty,' she demanded.

'No, my Lady, he denied any knowldge of the death of Overbury and placed all the blame on you.'

Frances drew in a quick deep breath. Her eyes flashed and her lips paled. 'Come this way, my lords,' she said, directing them to the library. 'I intend that you should witness my confession. I shall appeal to His Majesty for mercy.'

The following day the trial continued and a demure Frances appeared dressed in a black velvet gown and her ash blonde hair about her face to hide her real expression. As a courtier recounted the torture of old Abe and the death of Annabelle, Frances suddenly saw her friends before her eyes, and hid her face in her hands.

But Frances was not to die, nor was Robert Carr. At the end of the trial, they were both convicted but sent to the Tower, to await the King's pardon.

In 1616 Sir Walter Raleigh was released from the Tower and Frances and Robert, the Duke and Duchess of Somerset, moved in to his vacated apartments. There they fought each other every day for a whole year until they were finally reprieved. All the little birds had suffered, but predictably, the big ones had got away.

With Abe's tortured face burning in her mind, Marcelle ran from the terrible scene on the hill. 'Got to get to the brook,' she muttered to herself as she ran. Down the hill she went, away from the river scene, with people thronging about her dressed in gay colours and in a jolly holiday mood. There was talk of hangings and burnings and the excited crowds pushed their way through the dirty streets. Marcelle heard very little of what they said, seeing only a sea of strange, blurred faces before her. On and on she ran through the market place. Raucous voices roared out as stallholders advertised their wares. 'Hot pies! Soup! New bread!' they called. It was then the smell of food assailed her nostrils – the delicious aroma of hot soup. She had not eaten since she left home the previous day, and the smell was almost too much. Slowing down at one stall, she pulled her shawl tightly about her and gazed ravenously at the hot soup being ladled into bowls and handed out with big chunks of bread to dip into it. Various people sat around enjoying their meal. The huge red-faced woman serving the soup gazed suspiciously at her. 'Hi! You want some soup or don't you?' she demanded.

Marcelle did not answer, she just stood watching the soup bubble over the fire. 'Well, if you ain't got no money, be off with you. I can't afford to have beggars around.'

But Marcelle still did not move. She continued to stare wide eyed at the nourishing soup.

'Hoppit!' the woman yelled at her, waving the ladle. 'Hoppit! I said.'

Like a startled rabbit, Marcelle turned and ran. With her head dropping to one side as she went she looked a strange sight, hobbling quickly through the market, her wooden clogs clip-clopping over the cobblestones. Men called out obscene comments to her and the rough women laughed uproariously as her funny little figure stumbled past them. There were tears on Marcelle's eyelashes that refused to fall, and her feet were sore and blistered as the confused little creature ran away from these loud-voiced people.

'Where is the little brook?' she cried. 'Please God, let me find the little brook.'

By nightfall, Marcelle was still wandering the dusty streets weary and hungry and not daring to ask the way. At last she came to a tall church surrounded by a graveyard. It was the church of St John at Hackney, but Marcelle neither knew that nor cared. She just crept behind a tall gravestone and laid down her weary head to rest. The dark night covered the gravestones and only the dead knew that Marcelle lay huddled there among them.

Chalky was up bright and early that morning. He had much to do that day but first he had to see the parson and arrange for Betsy's funeral. He felt quite holy as he walked crisply up the long path leading to the church. 'Got to get her buried proper,' he told himself. 'She wasn't a bad sort, old Betsy, and, after all, I am a very responsible citizen with a good little business which might even improve after I'm married.' As he walked along with his hands in his pockets and that particular rolling gait reminiscent of his old days at sea, he stopped suddenly in his tracks as his attention was drawn to the little figure of Marcelle sitting on the edge of the path. Her figure was bent double as she clutched her stomach against the cramps of hunger that gripped her. She looked like a hobgoblin from another world.

'Cripes!' exclaimed Chalky. 'Who's this?'

A little moan came from the figure and as Chalky got nearer to her he recognised the signs of starvation, having suffered similarly himself – the stomach gripped with pain which would not allow the body to straighten out. He gazed down at this pathetic figure and his soft heart melted in sympathy. 'Gawd, blimey, you ain't half hungry, love. Here . . .' He held out a coin to her.

Marcelle's hurt, soulful eyes gazed up at him. She made no attempt to take the money but started muttering something about a brook.

Oh dear! thought Chalky. The poor cow's potty. She must have escaped from some place. 'Here you are, mate,' he said, trying to put the coin in her hand. 'Get some grub.' But still there was no response. 'Wait a bit,' he suddenly said, and went running back down the path. Along the road came a girl with the milk churns, her broad shoulders erect as they swayed each side.

'Quick, give us a can of milk,' said Chalky panting with exertion and handing her a coin. 'Lend us a can. I'll be back with it in a tick.' He went over the road to a stall that sold buns and bought a bag of them, and then he ran back to the churchyard where Marcelle still sat.

Gently he put the can of tepid milk to her lips. 'Come on, love,' he said softly. He persuaded her to drink the milk and then, sitting down beside her, he broke a bun into small pieces. 'Take it slow, ducks, that's it, not too quick.'

Slowly and surely Marcelle sat up as the slightly warm milk eased the cramp in her stomach. She sat nibbling the bun looking at Chalky with a grateful expression on her face, unable to speak her thanks.

'That's it, mate,' Chalky chattered to her. 'Feel better now?' he asked. He suddenly remembered his original reason for being in the churchyard, and he got up. 'Got to go now, love, must see the parson. Why don't you take a little walk and sit outside my inn? You might get a nice meal later on, and you can kip in the stables.' Saying this to her he was reminded of the day he himself had arrived in Hackney, cold and hungry. He helped her to her feet and pointed in the direction of the inn. 'I won't be long. I've got to go and see about burying me poor old stepmother.' Then having done his good deed, Chalky set off to the parson's house to do another, while Marcelle set off on stiff cold legs and swollen feet in the other direction towards the inn.

Across the fields at the end of a path stood the black-and-white structure of the Duke's Head Inn. Seeing it ahead, Marcelle hesitated. She was afraid of that place and of an unknown terror that lurked there. Limping quickly past, she headed towards the green pastures and then, to her utter joy, she came to the little brook which she had tried hard to find. Hurrying towards it, she knelt down as if in prayer. Taking off her shoes, she then splashed her feet and her face with the cool water. Afterwards she walked along the bank following the rippling brook as it wended its way over the fields. It ran under a little wooden bridge and there ahead of her was a magnificent park with soft rolling lawns and great trees. Marcelle decided to sit on the bank and dabble her feet in the brook, staring towards the big house with its turrets shining green and gold in the morning sun. 'At last,' she thought. 'I've found the little brook.' It was so cool and peaceful there, she decided to stay in this place. When night came she would lie down in the clear water to rest forever. She could go no further; this was the end of her journey. Suddenly she felt drowsy. And as sleep overcame her, she sat there with her head nodding only to be awakened by the sounds of children laughing and playing. It was like sweet music to her ears.

Marcelle opened her eyes and there they were, three children running over the hill towards the very place where Marcelle sat. As she watched them, a lovely smile came to her lips, and her pale, sad face lit up. They came running towards her – a sturdy little boy of about nine and a girl slightly younger who held a tiny toddler by the hand. The little one tripped along on chubby legs and the sun shone on his lovely red gold curls. The girl was very pretty – tall and slim with waist-length hair, the colour of golden sunshine. The older boy forged ahead a little; he carried a fishing net. Behind them and moving very slowly was a woman carrying a picnic basket. All the time she called out to them, urging for them not to get too far ahead. The boy with the fishing net had reached the brook just a few feet away from Marcelle. Kneeling down, he put the net into the water. The baby suddenly pulled away from the girl and came racing as fast as his little legs would carry him down the slope towards the water, quite unable to stop. Marcelle moved as quick as lightning to catch him. Jumping in, she waded waist deep into the centre to grab the little boy just as he reached the bank. Then she stood, holding him close. 'Roger!' she whispered. 'My baby has come back to me.'

Thinking it was a good game, the little boy twisted his fingers in her hair and smiled charmingly at her.

Soon the girl arrived followed by the woman who was very profuse with her thanks to this stranger who had saved little Popsi from falling in the brook. The strange lady was crying and holding on to Popsi but he seemed to like her.

'Thank you my dear,' said Mrs Powell, the lady in charge of the children. 'Every day I have dreaded that Popsi would do just that and my legs are so bad I find it hard work trying to keep up with these youngsters.' She produced a towel and gave it to Marcelle to dry her legs. They then ate beside the brook – cakes, sandwiches and sweet cider.

Marcelle spread her skirt out to dry in the sun while they watched the children at the water's edge. With the hot sun drying her clothes and warming her body, Marcelle suddenly felt supremely happy. She had known she would find her baby by the brook, and she had.

This was her son, she was sure, and with that thought in her head, her mind began to clear and her memory return.

The children rolled about with each other in the grass and the boy with his net fished for minnows.

'Who is that lady?' he asked Mrs Powell. 'Why is she so poor?'

'Hush, Robert, you must not be rude,' said Mrs Powell.

The golden-haired girl looked at Marcelle and demanded imperiously: 'What is your name?' And she held out her hands towards Marcelle's face. It was then that Marcelle suddenly realised that this beautiful little girl was unable to see her. And as the child pushed aside her long hair, Marcelle saw that one eye was sightless while the other eye was sunk deep in its socket. Marcelle gently took her hand and placed it against her cheek allowing the girl to feel the contours of her face. 'My name is Marci,' she croaked in a strange voice.

'Mousi,' giggled Elizabeth. 'Now that is a funny name. But I like you, you have a nice face just like a mouse. I will call you Miss Mouse. Do you mind?'

'Behave, Elizabeth,' remonstrated Mrs Powell. 'Do not pester the lady, she is very tired.'

Mrs Powell had noticed Marcelle's swollen feet. 'Have you walked a long way, dear?' she asked kindly.

'From Essex,' replied Marcelle. 'I have wandered for two days.'

'Have you no home, dear?' Mrs Powell asked.

'No, I left home to find my son who was stolen from me. But I am content now. I have found him again.' She smiled and put a protective arm about the baby.

Poor thing is a bit gone, thought Mrs Powell to herself, but she did save the boy, after all. Perhaps I ought to offer her shelter. 'You may come back to the house to rest if you wish,' she offered. 'The master is away but I am sure he will not mind.' She rose and began to bustle about. 'I could really do with a bit of help with these children now. Some days my legs are not as young as they used to be.'

The picnic was soon over and the little party made their way back over the green parkland. Marcelle carried Roger in her arms. Elizabeth skipped closely beside her. Behind them, Mrs Powell hobbled along very slowly with the sturdy Robert still clutching his net and helping Mrs Powell with the picnic basket.

So it was that a new nursemaid arrived at Brook House – Miss Mouse they all called her. The big house reverberated with the sound of children's happy laughter as they played and were fussed over by their new nurse. The old oak beams took up the sound and echoed it round the old grey stone wall as Miss Mouse called the children.

'Welcome to our home, Miss Mouse,' it seemed to say.

Chalky wiped the sweat from his brow with the back of his hand. 'Poor little cow,' he said as he went towards the parson's house. The street door with its brass knocker looked very imposing as it nestled under the creeper-covered walls. Chalky took a deep breath. He could handle most people but when it came to parsons and suchlike he was not so confident. Plucking up his courage he rattled the door knocker and waited. Seconds later, the door was open by a servant in a white apron who looked disdainfully at him.

Chalky looked her straight in the eye; he was not going to be thwarted. 'I want to see the parson,' he said in a loud voice. 'It's very urgent.'

The parson had heard Chalky's voice and recognised it as belonging to the giver of a nice bottle of dinner wine on his last visit to the inn. He came forward, his bulbous nose glowing pinky blue. 'Come in, young man,' he said. 'Come in and welcome.'

Chalky made much of wiping his feet on the rush mat and entered with much decorum, his hat in his hand.

'How can I help you?' asked the parson.

'It's me stepmother,' said Chalky. 'Died very sudden, she did.'

'Oh indeed? I am so sorry,' said the man of God. 'I will pray for her soul.'

'I'd like a bit more than that done for her,' replied Chalky. 'She was a most respected woman.' He spoke softly and furtively as though expecting to be contradicted.

The parson, however, did not connect Betsy with Chalky's stepmother. 'Well, what can I do?' he asked most obligingly.

'I want her to have a slap-up funeral,' said Chalky. 'I ain't short of money and I want a nice headstone. Will you see to that for me, sir?'

'Of course – you have already approached the undertaker, I presume?'

'Oh yes, and a damned nice coffin I'm getting for her, too, but I was thinking you might keep her in the church until she is buried.' Chalky was very anxious to get Betsy out of the house.

The old parson's eyes twinkled; he was beginning to get the picture. Still, it was not his business. 'What sort of stone would you like?' he asked. 'A cross, or an angel, maybe?'

'That's it,' said Chalky. 'A nice angel with wings outstretched. She'd like that.'

'Good, and how about the verse?' said the parson.

Now this question really foxed Chalky. He screwed up his eyes for a moment and then said: 'What about: "Here lies Betsy White. Died all of sudden on a Friday night."'

It was then that the parson's big Adam's apple went up and down in the most alarming manner and he started to cough as he tried so hard not to laugh.

Chalky banged him hard on the back. 'Nasty cough you got there, sir. Here, have a drop of the old fire water to take it away.' He pulled out a bottle and put it on the desk. 'Straight from the continent,' he said. 'Ain't been sold in England before.'

The beady eyes of the parson gleamed in appreciation as he looked at the bottle. 'I'll do what I can for you,' he said. 'Bring your stepmother into the church tonight and we will bury her tomorrow.'

'Thank you, sir,' said Chalky, pumping the parson's arm up and down like the village pump. 'Oh, wait a minute,' he said suddenly. 'There's another little favour you can do for me. I want to put the banns up for me wedding. Got to hurry it up a bit, if you knows what I mean . . .' He gave the parson a knowing wink which nearly caused the old chap to choke. 'And you wanna look after that cough,' Chalky said as he went cheerily to the door.

As soon as the door was closed, the parson sank down in the hall seat and laughed until the tears ran down his face. 'Oh dear, what a caution,' was all he could gasp as his servant came running to his aid.

Chalky felt on top of the world as he hurried down the leafy path to the inn and his beautiful Katy. He looked around for the little wanderer but there was no sign of her. She must have gone on her way. But there was lovely Katy at the door to welcome him, her dark hair shining and the little bump beginning to show under the apron.

'Katy, darling,' he said gaily, 'it's all sealed and signed. Come on, give us a kiss.'

Moments later they were making violent love on the little day bed in the sitting room, while Betsy lay in a coffin upstairs, stiff and white.

'Things ain't turned out so bad, after all,' remarked Chalky as he lay back relaxing, while Katy returned to her stall.

14

Homecomings

When Marcelle entered Brook House she had the wonderful sense of peace. She felt as though she had arrived home after a long absence. They entered by the south-west wing of the house, through a beautiful apple orchard where the trees formed cool archways and the heavy ripe fruit hung from the boughs. The children ran on ahead, laughing and prattling, and continued to laugh and chatter until they were all safely tucked up in bed by Mrs Powell and Marcelle.

Now Marcelle sat facing Mrs Powell in a wide, roomy kitchen lined with huge brass pots, which accommodated a stove that took up almost the entire side of the wall. Marcelle wanted to ask about the baby. She had undressed him and had seen the large crown-shaped mole on his bottom, and there was now no doubt in her mind that he was her baby. She waited to talk about him to Mrs Powell but was very wary of laying claim to him outright. The derangement of mind she had suffered had given her the astuteness she needed for such a situation. She so wanted to talk about Roger but she could anticipate what would happen if she did. They would say she was crazy and

shut her up somewhere. No, she had to remain quiet
and take her time, just like the mouse the children
liked to call her.

Mrs Powell groaned as she bent to undo the band-
age on her leg. Marcelle knelt down and with gentle
fingers took off the dressing. Then she applied the
cool balm to the ulcer on Mrs Powell's shin.

'Oh, thank you, my dear, that does feel better,' Mrs
Powell sighed with relief. 'I ought not to be on my
feet so much, but the children need me. You cannot
trust the servant girls these days. Agnes and Elsie are
always quarrelling.' She put her leg up on the foot
stool and sighed contentedly. 'Oh, I am glad that this
day is over.'

'Are they your grandchildren?' asked Marcelle,
anxious to hear all about her baby.

'Good Lord, no!' exclaimed Mrs Powell.

'Does their mother live here?'

'No, love, none of them are related. They are the
master's adopted children. The eldest boy Robert is to
be Sir Fulke's heir and the lovely Elizabeth, well, that
is a long story which I might tell you, if you stay long
enough. But the oddest one is the baby. No one really
knows where he came from. The master loves babies,
so when Elizabeth Howard brought him here one dark
night, the master welcomed him without hesitation
and handed him over to me. I have taken care of him
ever since. Ask no questions, you hear no lies – that is
my motto.'

A secret smile crossed Marcelle's face, and Mrs
Powell looked curiously at her. What a funny girl,

she thought, she looked as if she were in a dream all the time.

But Marcelle's dream had come true. Roger was indeed her baby. Her prayers had been answered and her worried harassed brain was gradually clearing. She could see things in a more normal way at last. 'Will you allow me to stay and work for you?' she asked eagerly. 'I would love to take care of the baby.'

Mrs Powell was puzzled. She knew nothing about this girl, but she did not look or speak like a common girl and there was an air of mystery about her. The way her head twisted to one side and her voice was deep and husky also helped to make this girl unusual. Mrs Powell was not one to take chances, but she pushed aside any fears she might have had.

Next morning, Mrs Powell dressed Marcelle in a black silk dress with a white collar and pushed her hair into a little white cap and sent her out into the little quadrangle to care for the children.

So began Marcelle's reign at Brook House, during the happiest and fullest days of her life. The little girl Elizabeth loved Miss Mouse and in spite of her limited vision, she took Marcelle by the hand and guided her on an extensive tour of the grand manor house, for the child knew every nook and cranny in the place. She took Marcelle along the portrait gallery to the lovely carved balcony which held a great golden organ and looked down over the carved balustrade at the black-and-white squares of the immense hall in which Queen Elizabeth had first held court and her father Henry had entertained her mother Ann Boleyn.

Marcelle knew nothing of these great people but listened enthralled as little Elizabeth related the history of this lovely house and its previous owners.

Behind the great organ was a door leading to a small apartment in which an old Jesuit priest had hidden for many years, since the time when Lady Cobham had lived in the manor. In these small chambers were many books. Elizabeth introduced Marcelle to Father Ben who sheltered there. He was now so thin and frail but his gnarled, twisted hands could still draw lovely pictures to amuse the children. He scrutinized Marcelle very closely and then said. 'Your mother was a good Catholic woman.'

Marcelle did not understand but she kept quiet, convinced that Father Ben must have mistaken her for one of the other servants. But it had been Father Ben who had buried the poor torn body of her mother whom the mob had drowned as a witch so many years before. Reaching out, he pressed into Marcelle's hand a little gold medal of the Virgin Mary which he had found sewn into the woman's clothing. 'Take care,' he whispered. 'Do not let anyone see it.'

Elizabeth pulled impatiently at her hand. 'Come on, Miss Mouse, there is more to see.'

So on they went to look at the lovely book-lined library, and then the elegant dining hall with its carved frieze and hand-painted ceiling, windows draped with blue velvet and cloth of gold, and massive walls covered by French tapestries. And on until Elizabeth had proudly shown Marcelle every little bit of her new home, and at every step they took,

Marcelle felt happiness building up as she had not felt for so long.

Marcelle had been at Brook House several months before Mrs Powell eventually presented her to the master. Sir Fulke was in his study surrounded by many books and papers and he did not look up as they entered. His head was bent and the candle highlighted the aristocratic profile of his face with the long nose and sensitive lips of the great family of Warwick. Marcelle noticed too the pain lines on his face.

'Come in, Poppet,' he called, thinking that Mrs Powell's knock was one of his adopted children. He called them all Poppet but with Roger it had stuck and become shortened to Popsi.

'It is I, sir,' answered Mrs Powell. 'I want to introduce our new young nurse maid to you.'

Sir Fulke glanced at Marcelle without much interest. 'Well, you take care of her, will you, Mrs Powell?'

The two women curtsied and left the room.

'He is always like that lately,' grumbled Mrs Powell. 'He is very busy writing the life story of his friend Philip Sidney, and he does too much, what with being a Member of Parliament as well,' she went on, defending her master's ill manners. 'Breastfed him as a babe, I did. Stinted my own babe to feed him.'

Marcelle was not very interested in Mrs Powell's grumbling. She loved it too much here with Roger and Elizabeth to care about anything else. The boy Robert had disappeared for a while, back to his school in Shrewsbury. Marcelle's cheeks glowed rosy from the daily walks in the big park. She no longer stuttered or stammered and her voice was no longer croaky, it was just low and husky. She was happier now than she had ever been in her life. In the mornings she knelt at the secret altar with Father Ben and cleared her soul of the dark misery that had hung over her in the past. She now felt as free and as happy as a bird. The stormy events of the world outside could not disturb or even interest Marcelle. In the peaceful sanctuary of Brook House it was almost as if she had entered a convent, the only difference being that with her was her beautiful sturdy son, a privilege that no nun could ever be granted. Surrounded by beautiful grounds that extended for miles, there was never any need to go outside the gate and no one could have persuaded her to. She had left the sad world outside behind to play in this beautiful garden with the children, her little Roger and the tall Elizabeth who walked so upright without ever complaining of her disability. Each morning Marcelle and Elizabeth with Roger by Marcelle's side would kneel and pray in the old chapel which had served many generations of great Catholic families. The tattered banners hung overhead; helmets and swords lay upon the marble tombs. The Reformation had destroyed the religious glory of England for which these knights of old had given their lives.

Most people had forgotten Father Ben, the old Jesuit priest, for he had been in hiding for so many years. He was so thin and his pale, deep set eyes seemed to stare into one's very soul. The sweet religious fervour he created entered Marcelle's heart and wrapped her soft and safe as a cocooned insect. With her mind now quite healed she began to look into the past with clear eyes and her memories returned. Marcelle knew that here she had a safe harbour for herself and her son, and that she would never go out of that gate again.

The old priest had, by gentle persuasion, managed to get the secrets of Marcelle's past from her. 'My dear,' he said gently, 'it is between God and yourself whether you lay claim to your son. You have made your peace with him. Now, stay, reflect on the wisdom of taking your son out of this safe place.'

Marcelle's hazel brown eyes glowed soft and gentle. She had grown so fond of this kind, clever old priest, whose thin hands traced the Latin words on the old manuscripts, and who had taught her so much of the beauty of religion. 'I will stay here, Father, because in this house I am so happy, and so is my son.'

'Then God be with you.' Father Ben made the sign of the cross and returned to his narrow hard bed in the paper-filled room where he had hidden for so many years.

In the morning they found him, his pale eyelids closed forever. He had died peacefully in his sleep, his hands were crossed clutching a rosary.

Marcelle was very sad at the loss of her friend and confidant, but was sure in her heart that he had left this sad world for a higher happy one. Death no longer held any mysteries for her.

They buried the priest secretly in consecrated ground at the back of the chapel beside the unmarked grave of Marcelle's mother, whom he himself had buried.

Each day, Marcelle and the children made little posies and laid one on Father Ben's grave and one on Grandmother's.

'But whose grandmother?' enquired Elizabeth. 'I have not got one. I am illegitimate, and so is Popsi.'

Marcelle smiled sweetly. 'Well, you and Popsi shall share this grandmother with me, because she was my mother.'

Elizabeth giggled. 'Oh, you are funny, Miss Mouse,' she said. 'But I do love you so.'

They would often run through the green woods down to the brook to dip their tiny feet in the clear cool rippling water. Very neat in her white hat and black dress, Marcelle sat on the bank sewing as the children played or tried fishing for minnows. Always on these outings they were accompanied by a big black-and-white hound called Prince who followed Elizabeth everywhere.

One morning in early summer they sat by the brook. Little Roger was becoming quite headstrong. He had acquired a fishing net of his own and started fishing quite independently, the dog beside him. On the opposite bank, a small fox terrier appeared and began to challenge Prince with his back erect and shrill bark. Prince rose up majestically and with loud, deep-chested growls, he seemed to be telling the little dog to be off. All this barking frightened little Roger who ran to Marcelle for comfort.

Soon the owner of the terrier, a little man with a

young child on his shoulders, came running along the bank calling the dog to heel. Seeing Marcelle, he called over to her: 'Hallo, mate, how're you getting on?'

It had been almost a year since Marcelle had seen anyone outside Brook House and this man calling out to her now with such familiarity scared her a little. In panic, she gathered the children and amid the noise of barking dogs they hurried on up the hill towards the big house.

Chalky stood scratching his head, quite astonished. 'Well, what do you think of that, Sam?' He directed his conversation to the little child on his back. 'Starving in the churchyard, she was, a year ago, and now she don't even want to know us. You can never tell with some people.' The little black-haired babe, so like his father and named after his grandfather, slept on.

Chalky's son was everything to him and although the child could not yet converse with his father he was always included in whatever his father had to say. Chalky loved being a father and was keen to have more sons. 'We will have another one soon, Katy,' he often said. 'Stock is as good as money, you know.'

Tall, magnificent Katy would laugh at him, when he said this, her white teeth flashing, her cheeks red and rosy. 'We will have a girl the next time, I hope,' she would say.

'No, we won't!' Chalky would argue. 'Sons is what I want and sons is what I'm going to get.' As dogmatic and business-like as ever, even in the raising of a family, Chalky had plans.

He was very happy with his Katy and was glad to have married her, despite their terrible wedding day which had ended in a riot. Katy's brothers had punched each other to a standstill and her uncles and aunts had drunk and danced until they fell. And it had taken Chalky many months of hard work to earn back the profits from the drink that Katy's relations had consumed.

Now that Katy was mistress of her own home, she had told her family to go to hell. She worked beside Chalky and was a real partner in every way.

'I've no regrets,' Chalky often boasted. 'I'm a happily married man.'

The inn was not such a prosperous place since the Lord of the Manor – rumoured to be ill – had moved to the town. The young gentlemen did not visit the inn so often, and Chalky did not care much for the sort of customers he got now – gipsies from the fair at Lea, stablemen from Brook House, and the villagers. The class of customers had deteriorated and this bothered Chalky somewhat.

'I ain't in this business for me health,' he would tell Katy. 'It's money I'm after, and these poor sods ain't got much.'

'Well, let's sell up and move further away,' suggested Katy.

'I might,' said Chalky, 'I'd better think about it.'

So with business being bad plus a son to take care of, Chalky's mind was well pre-occupied. He had completely forgotten Betsy and was much less likely to remember her brother Rolly. So when Rolly walked into the bar one day, Chalky got quite an unpleasant shock.

A white autumn mist hung over the harbour as little boats went back and forth from ship to shore. Out in the deep waters, lying at anchor, were the huge four-masted schooners, their white sails flopping loosely in the soft breeze. They were resting awhile, needing the time for the barnacles to be removed and a refit to be done before returning to the endless expanse of ocean. A shaft of sunlight filtered slowly through the mist lighting up the stone harbour wall and exposing the huddled shapes of the beggars who lay there out of the stiff Atlantic breeze which always blew around the harbour. Poor hopeless wrecks, they were, most of them disabled seamen, befallen fruits of the great sea battles. Once the sea had dispensed with them, there was no livelihood for them and they remained dirty ragged limbless men begging for a mere existence.

From the deep bow window of a nearby inn, a man looked down with compassion at these men. His dark eyes were angry and there was a frown on his brow. 'My God,' he muttered to himself, 'what a fate for these so valiant of British seamen! Surely no country on earth was so great, yet so morally impoverished as this?' He reflected on the fertile colony of Virginia, on its poor but happy settlers, each man was owner of his destiny and allowed to live and think freely. He would return to that land again and leave this battered country for ever, to the deep green valley where he had made his home. A dreamy smile crossed his lips as he thought of Marcelle, his little wife. He had not seen her in years, but now he would take her and her child to this clean new world and maybe have children of his own. His sons would inherit his green valley. He stroked his little black pointed beard thoughtfully as his mind wandered over these matters.

Yes, this was our friend, Thomas Mayhew, back home in England on what was not a happy homecoming. His deep-set unfocused eyes stared out to sea. Out there in the Atlantic a ship was sailing steadily towards England and aboard was a great man, a heart-broken man who had lost his much-cherished eldest son, slain by the Spaniards. The great Sir Walter Raleigh was sailing home from a disastrous voyage to the New World, a broken, defeated man.

A silent brooding atmosphere hung over the port. It even pervaded the inn, and had affected those poor devils crouched by the wall out there. The secret was out: everyone knew that the King's men were out there waiting for the great man to come ashore. They could see the glint of steel and hear the impatient clamp of the horses' hooves echo through the misty air. The escort was ready to take Sir Walter back to the Tower, where he had already spent thirteen years. It was a hard and bitter fate for a man so great, but there was no gold in the hold of his ship and King James considered this to be treason.

As Thomas watched and waited for the arrival of that little ship called *Destiny*, he thought of Raleigh's son Cary, who had been his own best friend, and of how good a master Raleigh had been to him. At least he was here to lend support to Sir Walter now.

Thomas' face was well tanned by the sun, his body hard and virile after two years at sea. The travel had been well worth it; many Spanish prizes had been taken and there was plenty of money to share out when the crew of the privateer ship disbanded. Now all he wanted to do was to find his wife and sail away again back to Virginia far from the injustice of this English way of life.

In the room behind him, not two feet away was Rolly. In the last two years he had never been far away, sticking as closely to Thomas as his own shadow. Many a knife thrust and sword length Rolly had taken instead of his master, but it seemed that Rolly's wounds healed very quickly and he always returned to full health, hale and hearty as ever. Thomas was eternally grateful for Rolly's loyal protection of him and had kept him by his side.

Now Rolly stood, his long body propped against a table as his strong white teeth crunched the fine red skin of an apple. In appearance Rolly was now a very handsome fellow, and well-dressed in a black satin suit trimmed with gold braid. His tremendous feet were shod in a long pair of highly polished boots with wide tops, Spanish style, his hair bleached almost white by the tropical sun and the gold rings in his ears made him look part of the swash-buckling pirate he fancied himself to be. There was still a remote look in his eyes and often, for no reason at all, his mouth would hang open, but mentally and physically Rolly had improved immensely. The ship's crew had known that Dour Thomas' man was a fellow to be reckoned with in any battle. His life at this time and his only love was his master, Thomas Mayhew, who understood perfectly that just the bat of an eyelid would bring Rolly to his side, always ready and able to serve or defend. Thomas and Rolly had a great respect for each other.

It caused much amusement among the other servants that Rolly liked to dress up and would be decked out like a bird of paradise while his master had no taste for fancy clothes and was likened to a dowdy little sparrow. But they were a grand team together and their adventure had been very profitable. Life had bound them very close but now they were back in the homeland. Marcelle was uppermost in Thomas' mind while Betsy was in Rolly's.

Thomas turned from the window. 'Watch for *Destiny* to come into view,' he instructed Rolly. 'I'll attend to the mail.'

On the table was a large pile of correspondence, parcels and letters newly arrived from the trading company that had collected the mail during his absence. Thomas sat inspecting them, turning the papers over and over as he searched for letters from Marcelle in her neat handwriting. But there were none, only bills and pamphlets concerning all sorts of legal matters but not one letter from Marcelle. His face showed his disappointment as he picked up one big legal document and broke the seal. It contained news from his solicitors at the Inns of Court, and the legal draft of a will that contained a small legacy from a

departed uncle. Thomas put this aside with little interest. He was more interested in a letter from Mr
Spenser, the clerk who had been left in charge of
Marcelle's affairs while Thomas was away. He read
this letter with puzzled bewilderment which showed
on his face.

> I have been many times to your wife's home in
> Essex. The whole place is empty and dilapidated. I
> cannot glean any information from the villagers, as
> they appear to be afraid to talk. Both your wife and
> child have disappeared from their home. It is as if
> they have left the face of this earth, for I can simply
> find no trace of them. I am indeed sorry to be the
> one to have to give you this information but I do
> assure you I have not given up my search for them
> and may have better news for you on your return to
> England.

Blood rushed to Thomas' head and he covered his
face with his hands. In a loud voice he cried out: 'Oh
God! What has happened to her?'

Hearing the anxiety in his master's voice, Rolly
came over to his side. Now Thomas was reading the
letter from Betsy, written just before her death. He had
come to the postscript. In strange uneven writing, so
different from the neat hand of the clerk, the words
seemed to dance before his eyes: 'I saw Marci. She was
walking by the brook.'

The mystery deepened. Why should Marcelle be
walking by the brook in Hackney more than ten miles

from her home? Thomas began to sort out the rest of the mail with his brow puckered in puzzlement.

Rolly came to stand beside him and looked at him quizzically. 'What is it?' he enquired.

Thomas looked at him. 'I have received a letter from your sister.' He handed Rolly the sheet of paper but Rolly only grinned from ear to ear and stared at the missive in wonder. 'You know I can't read,' he said. 'And Betsy can't write either.'

But Thomas was not listening. He was staring at a pamphlet which lay open on his desk. He had gone pale under his tan and looked a sickly yellow. Staring up at Thomas was the face of Annabelle standing on the gallows with a rope about her neck. It was a life sketch, the artist had coloured yellow the ruffs and frills of her dress and underneath the illustration was a foul and very detailed description of the way in which poor Annabelle had died.

Rolly had returned to his post looking out of the window. Suddenly he called out: 'She's here! Just caught sight of her, but it's the *Destiny* all right.'

Thomas gathered his papers quickly. 'We cannot wait for the *Destiny*,' he said grimly. 'Our own destiny is at stake. We must go quickly to London now. Go saddle up, and hurry.'

Within an hour they were galloping along the west country roads. They were miles away when Sir Walter Raleigh finally stepped ashore only to be arrested instantly by the King's men. Thomas Mayhew was not there to try to save him, for he was away out on the moors riding as if the devil was behind him, scared for the wife and child he had left in the care of Annabelle whose distraught face had stared out at him from the news sheet.

By dawn they had entered the deserted city streets and arrived at the Temple to await the clerk outside his offices. Thomas and Rolly were dusty and saddlesore, and the sight of them was a shock for Mr Spenser when he came from his lodgings to work. He greeted them and he begged them to take breakfast with him but Thomas gruffly refused. He had to know at once what all this was about and he would not rest content until all the facts were laid before him. The clerk fussed and fidgeted with an eyeglass which he wore hanging round his neck and was trying hard to fit it into the front of his eye, while at the same time keeping a wary eye on Rolly, who in turn stared aggressively back at him because he sensed that this red-faced little man was upsetting his master.

'Wait by the door, Rolly,' Thomas ordered.

Rolly immediately took up a position by the door with his hand on his sword hilt as if he were expecting Mr Spenser to make a bolt for it.

Then with a rustle of papers, Mr Spenser began to explain. 'This is a very sad business, sir,' he said. 'I suppose you have heard of the case of Mistress Annabelle?'

'All right, get on with it,' Thomas retorted abruptly.

'Having thoroughly investigated the case I fear that the report I had from the village in Essex is true.' Mr Spenser was sweating and seemed ill at ease.

Thomas' voice rose in temper. 'Well, what *is* it man?' he bellowed.

'That your wife lost her wits and did away with herself and the child,' Mr Spenser said timorously.

Thomas drew in a deep breath of horror. 'What proof have you of this?' he demanded.

'I was fortunate enough to trace a servant who was with her on the day she disappeared. Her name is Wanda – a nice homely girl.'

'Well, where is she? I would also like to talk to her.' Thomas got up impatiently, ready to go.

'In her old home in Essex. The poor girl has just recently recovered from smallpox so I would not advise you to go there, sir. There has been quite an epidemic in that part of the country.'

But Thomas held out his hand for the written address. 'You don't seem to have made much progress so maybe I will do better,' he muttered hoarsely, choked with emotion. He knew that once outside this office he would have to give way to the grief which had suddenly assailed him.

With Rolly at Thomas' side, they rode east, stopping only to change mounts and to eat a quick meal, then on they went over the Weald to the little village where Thomas had first taken Marcelle.

The day was still young when they came to the forest. Leaves had already started to fall from the huge horse chestnut trees and hissed and crackled under foot. Still and silent, the forest shaped a tall, tree-lined avenue. Thomas was engrossed in thought as he rode but Rolly beside him had his eyes on their surroundings always on guard, for those days in the Spanish colonies had taught him to be forever alert.

Thomas was day-dreaming of Marcelle, of her nut-brown hair and rosy cheeks, remembering the feel of her young body pressed close to him when they first rode out to Essex from the inn at Hackney. Could she really have gone crazy and destroyed her own child? No, it was quite impossible, she was too like a child herself. Marcelle had been so timid on her wedding day – perhaps he should have stayed a while to unite themselves closer, but the thought of that child in her womb had sickened him. Poor little Marcelle, she never had a chance. She had been so young and her life, apparently, was finished. He had to try to put that thought from his mind; it did not bear thinking about.

At last they came in sight of Craig Alva. The black-and-white timbers seemed to stare desolately at them as they rode up the weed-covered drive. The once bright windows were dirty and drab and the lawn grass was waist-high. It did not take much to know that the house was empty. They searched the stables but found nothing there but a family of rats. And the farm cottages were deserted too. They rode on a mile or two down the road to the little village of Beauchamp Riding where Wanda lived, and pulled in at a small inn called the Red Lion. Leaving the horses with the groom, they went inside.

Inside it was cool and dark. The low ceiling with its blackened oak beams told its age. The wide polished bar was welcoming and Thomas would have liked to have stayed. But at the moment his mind was preoccupied and the hospitality of the inn would have to wait.

The landlord was fat and of florid countenance. Thomas knew he had met him before at his own wedding. At first the landlord did not recognise Thomas but when the younger man mentioned Craig Alva and Abe and Annabelle, the landlord's face turned a sickly white. He lifted the little flap in the counter. 'Come through,' he whispered hoarsely, looking from side to side. 'Who are you, sir?' he asked furtively once they were inside.

'I am Thomas Mayhew. I am seeking information regarding my wife. This you should know, since you were a guest at my wedding.' Thomas spoke in a clear cold and precise tone looking angrily at the quivering landlord around whose neck rings of fat wobbled like jelly.

'Oh dear, oh dear!' he replied. 'Terrible business, that was, and not over yet,' he added nervously. 'Denouncing people as witnesses every day they are, indeed, sir.'

'What's that to do with my wife?' demanded Thomas.

'Oh, you don't know, sir? It was terrible – corrupted that little girl, they did. She killed herself and done away with her own baby.'

Thomas' fist crashed down on the table. 'Stop this nonsense!' he yelled. 'I came here for facts, not some damned yokel's ravings.'

'It's true, sir, I swear it's true! I went up to London to the trial. Made contact with the devil, he did, that crazy fellow who used to live there.'

Thomas had drawn his dagger and with its point at

the landlord's throat he held him against the wall. 'Oh, shut your damned foul mouth!' he snarled. 'Tell me, where does the servant girl Wanda live?'

The landlord pointed with trembling hands to the shack down the road. 'Down there, sir, that old wooden place on the corner.'

Thomas released him, put his dagger away and strode out with swift step down the dusty village street to where a slated dwelling leaned crazily to one side. In the doorway with her arms folded stood Wanda.

Life had not been very kind to Wanda over the last few years. For many nights she had waited at Craig Alva for Marcelle to return, quite heartbroken at the loss of her beloved mistress. Then one night the king's men came and arrested her along with the farmer and his family, and they were all shut in the courthouse for a night. The next day, they were questioned about the activities of the family that had lived at Craig Alva, but then were released the next day. Although they were innocent, rumours of black magic and witchcraft gripped the village. With righteous indignation, the villagers waited outside the courthouse ready to aim stones and filth at Wanda and the farmer's family. Then they put the farmer in the stocks. The following day, the whole lot of them were driven out of the village, these blameless people whose only fault had been to live in a cottage on the land belonging to Craig Alva, now reputed to have been a den of iniquity. A stone had hit Wanda in the eye and she had gone screaming to her mother, who hid her until the wrath of the villagers had died down.

Wanda had never been much of a beauty and now she had a vivid scar above her eye as a result of the injury. Then, to add to her trouble, came the small-pox epidemic. She lost her poor old mother but survived the epidemic herself. Now she was pock-marked as well.

After all this bad luck, Wanda's mind had turned nasty and she was always at odds with her neighbours. Now she stood in the dark doorway as Thomas came up the path but as he approached she darted indoors with a scared look. As Thomas reached the rickety door, it was slammed in his face.

'Come out, damn you!' roared Thomas impatiently, beating on the door with his fist. But not a sound came from inside. Thomas motioned to Rolly, who knew what to do. Marching up, he put his huge shoulder to the door and pushed hard. There was a sharp sound of splintering wood as the door fell inwards.

The two men stepped into the darkened shack to find Wanda crouching down in a corner sobbing with terror. She was convinced that she was about to be arrested as a witch.

Thomas put a gentle hand on her shoulder. 'We don't want to hurt you,' he said. 'We only want to find out some knowledge that you might have about my wife.'

Wanda's big, disfigured face stared up at Thomas in wonder. 'You are little Marci's husband?' She jumped to her feet. 'Oh, thank God you have come!' Her big hands held on to his arm. 'Oh, God, how I have prayed for you to come home!'

Thomas pulled her into a chair. 'Now,' he said kindly, sitting down in front of her, 'tell me all about it.'

As Wanda unfolded the story of Marcelle's last days at Craig Alva before she disappeared at the height of a storm one afternoon, Thomas listened and his expression became darker and his brow creased. Occasionally his lips twitched as if he were in pain. She told of the decoy, the boy who had knocked at the door on the evening that Roger had been taken, and of finding her mistress' crumpled little body, her head all twisted to one side, and the despair at the sight of the empty cot.

'Do you honestly think that Marcelle was mad the day she left?' Thomas asked Wanda.

Wanda shook her big head. Her thin, sandy hair stuck out from under a large cap and her strange blank eyes looked vaguely at him. Despite her look, honesty was there in her face and Thomas was sure that this homely girl would give him the untarnished truth of Marcelle's disappearance.

'My mistress was not mad,' said Wanda indignantly. 'She was lost and bewildered, so young and alone, and the terror of that night was always there to haunt her.'

Thomas looked relieved and patted Wanda's shoulder. 'So you think she went off by herself, or did someone abduct her, as they did the child?'

'It was not possible, sir, for anyone to approach the house unnoticed in daylight,' replied Wanda. 'At the back is open country and I was down at the cowshed with Daisy who had just given birth to a calf. The boys were outside, so no stranger could come past the gate without being seen.'

'So she went out the back way towards London, is that what you are saying?' Thomas asked.

'Yes, there was no other way she could go.'

'Well where would she go?' he enquired.

'To find Roger,' Wanda was most emphatic. 'She went to the King's palace to ask him to find Roger for her.'

Thomas rubbed his beard thoughtfully. Did Marcelle know the identity of her child's father? Was it possible that the secret was out? Why else would she go to London? If she were still alive, he would find her and God help the fiends who had harmed her. He gripped the hilt of his sword and stared out of the broken doorway to where Rolly sat squatting in the sunshine, his eyes fixed forever on the road. With his loyal servant beside him, Thomas would search for Marcelle to the ends of the earth. He rose to his feet and smiled at the distressed girl who sat slumped over the table. Pulling a leather pouch from his doublet, he poured some gold coins out on to the rough wooden surface of the table. 'Don't you fret, my dear,' he said kindly. 'This money will repair your doorway and give you some extra comforts.' He then wrote down an address. 'You will find me here if you learn of anything new.' Then with a warm gesture, he put his arm on her shoulders. 'Many thanks for the care you have given my family. Don't distress yourself, what happened was not of your doing.' Then, with a final farewell, they returned to the inn to collect their mounts and were soon riding back towards London.

'Where to now, sir?' enquired Rolly.

Silent and brooding, Thomas turned and looked at his servant with a distant expression on his face. He really did not know the answer to that question. 'We had better go and visit your sister, I suppose,' he said.

'Good,' Rolly's white teeth showed in a happy smile. 'Yes, we will go home to Betsy. She will know where your wife is,' he said.

Thomas smiled affectionately at him. 'Come on, then,' he dug his spurs into his horse's flank. 'Let's get going.'

They set off at a fast gallop towards the inn at Hackney. As they rode over the rickety bridge which crossed the River Lea, the sun hung like an orange ball in the sky. The little brook, a silver strip, went babbling past the tall building of the Duke's Head as the shadows of the evening played hide and seek around the ivy-clad walls.

Rolly's suntanned face beamed as he pointed towards his old home. 'Here we are, sir, there is the inn. I'll bet Betsy will be pleased to see me.'

As they approached, they saw a little man dressed in a blue striped apron and whistling merrily as he swept the flag stones in front of the inn. With great agility Rolly sprang from his horse and yelled out: 'Betsy, I'm home!'

The man in the courtyard looked up with his mouth open. Then, dropping the broom, he darted inside like a rabbit into its warren.

Katy was behind the bar polishing the pewter tankards when Chalky came belting in and crouched down beside her. 'I'm not in,' he said hoarsely. 'You ain't seen me today.' He held on to her dress with one hand and gave it a hard tug. 'Go on Katy,' he pleaded. 'Do try to get rid of them.'

Rolly's huge shape had darkened the doorway and Katy looked up in amazement at the sight of this flamboyant figure whose black-and-gold suit was still dusty from the long ride. Rolly's big mouth gaped open as he saw another woman behind the bar. After all, he had been so expecting to see his beloved sister Betsy.

Katy looked up at this stranger with amusement. 'What can I do for you, sir?' she asked sharply.

Thomas who was only a step behind Rolly, took in the situation at a glance. The inn had changed hands. It was clean and bright and shining, and this tall, dark young woman standing with a jug in her hand was not Rolly's sister. He stepped inside and bowed graciously to her. 'Pardon the intrusion madam, but I believe we have come to the wrong inn.'

'Who were you looking for?' Katy asked. 'Did you want a glass of ale?' Katy's business sense was always there.

'Might as well,' replied Thomas, seating himself on the bench at a scrubbed wooden table and motioning Rolly to be seated.

Katy came round from behind the bar, tall and regal. Her shining hair was tied up under a white lace cap and she wore a neat black dress with a locket of gold about her neck. She is certainly a striking-looking woman, thought Thomas, as she placed the two

foaming tankards of ale on the table and stood loom-
ing over them waiting for the money.

Thomas handed her a coin. 'Is your master at home,
madam?' he asked.

'If you mean my husband,' Katy returned imperiously, 'he is not. And may I ask what you require of
him?'

'We are looking for Elizabeth, a fair buxom person.
She is the sister of my servant.'

Katy looked incredulously at Rolly who was almost
choking as he quickly gobbled down the ale. With a
glance behind the bar where the sweating Chalky
grovelled, she leaned over and grabbed hold of his
collar. 'Come out, you fool,' she said firmly. 'They
came to ask about Betsy.'

Avoiding Rolly's gaze, Chalky emerged from behind
the bar. He looked quite ashamed and very nervous of
Rolly, who stared at him with narrowed eyes. 'This is
my friend,' Rolly said to him through clenched teeth as
he introduced Thomas.

With a wry grimace Chalky seated himself opposite
Thomas to face the music. His quick mind was working out the best way to tell Rolly of the death of his
sister and still remain alive himself. Taking a deep
breath, he told the visitors of the demise of poor Betsy
and of how he had looked after her. In a very plausible
manner, he told of the care he had taken of her and
then of the magnificent funeral he had given her. 'As
gawd is my judge, sir,' he whined, 'never a hair of that
gel's head would I have harmed. Thought the world of
me, she did, and very fond of her, I was too.' But as he

wiped his eyes on the sleeve of his coat, Rolly put his head on the table and blubbered like a baby.

Thomas had almost fallen asleep. The warmth of the room and the strong ale were almost too much for him. It had been a long tiring day and Chalky's whining vice seemed to be fading farther and farther away. He felt his eyes closing as he sat there trying desperately to stop his eyes closing.

The wily Chalky realised that he had the situation in hand. 'Prepare supper!' he called to Katy.

Katy stood watching this charade with a smile playing about her face. With her dark eyes inscrutable, she obediently went to the kitchen to prepare a meal for the travellers.

'You are travel weary, sir,' said Chalky. 'I beg of you to stay and partake of our hospitality.'

'Might as well,' said Thomas, rising. 'Conduct us to your guest chamber. We will wash and come down late for a meal.'

Chalky bowed low and showed them upstairs, chatting and laughing all the while. But Thomas and Rolly were too weary to listen. They washed and lay down on their beds for a rest but in the end slept through the night, without even appearing for a meal.

The daylight filtered through the leaded casements and the flowered curtains fluttered in the breeze when Thomas awoke the next morning. He had had a strangely disturbed night, with many vivid dreams. He was slightly embarrassed by these dreams for they had been quite intimate and about himself and Marcelle. He dreamed that they had lain beside the brook together and he had held her close, as he had always wanted to. The soft, sweet feeling of love still lingered now as he opened his eyes and looked over the room. There was something very familiar about it, he thought. He eyed a light on the shelf where a little blue sandlewood virgin stood. This must be the room in which Marcelle had once slept. Some old trick of fate had brought him back here. Did the secret lie in this room?

Thomas sat up and looked around him. There were just the plain painted walls, a fireplace, and this dingy-looking four poster bed – nothing of interest. The little blue virgin provided the only spot of colour in the room, and she smiled at him, it seemed, with familiarity.

On a trestle bed in the corner was Rolly. He was lying on his back with his great feet sticking out past the end of the bed. Thomas picked up his boot and threw it at his servant. 'Get up!' he called irritably. 'The day is almost gone.'

Rolly staggered to his feet and was pulling on his breeches just as Chalky knocked on the door and sidled in.

'Good morning, sir. Nice day,' he began conversationally. 'I'll get some hot water for you in a tick. Now, what would you like for breakfast?'

Thomas looked distastefully at this cringing little man. There was something very unattractive about him. 'My man will wait on me,' Thomas replied shortly. 'Have your wife prepare a meal and in half an hour I will be down.'

Chalky scuttled off. 'Sour-faced bastard,' he muttered, as he scrambled downstairs. 'I wonder how Rolly got in with him.'

Katy was in the kitchen and not in too good a temper. She was pregnant again and suffering from morning sickness. Sitting in a tall chair at the table was Sam, Chalky's son, banging a wooden spoon. His father immediately went over to play with him.

'Never mind all that larking,' said Katy sharply, 'and give me a hand with these breakfasts. I hope those two are going to pay?' she added.

'Of course he'll pay. What a suggestion!' retorted Chalky.

'Well, seeing as that great oaf was a relation of Betsy's you might be trying to ease your conscience,' she added spitefully.

'Don't know what you mean, Katy.' Chalky looked indignant. 'I took care of Betsy, didn't I?'

'Not arf, you didn't,' replied the truculent Katy. 'Helped her to break her bloody legs, you did.'

'Now don't be so nasty, love,' said Chalky woefully, as he scuttled off to lay the table for their guests.

An hour later, Thomas and Rolly sat in the window seat enjoying the well-cooked meal that Katy had produced. Rolly seemed to have forgotten his sorrow that morning and was tucking into the good food with one eye on the toy he had been playing with all morning. It was a little artificial bird in a cage. At the turn of a screw, it twittered and flapped its wings and sweet music came from it. It was a very valuable toy, for the cage and bird were engraved in gold, and it had been a gift for Betsy. Rolly played with the toy and his infectious loud laughter affected the others around him and soon they had all joined in. Even Thomas managed a wry sort of smile.

Sam cooed loudly at the little bird and Chalky stared at it fascinated. 'Ain't it marvellous!' he said. 'Who thought of that? Clever bloke I reckon. Look, Sam, here he goes,' he called as the wheels could be heard whirring within.

Tall and graceful, Katy served the meal with amusement in her dark eyes as she surveyed the scene. 'I wonder what Chalky is so scared of,' she thought to herself as she looked at her husband. Her swift hands swept the dishes from the table and she caught Thomas' eye.

Thomas looked back at her. He liked the look of Katy; she was a woman to like and respect, this tall beauty. What was she doing with this whining little rat of a husband? Thomas could not even bring himself to be civil to the man.

'Go on, Chalky, take Sam out for a while,' Katy commanded.

Sam went reluctantly with his father. Really, he wanted to stay and look at the little bird that sang. But soon the inn was quiet again, when Sam had gone with Chalky to the brook and Rolly sat outside on the cobbles still playing with his toy.

Katy lazily poured Thomas and herself a glass of wine, she then sat down facing him, her elbows on the table. 'Come on,' she said coaxingly, 'let's talk, I know you want to.'

Thomas' sad face softened for a moment. Here was a woman who was not only beautiful but also intelligent. He guessed that she was also very courageous. His admiration for her showed in his sad, deep-set eyes.

'Why are you here?' asked Katy, wasting no time over niceties. 'And what is that great oaf you are travelling with to you?'

'That great oaf is my servant, and this is his home,' Thomas returned quietly.

'I know all that,' Katy retorted impatiently. 'But what is this air of mystery that surrounds you all? Even my husband is afraid. What is it? I intend to find out.'

Thomas' respect for her deepened. 'Madam, we will perhaps be able to solve it between us. I met my future wife here some years ago when she was just a child and this was her home.'

Katy's eyes opened wide with surprise. 'A girl? I never heard of one living here. There was Betsy, but she was Chalky's stepmother. At least, so he says!'

Thomas approached the subject of Betsy warily. 'When did Betsy die?' he asked.

'Last year,' replied Katy. 'I married Chalky three weeks after she died. I remember, 'cos he told me he put the banns up the same day.'

'You never heard her mention Marcelle?' Thomas spoke the name very sadly.

'No,' Katy shook her head and pursed her lips in thought. 'I don't even remember hearing of her. As a matter of fact, Betsy was bedridden all the time I was courting Chalky. I thought she was an old lady, so I got a shock when they said she was only a few years past twenty.'

Thomas relapsed into silence. Marcelle was remaining as elusive as ever; no one had heard of her. As he looked at Katy, he caught a glimpse of diamonds in the locket around her neck. On the front was a painted miniature which was surrounded by diamonds and set in gold. The sweet face of a child of about seven looked out at him. It was quite remarkable. There was no doubt they looked like Marcelle's eyes, staring sad and sweet into his very soul. He closed his own eyes for a moment and then opened them quickly again. That little girl *was* Marcelle! She had the same thin nose and pointed chin and that unusual elf-like expression which was seldom seem in England.

Katy had noticed the strange look on Thomas' face as he stared at her and her hand went nervously to the locket as she twisted the chain in her fingers.

'Where did you get that?' Thomas' words came out sharp as a knife.

'My locket, do you mean?' asked Katy.

He nodded.

'It was a wedding present from Chalky. Why?'

'Because I am almost sure that it is a miniature of my wife as a child.'

Katy undid the clasp and placed the locket on the table. They both scrutinised it carefully.

'It's a pretty little girl aged about seven or eight,' Katy spoke at last.

'It is Marcelle all right,' said Thomas. 'I'm sorry,

Katy, but your husband must know more than he cares to say.'

'Don't worry,' said Katy. 'When he comes back he'll talk, I'll see to that. Anyway, why are you so worried over her?' she asked.

'She disappeared, as did her child, though separately. I intend to find out what happened to her or die in the attempt,' Thomas replied emphatically.

Katy's face paled, 'God,' she said anxiously. 'I know Chalky's a rogue but he would not hurt women and children.'

It was not long before Chalky came trotting back up the path with his son on his back. He glanced at the pendant on the table and took in the angry look on Katy's face. 'Gawd,' he said nervously. 'The cat's out the bleedin' bag, then?'

'I am afraid it is, love,' Katy spoke quietly. 'I think you owe this gentleman an explanation.' She whisked Sam away and left the room.

Chalky sat down facing Thomas, his eyes on the locket. 'I never nicked it,' he began. 'Found it, I did, and that's the God's honest truth.'

Thomas passed his hand wearily over his brow. 'I don't care how you got it,' he replied. 'What I want to know is where you got it from.'

'Down in the cellar,' said Chalky brightly, pointing downwards with his hand.

'You mean you found it there, but when? It is a miniature of my wife as a child and it may be a clue to her disappearance.'

Chalky told Thomas of how he had come back to

the inn cold and hungry to find his father gone and Betsy his mistress in charge.

Thomas raised his eyebrows and looked very thoughtful. So this was old Sam's son, after all. And since it had been Thomas' own sword that had ended old Sam's life, Thomas knew that he had to approach this subject very carefully.

'Down in the cellar, in an old jar, that was,' said Chalky, eager to seem helpful. 'There was letters too. But I burnt them. Written in French, they were.' He chatted on endlessly.

Thomas was getting desperate. 'Chalky, I must appeal to your honour. I have lost my wife and child. Think, man, how would you feel if the same happened to you? You must try to be honest with me. Did Betsy ever talk about Marcelle?'

Chalky scratched his head. 'Wait a bit. There was something, the day she died. She made me write a postscript to the letter, something about seeing Marci.'

Thomas produced the letter. 'Is this that letter?'

'Yes, that's it! I wrote on the bottom of it,' Chalky added proudly.

Thomas picked up the locket and stared at it. 'This must have belonged to Marcelle's mother,' he said.

With his lank hair hanging in his eyes, Chalky bent over to look at the little girl in the picture. 'Tell you what,' he said. 'She ain't half like some poor soul I once saw in the churchyard last summer. Was on her last legs, she was. I got milk and bread for her but where she went, Gawd knows. I think I did see her again once, but I'm not sure.'

But Thomas was reading Betsy's letter again. There was nothing new to see, but he looked again at the scrawl at the bottom of it: 'Saw Marci near the brook.'

'Where is the brook?' he asked Chalky.

'Just down the bottom,' he pointed out the back door. 'It runs from the Lea past the inn, through the grounds of Brook House.'

'Come on,' said Thomas. 'Let's go and look.'

They walked beside the swift flowing brook which rippled and ran through the green meadowland. They followed its path until they came to the wooden stile from which the magnificent green parklands stretched out before them. They could see a house in the distance in the valley but the little brook left it behind, wandering on through the woodlands until it met the River Thames.

'What house it that?' Thomas asked.

'That's Brook House, sir,' replied Chalky. 'Posh place, it is, and a lot of royalty lived there.'

Thomas nodded. 'Yes, of course, I know it,' he said.

The November mist swirled about them and the air had suddenly become chilled. Thomas looked over the immense park towards the house, and a shiver came over him as if he were catching a chill. 'Let's go,' he said. 'There's no sense hanging about here in this cold air.'

Both men looked despondent as they returned to the warmth of the inn. Katy prepared spiced drinks for them and they drank these sitting by the fire. Rolly and Thomas remained very quiet when Chalky left to serve at the bar.

'Got to go, mate,' he said. 'I've got an awful lot of customers to see to, I have. I hope you will decide to stay the night.'

Thomas was uncertain about staying. He had almost decided to leave that evening, having decided to make for France. It was possible that Marcelle had found her own family in France. Perhaps there was a chance that she had returned there. But he felt very tired and, besides, there was a fog coming up. It would be better to start early in the morning, he decided. 'Come on, Rolly,' he said with a yawn. 'Let us retire and make an early start tomorrow.'

So the two men left the warmth of the fire and went up to bed. Another day had been wasted and there was still no real hope of finding Marcelle.

15

Alone at Brook House

The long warm summer weather had been kind to Marcelle; the outdoor life she spent in the gardens with the children had brought her back to good health in every way. The strength of her religious feeling gave her peace of mind and the love of the children brought great happiness. Yes, Brook House was her Garden of Eden while she was in the company of the son she loved so much – little Roger, so sturdy and strong – and young Elizabeth who clung to her skirts so lovingly. There was an affinity between the golden-haired Elizabeth and her beloved Miss Mouse. The rest of the household agreed that little half-blind protégée of the Brook family had never been so happy.

Mrs Powell had informed Marcelle that the disease that Elizabeth had been born with, and which had destroyed her precious sight, would also eventually kill her. Many doctors, including the royal physician, had examined her but they were all of the same opinion that she would not reach maturity. And the fact that the disease was hereditary was not discussed because of the mystery of Elizabeth's birth.

One evening, shortly after her entry to the big

house, Marcelle discovered how Roger came to be there. She was sitting in the large kitchen with Mrs Powell and the tall, prematurely white-haired Ralph, the master's personal servant, who talked of the children – of Robert, now away at school, who was Sir Fulke Greville's nephew and heir to the estate, and of Popsi, the mysterious child who had been brought to the house by Lady Elizabeth Howard, who was now travelling abroad.

Marcelle listened quietly and keenly. So, she thought, it was the fair countess who had stolen her child. Her eyes widened but her lips remained sealed. And it was Frances Howard, who was responsible for this present state of affairs . . .

As Marcelle's relationship with the young Elizabeth grew, the girl became more and more dependent on her, especially as her eyesight faded. 'Stay, Miss Mouse,' she would say. 'Tell me what colour the Virginia creeper in the courtyard, is this morning.'

Marcelle would then describe the gold and orange of the creeper which adorned the old stone walls. She would brush Elizabeth's golden hair and smooth it with her fingers. Every comfort and need Marcelle gave to this lovely, sick girl, including her morning prayers in the little chapel. There was no longer a priest but Marcelle would light candles and decorated the altar for the two of them.

Sometimes it seemed to Marcelle that in this old historic house the spirits from another world reached out to touch her. But she was not afraid; she had defeated the evil one and these were her friends. One evening at twilight on a day when Elizabeth had been quite ill, Marcelle knelt to pray to the Holy Mother to help this afflicted little one. Suddenly she became aware of a white-haired lady kneeling beside her. Marcelle made no movement but she knew the lady was there. Then as Marcelle left the chapel, the lady stood up, tall and majestic. She wore a Spanish black lace mantilla on her white head, and in a voice that was not really a voice but seemed to be inside Marcelle, she said: 'I have known much sorrow in the world, too. Here you will find peace, little one.' With that, she disappeared as if she had faded into the old grey walls. Marcelle was not afraid, and when she told Mrs Powell about seeing this lady, the housekeeper did not seem a bit surprised.

'That was Lady Lennox, the Scottish Queen's mother-in-law,' said Mrs Powell. 'She died here. Some say that Lord Leicester poisoned her. Well, you are favoured indeed. She only appears to the family, as a rule,' she smiled. 'Don't let it worry you, dear. I've lived here for many years and I have never seen any ghosts. But I do know there are plenty about, as I've often heard about them.'

Marcelle smiled gently, and after that day, she would include poor Margaret Lennox in her prayers, acknowledging the fact that although King James had taken her bones from Hackney to Westminster, her spirit remained at Brook House.

Towards the end of the summer a serpent arose in Marcelle's Garden of Eden. It concerned the two servant girls Agnes and Elsie who were always quarrelling and whom Mrs Powell only tolerated because their parents were old family retainers and lived in cottages on the estate. The trouble had started seven years earlier when a good-looking young man had made love to both of them, and then gone off and got killed in France. The girls did not marry, but continued to hate each other from then on.

But this summer, Mrs Powell's patience ran out. Unable to stand their bickering any longer, she persuaded Sir Fulke to get rid of Elsie who was getting lazy in any case. But the rejected Elsie became vindictive. She accused Agnes of stealing her betrothal ring and brought the law to investigate. It turned out that Elsie was telling the truth. Poor Mrs Powell who was forced to admit that the ring was Elsie's property, so they took Agnes away and hanged her. Poor Mrs Powell was so distressed by the whole incident, for which she blamed herself, that her health deteriorated. Her legs became very stiff and she was no longer able to cope with the great house. The bother of keeping servants in order became too much for her, so it was decided to close the house up and move the household to Alcaster House, the family's country home in Warwickshire. Sir Fulke was very keen on the idea as he found that maintaining an extra house in London was too much since he had become the Speaker of the House.

It was Ralph who brought the news that Brook House was to be let to strangers, that all the best pictures were to be taken down and the richest of the tapestries taken to Warwickshire. Marcelle and

Elizabeth looked sadly at the walls, which were now bare apart from the fine religious wall paintings which had been done a hundred years before by the monks that used to reside there.

'Tell me, Miss Mouse,' said Elizabeth, 'is St Augustine still there? He has not faded, I hope.'

'No, dear,' replied Marcelle. 'His hands holding the cross of gold are as bright as ever.'

Suddenly Elizabeth threw herself into Marcelle's arms. 'Oh, Miss Mouse!' she screamed hysterically. 'I won't go! I won't leave my lovely home!'

Cuddling her with soft gentle arms, Marcelle tried to calm her. She led her to the doorway and they sat on the wide stairs together. 'It is beautiful country up in the hills, so Ralph says,' said Marcelle reassuringly. 'Perhaps you will like Warwick as much as you like Essex.' She tried to calm the little girl but she could feel her own fears mounting as she wondered if they might separate her from Roger.

'What about you, Miss Mouse? I will not go without you and Popsi,' insisted Elizabeth.

'Don't fret, darling, we may not have to go.' And a very strange feeling told her then she would never leave Brook House again.

Marcelle had failed to reassure Elizabeth about the move, and soon the girl was having nightmares and tantrums about it. Her screaming fits were very disturbing and she often refused to eat, or would smash the fine china in a screaming rage until at last it was decided to let Elizabeth, Roger and Marcelle stay on for a while more. One wing of the house was to remain open – the south-west wing, which opened out to the courtyard where the white doves flew up and down from the picturesque dovecot and the Virginia creeper climbed the walls. This courtyard was Elizabeth's favourite spot, and Marcelle was delighted to be staying on to take care of the children. The stables were to remain open and maids would come in daily to cook and clean.

Once the final arrangements had been made, Elizabeth settled down. 'We will have a lovely time on our own, Miss Mouse,' she said. 'With just you and me and little Popsi.' She snuggled up to Marcelle, who stroked her golden hair and sent up a prayer of thanks that she did not have to leave this safe haven so quickly after all.

In October, when Ralph came with a carriage to take Mrs Powell to Warwick, the poor woman wept continuously. With her bonnet and black shawl and a little basket of provisions for the journey, she limped down the drive, with only one pathetic glance back. She knew she would never see her old home again.

'Goodbye, my dear,' she kissed Marcelle. 'God will reward you for the care and love you give these help-less babes. Take care, Elizabeth, don't wander, will you, dear?'

'No, I have got Miss Mouse and Prince, haven't I?' Elizabeth put her hand on the head of the great hound who was always at her side.

The horses sped off down the drive and Marcelle was left alone, more or less mistress of this lovely house. With an arm over each child, she said: 'Come inside, and we will think of a nice game to play.'

Chalky was feeling very unsettled. He wiped the sweat from his brow as he screwed the taps more securely into the large wine vats and lined up the pewter pots under the barrels of beer. He was getting ready for the big rush; it was Saturday night and soon the bar would be full of customers.

'Been quite a day, ain't it?' he spoke to Katy who sat with the child on her lap, her legs spread wide as she watched her husband with fond amusement in her lovely dark eyes.

'Gawd, Katy,' said Chalky. 'I dread this bloody lot tonight. It's Guy Fawkes Night, the anniversary of the Gunpowder Plot, and they go bloody mad.'

'They don't bother me,' said Katy, 'so long as they pays up.'

'Believe me, Katy, I'd sooner have a nice young gent who likes a bottle of wine and a bit of the other than this scum.'

'Don't let them bother you,' said Katy, placidly getting up to take the sleeping child to bed.

In fact, the crowd did not bother Chalky much that night; mostly it was Holkin, a big brute of a man who had once worked for Topcliffe, the evil agent who had hanged and tortured the Catholics who did not pay their fines. Chalky had no religious beliefs but the stories of persecution he was forced to listen to made him sick.

That evening Holkin with his two companions,

Welkin and Jenkins, were standing at the bar talking very loudly as usual. Holkin was in his element, having got on to the subject of his late master Topcliffe. He held forth with lewd stories about the late Queen Elizabeth. With his mouth opening and shutting like that of a fish and his blue bulbous nose and mop of greasy hair shining, he shouted out to all and sundry. 'Showed him her arse, she did, dirty old cow.'

Chalky was very shocked by this man's stories. He had great respect for the late queen and had once seen her riding the forest on a white stallion with all her grand courtiers around her.

Holkin's loud voice continued: '"'Ere, 'ere," she says, "does this look like Henry's arse?" It always worried her, being a bastard, it did.'

Chalky certainly did not know where he got the courage from but, banging on the counter, he called out: 'Hi! Shut your foul mouth! Don't want talk like that in here.'

Holkin was on him in a flash, dragging him over the counter like a stunned rabbit and proceeding to give poor Chalky a good beating. He would have made a fine job of it, too, but a pewter pint pot hit the thug on the side of the head and Holkin went down like a sack of potatoes. He sat there on the floor with a ludicrous expression on his face as he stared up at Katy's tall, splendid figure.

Waving the pot over his head, Katy warned: 'Keep your dirty hands off me husband or you will get a harder one the next time.'

'All right, Katy, don't want to offend you.' Holkin

pulled himself up and backed towards the door, Katy's entire family was well known for its methods of disposing of enemies, and he, Holkin, was not taking any chances.

But later that night, Holkin returned, louder and viler than ever, with a knot of companions with him. There was the tinker – a dirty sly fellow wearing a bright yellow cravat about his neck and dusty cap on his head. He talked only of the women he had raped and other equally unpleasant matters. One of the members of this foul-mouthed group was a tall young man wearing a black suit with a small white collar. After drinking gallons of beer, he began to spout religion. He was a blood-thirsty, fanatical young man called Robert of York, who listened avidly to Holkin's lewd stories of execution, the cutting down of men and dismembering of them while they were still alive, and then he would start raving: 'Repent you sinners,' he shouted. 'In the fire of hell you will perish! Kill the Popish bastards!'

'Bleeding maniac!' Chalky muttered, regretting that he had ever allowed such a crowd to feel at home in his inn. 'Think I'll sell up and get out,' he muttered to himself. 'Wonder if Katy would like to go to the new colony.' Then he remembered Thomas who was asleep upstairs. 'I will have to ask him about it. And I hope he finds his little woman, he don't seem like such a bad bloke.' So reminiscing, he served up the jugs of porter as the customers got louder and more rowdy. His thoughts wandered and suddenly he remembered his walk down by the brook so many months ago when he had seen that frightened young woman with the children. Of course! Chalky clapped his hand to his head. 'Gawd!' he cried. 'Katy, come here, and take over quick!'

Katy came up to him at the counter and stared at Chalky with some surprise as he suddenly darted upstairs as though the devil was behind him.

Thomas was asleep when Chalky knocked rapidly on the door, but the noise woke him up and he sat up quickly. 'What the devil do you want?' he shouted irritably.

'I saw her! I remember now, I saw her!' Chalky gasped excitedly.

'Saw who?' asked Thomas.

'Why, your little woman! She was at Brook House. I saw her by the brook, months ago.'

Thomas looked anxiously at him. Was this man drunk and sending him on another wild goose chase? Wearily, he got up and began pulling on his breeches. 'Why did you not tell me this morning?' he enquired.

'I dunno, I must have forgotten. It came to me just now, like a flash of lightening. She was dressed as a nursemaid and there were two children with her. I'm sure it was the same girl I saw in the churchyard, but she looked much younger this time.'

Thomas looked doubtfully at him. 'Can you be sure? Perhaps it was just someone like her.'

'No! No!' Chalky shook his head. 'I am sure of it!'

A lot of noise was coming from downstairs. 'I've got to get back,' said Chalky. 'Katy's in charge down there, and I don't trust that lot. I'll go over to Brook House with you when the bar's shut, or leave it to the morning if you like.' With that he darted away.

Thomas buttoned up his shirt. He looked very perplexed. Could he rely on what this man said? After all, he might get him out there in the dark and then jump on him and rob him. No, Thomas did not trust anyone these days. He would ignore Chalky for the time being and investigate in the morning. Having made his decision, he turned to Rolly, who was staring at him, open-mouthed. 'Get back to sleep,' he ordered.

But on seeing his master lying fully clothed on the bed, Rolly had got up and dressed. Now he was buckling on his trusty sword, and wondering if they were going out to look for Marcelle.

From outside came the sound of fireworks and a red glow appeared in the sky from the big bonfire on the Lea fields. Wild uncanny cries came through the window and the air was suddenly thick with smoke. Thomas felt restless and apprehensive. Something terrible was happening out there. His mind drifted to the burnings in Smithfield, the Bartholomew massacre, and all other kinds of ill-fated memories.

Outside they were celebrating the death of a gallant man. He recalled the awful blood-stained ground around St Paul's and the screams of the dead and dying. Eight men had been butchered in one day. Was that such a thing to celebrate? He tossed and turned. The smell of blood was in his nostrils. Oh God, he thought, he had to move on tomorrow. His mind was becoming so morbid. He closed his eyes. For a long time he had never felt so afraid.

As the night got wilder, the air thickened. A bright yellow fog floated overhead, and the noise downstairs was becoming worse. Now it sounded like the angry buzz of an army of flies. Unable to get to sleep, Thomas got up and walked around the room and then stared out of the window at the big fire on the fields and the weird, unearthly shapes dancing around it.

'Go down and get me something to drink,' he ordered Rolly. 'I cannot stand being cooped up here. We will move on as soon as dawn breaks.'

Rolly went downstairs. There was nobody in the kitchen so he looked into the bar. There an astonishing sight met his eyes. Tables were upturned, beer was spilt all over the floor and, jammed in the doorway, was a knot of fighting men. Inside the door was Chalky, pushing and puffing with all his might in an effort to close the heavy door on them. His face was red and sweat poured down his brow as he strained to get the combatants outside.

With long strides, Rolly crossed the room in a split second. His huge boot went into action, kicking the fighting men straight out into the courtyard, punching and kneeing them and then hurling them away from the doorway, one by one. The great door then closed and bolts were shot as Chalky collapsed on the floor.

'Oh dear! that was a close one,' Chalky gasped. 'Thank God you came down in time. They ain't arf in a mood tonight. Look at the bloody damage they've done.' He got up and started to pick up the stools and splinters of glass from the broken lamps. Rolly just stood looking around at him: nothing disturbed him. 'My master needs a drink,' he said simply.

'We all need a drink,' replied Chalky, reaching for a thick earthenware bottle of spirits.

'No,' said Rolly. 'I must not drink. My master is not feeling so good.' He snatched the bottle and went.

'Social sort of sod,' sniffed Chalky. He got up on a bar stool and looked out of the top of the door to see what the crowd outside were up to. Women had joined their men and there was plenty going on out there. Then his attention was focused on a ring of men in the centre of the yard. He could clearly see Holkin's great hulk and the small shape next to him of the horse thief, Jenkins. Behind them milling about in the crowd, was the tinker, but the central figure was that of Robert of York, the crazy revolutionist. He was waving his arms and screaming, and the people around him joined in.

'What are they up to?' muttered Chalky to himself. 'They are all there, the whole vile damned crew. I wonder what's going on?' He put his head out a little further and saw, to his surprise, leaning against the wall, young Tim, the boy who helped occasionally down in the cellar.

'Tim!' he whispered urgently. 'What's up? Why are they all hanging about?'

Tim had his cap cocked on the back of his head and he stood nonchalantly against the wall, looking on with a naive curiosity at the antics of this drunken lot of rogues. 'They are going to do in the old priest,' he informed Chalky. 'They've gone down to get some more men and torches from the bonfire.'

'What old priest?' asked Chalky.

'The one that's at Brook House hiding.'

'But he's dead,' replied Chalky in puzzlement.

'We know that,' said Tim, 'but they don't.'

'Crikey! Stop them!' cried Chalky very alarmed. 'There's women and children in that house!'

Tim shrugged. 'I can't stop them,' he said. 'That preacher's got them all riled up.'

Just as he spoke, a procession of people came along the lane – men and women, even children. Most were drunk, and screamed anti-Popish slogans and all carried lighted torches. Other men joined them and with the crazy preacher leading, they all moved off in the direction of Brook House.

'Christ!' shouted Chalky. 'Quick, Tim!' he hissed. 'Get your old man and brothers to help.'

'Ain't our business,' sulked Tim, shoving his hands down into his pockets.

But Chalky was outside in a flash and pulling Tim by the collar. 'Get moving or you'll get my toe up your arse,' he bellowed. 'Now quick, move! There's little children over there and the rest of the house is empty. There's no one to defend them.'

At last realising that the situation was serious, Tim ran off to the line of cottages to get help. Then Chalky began yelling at the bottom of the stairs until Thomas, half-dressed and with a lot of rum inside him, opened his bedroom door. Chalky rushed up the stairs shouting. 'Quick! Hurry! They're going to raid Brook House,' Chalky had almost burst a blood vessel in his excitement. His face was purple as he called out:

'The mob! They're attacking Brook House. My Gawd, there's women and kids in there, and no one to protect them – only the old gatekeeper, and he's about ninety!'

Thomas stood in the doorway looked disdainfully down at the landlord. He was feeling less depressed now that he had taken a drink and this sprat of a man was becoming a nuisance. 'What the hell are you jabbering about?' he demanded aggressively.

'That lady, sir, your little wife, I'm sure that's where she is – Brook House.'

Thomas grabbed him roughly. 'Say that again!' he shouted.

'In Brook House! That's where I saw her some time back, in the grounds, and now a bloody lot of awful villains are heading up there too.'

Thomas was buckling on his sword and Rolly had already gone to get their horses.

'How many men are there?' Thomas asked Chalky.

'All told I should think about fifty, with the women too,' replied Chalky.

'Well, three of us, won't be much good,' said Thomas. 'Send for the watch and arouse the men in the cottages around.'

'I did that, sir, and the boy has gone for the soldiers.'

'Good, let's go then.'

With Chalky perched behind Rolly, they galloped down the road to where a knot of men armed with rusty bits of farm implements waited.

'Right!' said Thomas as they rode up. 'We must

attack and make plenty of noise so they think that there are many more of us than there really are.'

And so they rode to the rescue, little dreaming that here was the beginning and end of the search for little Marcelle.

16

That Many-Headed Monster

At Brook House the evening had been very long. Elizabeth had not been well that day; she had run a high temperature and been rather restless. Marcelle sat by her bed watching her sweet little face and stroking the golden hair spread over the pillow. Two bright spots of colour had appeared on the child's cheeks as she tossed and turned, and muttered: 'Are you there, Miss Mouse?' Each time she called out, Marcelle took her hot feverish, little hand and held it tight.

The house seemed full of noises that night as though all the ghosts had come out to walk together, and from outside came the noisy sound of fireworks. Her nostrils caught the smell of burning in the air. Marcelle shivered. It must be the anniversary of the Gunpowder Plot. How she hated that night and the dreadful things people did to the priests and their Catholic followers!

In the distance came a buzz of voices floating in through the night. Suddenly the memory of the mob that had come and dragged her mother out of her bed flooded her thoughts. She gasped. 'Oh God! Please do not let me be afraid,' she prayed. 'Give me strength and courage to protect my little son and this little sick girl if the need arises.'

A sweet peaceful feeling wafted into the room like a gentle breeze. The white silk cover upon the bed where Elizabeth slept seemed to have an indentation as though someone were sitting there. There was nothing to see, but Marcelle had the strongest conviction that Father Ben was there giving her comfort. No more was she afraid, but she sang softly to Elizabeth who had now dropped into a peaceful sleep.

While the child slept, Marcelle took a wander along the corridor taking a peep at Roger on the way. Behind her strolled Prince, the great hound, who suddenly darted to the window and leaped up with a loud bark. Marcelle knew that someone was out there, for Prince would not worry over ghosts. Out there was some evil person. She stood quite still and through the garden came that terrible sound of the drunken cries of the mob. Through the window she could see a long line of lighted torches; it was just like the time when they attacked and took her mother away.

Quickly she ran to wake Elizabeth, who got out of bed protesting all the time. 'Whatever is the matter, Miss Mouse?' she asked fretfully. 'It is only Bonfire Night – it is always noisy out there.'

But Marcelle was sure that there were people in the grounds, and so was Prince, who was dashing up and down the corridors barking furiously. She picked up the sleeping Roger in her arms and they all ran to shelter in Father Ben's old room behind the altar. The noise in the grounds got louder. Distinct cries could be heard as the crowd chanted slogans and yelled for Father Ben, the Jesuit priest, to show himself.

The three fugitives sat on the steps of a small alcove. The room was still littered with Father Ben's old manuscripts. Marcelle shuddered as she listened to the howling of the mob, and she felt almost responsible, as though she were to blame for her wicked ways. Turning to the statue of St Augustine, which stood in the niche in the wall, she prayed fervently.

Roger did not seem very upset by being turned out of bed and now he returned to sleep rolled up in his blanket on the floor. Elizabeth, however, sat beside Marcelle and shivered, pulling the white silk bed cover tightly around her. 'You are becoming alarmed unduly, Miss Mouse,' she remonstrated with Marcelle. 'Let us return to our beds. It is cold in here.'

Marcelle's face was white and her eyes wide open with terror as she placed a finger to her lips. 'Hush dear, or they will hear us. Remain perfectly quiet, and they will not find us in this room. Father Ben – God rest his soul – hid here for many years.'

'As you wish, Miss Mouse,' Elizabeth replied sulkily, and hunching up her coverlet, closed her eyes.

Marcelle listened, as tense as a wild animal, to the noises outside. Suddenly she heard a splintering noise and a terrible yelp from Prince. A hand had broken a window in the corridor and Prince had pounced at it, tearing the flesh with his great jaws. Another man came to the window and threw a lighted torch into Prince's face causing the dog to retire with a loud yelp of pain. He backed away but then stood there by the window snarling and snapping so loudly that the men changed their minds about climbing in.

Outside by the window were Holkin and Jenkins. Their idea had been to sneak into the house while the rest of the crowd danced wildly on the lawn, and loot the house. Now Jenkins was holding his bleeding arm and Holkin, whose clothes were ripped and chest was badly mauled, stood over him.

'I told yer not to try and get in by yerself,' he snarled at the tinker who had thrown a lighted torch at Prince. The fire had set a carpet alight and now the corridor was beginning to fill with acrid smoke. Prince quivered and whined loudly.

'There's gold candlesticks on that altar,' growled the fallen Holkin at his partner. 'Won't get a chance for that sort of thing once they all get in.'

The tinker re-emerged from out of the shadows with another lighted torch. 'Here,' he called to Holkin in a cracked voice. 'Come round the corner, I'll show yer where we can smoke the bastards out. Once we get the old boy and give him to the crowd, we can have a good rake about. There's plenty of good stuff inside.'

The people in the crowd on the lawns were screaming more wildly than ever. They had lighted a pile of brushwood, and now cavorted around it. The tall thin figure of the crazy preacher in the centre called down hell fire on the Papists.

The two men crept around the old grey walls until they came to the tower. The gold cross on the top shone brightly in the light of the fire as though the power of good showed up against all this evil.

'That's it,' whispered the tinker. 'That's where the old devil hangs out.'

'How do we get up there?' asked Holkin.

'We don't. I'll smoke the old swine out. Give us a lift up.'

He climbed on Holkin's wide shoulders, and through little vent near the top of the tower, he pushed the lighted torch and quickly slid down again.

'Come on!' he shouted as he ran round to the front door. 'That will roast him out.'

Marcelle was sitting still with the children beside her when the blazing torch descended upon them, landing on the table where the dry parchments lay. They all went up in a sheet of flames.

Grabbing Roger in her arms and pulling Elizabeth behind her, Marcelle ran in utter terror from the room which quickly became wreathed in flames. She almost flew down the smoke-filled corridor to where the howls of Prince the faithful hound, could be heard through the thick smoke.

Different sounds were now coming from the crowd as they scattered in panic. Thomas Mayhew and Rolly rode in among them at the gallop and using their swords. The old boys from the cottages arrived and prodded and poked the mob with sharp hay forks, rakes, sickles and anything available. The crowd was dispersed in minutes.

Holkin had managed to break the locks on the heavy front door and he was just pushing it open, when Thomas' sword came slashing down by his face and cut off an ear. Holkin fell to the ground screaming in pain.

Meanwhile Rolly disposed of the tinker and tried to

dash into the house but was forced back by the smoke and flames.

'Oh my God!' cried Thomas. 'The whole place is ablaze!'

Trapped in the burning corridor, Prince howled loudly to catch Thomas' attention. With Rolly close on his heels, Thomas ran to a side window. Suddenly the smoke-blackened, terror-stricken face of Marcelle appeared, and in her arms lay a crying kicking little bundle. 'Take my son,' she sobbed. 'Take care of my son.'

'Marcelle! Oh my dear!' Thomas took the crying child and handed him to Rolly. Then he leaped into the burning building to rescue his long-lost wife.

Piercing screams came from Elizabeth behind her. The girl had run to her beloved Prince, who was howling in pain.

Marcelle screamed too. 'Elizabeth! Come back!' She turned and ran after her with Thomas calling behind them.

There can be no fate more terrible than to be trapped in a burning building but Marcelle thought only of little blind Elizabeth running frantically into the thick black smoke to find her dog. Prince's howls ceased and a great pile of blazing wood crashed down into the corridor.

Thomas was frantic. With bare hands, and his clothes alight, he tore at the burning timbers, but could find no trace of anyone. Others had joined him, including Chalky and Rolly, who had handed Roger to Katy.

All through the night they searched, and by the time dawn broke, there was little left of the house but smouldering timbers. It was then that they found them. One of the men from the cottages was Ralph, who had been an old retainer at Brook House. He remembered the priest's hole and its secondary niche high up in the gables which was used in times of danger, and it was there that they found Marcelle and the lovely little Elizabeth. Death had given them the peace they never had found on this earth. Their hands were clasped together and in between their hands was a little gold medal that had belonged to Marcelle's mother. They had been suffocated by the dense smoke.

The two delicate bodies were laid out in what had been the great hall, where Henry VIII had once held court. They all knelt to pray, Thomas and Ralph side by side. Deep sobs racked old Ralph's thin body for he had loved Elizabeth and was the only one who knew the secret of her birth.

Thomas felt too numb to cry. He could not believe what had happened. Then a strange coldness came over him and a soft hand pulled at his sleeve. In his ear he heard a voice whisper: 'Go now, and take my son from danger.' Thomas passed his hand over his eyes. Leaning forward, he wiped the soot from Marcelle's white lips, thinking for a moment that by some miracle she was still alive. But now, her small thin face was set in a mask of death but there seemed to be a soft secret smile on her lips. Then it came again, this tug at his sleeve and Marcelle's voice more urgent this time: 'My son! Save my son!'

Thomas stood up quickly. Voices buzzed around him. 'There was another child,' he heard a voice say. 'A little boy. He must have perished in the flames.'

With a quick sign for Rolly to follow him, Thomas strode quickly away. Marcelle was not dead; she lived on in her son. Thomas had to get him to safety.

Katy was waiting for him at the inn, her dark eyes wet with tears. Roger was tucked up in bed beside her own babe and for once in his life Chalky was silent. He sat beside the two babes as they cuddled up together, with tears running down his blackened face.

'Will you not rest awhile?' Katy asked Thomas anxiously.

But Thomas shook his head. 'No! We ride before the dawn. Wrap the child well and pack food for him. We have a long journey ahead of us.'

Katy stared in wonder at this unemotional man whose wife had just died a terrible death.

Upstairs Rolly packed their belongings, and huge tears rolled down his cheeks.

Thomas' eyes were sad but dry as he said goodbye to Katy and Chalky. 'One favour I ask of you both,' he said, placing a heavy purse on the table. 'This is for your kindness and assistance, but I must ask only one more favour of you – that you forget I was ever here. And forget the child too. I cannot explain, but it is for my son's well-being I must beg an oath of secrecy from you both.'

'Anything you say, sir,' Chalky assured him. 'You are a fine gentleman and I'll never doubt your word. No one's ever going to get anything out of me or Katy.'

'I thank you from the bottom of my heart,' replied Thomas. 'We will ride before daybreak.'

Back at Brook House, the sad villagers still searched the ruins for a body of a child, a strange little boy who had come into the family as the great Henry Howard had died, and disappeared when their youngest member Elizabeth left the world. It was a mystery they were to discuss for generations – about the lovely child who was here when the great comet hung over the town.

Epilogue

The little ship battled on, its white sails blowing in the wind as it braved the Atlantic gales. Suddenly the hoarse welcome cry of the sailor aloft was heard: 'Land Ahoy!'

The murmur of voices came from the hot sun-baked decks as the weary travellers spotted that wonderful haven, the New World. Those on board gathered around to pray to give thanks to their God and to their wonderful captain who had piloted them through thousands of miles of treacherous seas, past the dangers from Spaniards who prowled the waters protecting their new colonies from the hoards of pilgrims sailing from England and the horrors of persecution. The little party knelt and prayed together – the men soberly dressed and the women in plain dresses with bonnets and shawls.

High up in the wheelhouse the captain read aloud from a heavy bible.

Thomas Mayhew was looking much older. His dark beard was long and thick. Beside him stood his sturdy young son Roger, and behind him, his loyal servant, Rolly. Quite near to them, stood a young woman whose face was terribly disfigured, with a sightless eye and pock-marked face. In spite of her scars, a sweet calm serenity glowed from her face as she gazed upon her charge. It was Wanda, who had travelled to the New World with Thomas to take care of Roger. She held a little girl by the hand.

'Hush, Virginia,' she whispered. 'Be a good girl. We must listen while our captain prays for a safe landing.'

'I want to get my flowers,' declared the child.

'Be still, Virginia,' ordered her mother, the tall Elizabeth Washington. Her husband, George Washington, was the First Officer on board ship and they were going to join her family who had settled three years earlier in the new colony of Virginia. Her first-born, now nearly three, had been named after England's first Colony and now, after a year of travelling, the New World was in sight. They had reached their journey's end.

The strange and beautiful shore came nearer. Multi-coloured birds flew about the ship's masts and as they drew nearer to the shore and sailed inland, tropical plants of glorious colours aroused the interest of the pilgrims.

Virginia was clinging desperately to a withered bunch of dandelions that had gone to seed. 'They are for my auntie,' she told little Roger Mayhew who was staring at them in wonder. 'I have brought them from England for her.'

'But they are dead,' he lisped pointing at the silken fluffy seeds. 'Look,' he said, blowing on them. 'They will sail away.'

As the dandelion seeds rose up in the air and sailed towards the shore, Virginia wept. 'You are a naughty boy,' she told Roger.

Roger's blue eyes followed the seeds as they floated to the shore. 'Look!' he cried. 'They will grow again, Virginia!'

Do you wish this wasn't the end?

Join us at www.hodder.co.uk, or follow us on
Twitter @hodderbooks to be a part of our community
of people who love the very best in books and reading.

Whether you want to discover more about a book
or an author, watch trailers and interviews, have the
chance to win early limited editions, or simply browse
our expert readers' selection of the very best books,
we think you'll find what you're looking for.

And if you don't,
that's the place to tell us what's missing.

We love what we do, and we'd love you to be part of it.

www.hodder.co.uk

@hodderbooks

HodderBooks

HodderBooks